Lord Henry made a slight, dismissive gesture

"What could a rake wish for from a lady on a providentially empty terrace?"

"Oh!"

Understanding came to Polly at the very last moment. She had once quite ached for Lord Henry to kiss her as long as it had been in a completely undemanding fashion. Some chaste but impassioned salutation had been the height of her aspirations.

This kiss might have been impassioned, but in no way could it be described as chaste. Lord Henry brought her into sudden, shocking contact with his body. His mouth captured hers with the ruthless skill of the expert, parting her lips so that her gasp was lost.

* * *

Lady Polly
Harlequin Historical #574—August 2001

**Harlequin Historicals is delighted
to present author Nicola Cornick
and her sparkling Regency
LADY POLLY**

Lady Polly

NICOLA CORNICK

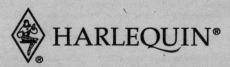

HARLEQUIN®

TORONTO • NEW YORK • LONDON
AMSTERDAM • PARIS • SYDNEY • HAMBURG
STOCKHOLM • ATHENS • TOKYO • MILAN • MADRID
PRAGUE • WARSAW • BUDAPEST • AUCKLAND

ISBN 0-373-29174-4

LADY POLLY

First North American Publication 2001

Copyright © 1999 by Nicola Cornick

Visit us at www.eHarlequin.com

Printed in U.S.A.

Nicola Cornick is passionate about many things: her country cottage and its garden, her two small cats, her husband and her writing, though not necessarily in that order! She has always been fascinated by history, both as her chosen subject at university and subsequently as an engrossing hobby. She works as university administrator and finds her writing the perfect antidote to the demands of life in a busy office.

Available from Harlequin Historicals and
NICOLA CORNICK

The Virtuous Cyprian #566
Lady Polly #574

Prologue

1812

"**Y**ou're a damned fool, Henry!" Simon Verey leant on the table and addressed his friend in tones that would have led Henry Marchnight to call him out under any other circumstances. "Leave it a few weeks—a month, even—for everyone to lose interest in Miss Jacques's vicious rumours! If you go to Lady Paulersbury's rout tonight, they'll make mincemeat of you!"

Lord Henry's only response was a rather lop-sided grin as he tilted his head to consider the intricate folds of his violet cravat in the mirror.

"The Napoleon," he mused. "Rather a neat style, don't you think, Simon? Languishing and romantic, as is appropriate for this evening! Do you think that it will bring me the luck of the French?"

"In love or in war?" Verey asked drily.

Lord Henry's only reply was another smile. "I regret that I cannot take your advice, Simon," he continued. "I must see Lady Polly Seagrave tonight. I am hoping that I may still persuade her to consent to be my wife.''

Verey's lips tightened. He had seen that reckless look in his friend's grey eyes before and knew it promised trouble. There was something both tense and watchful about Lord Henry's elegantly clad form, some element held under the barest control. And Verey understood his desperation, but he thought Henry had miscalculated.

''They'll never let you near her,'' he prophesied grimly. ''Good God, the whole Town thinks that you have tried to debauch Miss Jacques, then proposed marriage to Lady Polly for her fortune only a day later! You'll be ripped to pieces, Henry!''

Lord Henry shrugged. ''Lady Polly would never believe such a thing of me, Simon. I *know* she would have accepted my suit had the Earl not refused to countenance it!''

Verey shook his head. What madness could have possessed Lord Henry to ask the starchy old Earl of Seagrave for his daughter's hand in marriage whilst such unsavoury, albeit untrue, rumours were being circulated? He must have known that the Earl was so high in the instep that he would never sanction a match between his only daughter and a man who had been branded a philanderer and deceiver.

With its usual appetite for scandal, Society had been quick to seize upon the accusations of Miss Sally Jacques that Henry Marchnight had promised her marriage and then attempted to seduce her. Verey knew that Miss Jacques was the daughter of a Cit who had attempted to establish herself amongst the *ton* and whose disappointment at being unable to bring Henry up to scratch had led to this ill-considered revenge. Verey also knew that most of Society thought Miss Jacques an ill-bred mushroom and that interest in the story would wane very swiftly. If only Henry had exercised his usual cool detachment! But in his very real passion for Lady Polly Seagrave he seemed uncharacteristically hasty, unable to wait even a few days for matters to cool. Simon was prepared to support his friend, but he was certain that the evening would be deeply unenjoyable.

Their reception at Lady Paulersbury's was everything Verey had predicted and worse. Silence fell as Lord Henry Marchnight was announced. Men whom he had counted his friends pointedly turned their backs. Some women whispered maliciously behind their fans, whilst others drew aside from him with disgusted expressions. There was a moment when Lord Henry was certain Lord Paulersbury was about to have him horsewhipped from the house before his wife's more temperate counsel prevailed. But he was treated as a social pariah, ignored or ridiculed, and it was a profoundly unpleasant and uncomfortable experience.

Lady Polly Seagrave saw Lord Henry's tall figure across the ballroom and was immediately certain that he had come to seek her out. She caught her breath. To have dared so much public opprobrium, just for the chance of speech with her! He must know that her father had forbidden them to meet and the entire Town was reviling him over the scandal of Miss Jacques.

Polly burned with outraged fury at the treatment
Sally Jacques had meted out to Lord Henry. Sally
and Polly had once been friends, before Miss
Jacques's jealousy at Lord Henry's partiality for
Polly had driven a wedge between them. Sally had
contrived that her carriage had broken down in the
vicinity of Lord Henry's home at Ruthford and had
imposed on his hospitality overnight so that she had
compromised them both. In vain had Lord Henry argued that Miss Jacques's companion and his own
servants had provided ample chaperonage and that
nothing untoward had occurred. Public opinion, carefully encouraged by Miss Jacques and her chaperon
with their hints at false proposals and attempted seduction, was firmly of the belief that he should have
made her an offer. His refusal to do so proved him
to be no gentleman. It was not long before the true
facts of the case had been turned inside out and
Henry Marchnight was denounced as a scoundrel and
seducer.

A few days before, when Polly had heard the
harmful gossip repeated by two salacious matrons,
she had burst out that it was all malicious lies. Immediately their watchful gaze had turned thoughtfully on her. Her mother had pulled Polly to one side.

"Be quiet, you silly girl!" Lady Seagrave had
hissed in Polly's ear. "You will have them thinking
that Lord Henry has debauched you too!"

"Lord Henry has not debauched anyone!" Polly
had muttered furiously, but she kept her voice dis-
creetly low for all her vehemence. "He is an honourable man!"

For a moment Lady Seagrave had looked almost

sorry for her daughter. ''Lord Henry may be as honourable as you please, but no one will believe it now! And that is because they do not *want* to believe it, for the tale is so much more interesting than the truth. So you will be a good girl and have no more to do with him!''

For a moment Polly had looked mutinous. Lord Henry had always behaved as a perfect gentleman towards her. She was more than half in love with him. But she had already had her father explain, very clearly and kindly, just why he could not entertain Lord Henry's suit. And Polly was only eighteen, and accustomed to obeying her parents unquestioningly in everything…

And now Lady Seagrave had caught her arm, turning her away so that Lord Henry's curiously compelling grey gaze could no longer disturb her so.

''You must *not* acknowledge him,'' she murmured, whilst keeping a spurious social smile fixed on her face for the benefit of those about them who were watching with a keen interest.

Polly knew her mother was only acting with the best of intentions. A young lady's good name was so fragile and scandal so contaminating. She had seen how a reputation could become so tarnished that a girl would become quite unmarriageable. But she was torn by her burgeoning feelings for Lord Henry. She had never been in love before and he had wooed her throughout the Season, so gently, so carefully. His attentions had never overstepped the mark and when he smiled at her with all the warmth and tenderness that spoke more clearly than any words, Polly felt deliciously safe and cherished.

She reluctantly allowed her mother to shepherd her away, but could not resist a quick glance over her shoulder. Lord Henry was still watching her. Polly gave a pleasurable little shiver of excitement, but at the same time a *frisson* of nerves prompted her to hope that he would not make a scene or press his attentions on her. That would be deliciously romantic but rather difficult to handle. Polly was not at all sure that she could cope with impassioned protestations of love.

It was much later in the evening when Lord Henry finally managed to get Polly on her own. Throughout the ball, she had been aware of his presence, the deceptively casual way in which he was watching her all the time. But she was never left alone. Lady Seagrave, a very dragon of propriety where her only daughter was concerned, seemed to follow her everywhere until Polly told her with asperity that she was quite capable of visiting the ladies' withdrawing room alone.

It was on her way back that Lord Henry seized his chance, materialising in the deserted corridor and drawing her into an empty room before Polly even had time to catch her breath. It was vastly exciting, but also rather frightening. There was something driven about Lord Henry that evening, Polly thought, something so resolute that it made her quail and find him almost a stranger. She was not accustomed to strong emotion. The Seagrave household was run with apparent harmony and the Earl would never have countenanced any vulgar display of feeling.

Polly knew very little about love; she loved her

parents with a dutiful respect, and knew, far more
scandalously, that her brothers had both at one time
or another had in keeping certain ladies on whom
they lavished their affections. That, Polly had once
overheard her mother darkly telling another matron,
had very little to do with *love* at all. And here was
Lord Henry Marchnight, burning with another type
of romantic passion. His intensity frightened her.

"Lord Henry!" Polly's voice trembled a little.
"You know my father has forbidden me to speak
with you—"

He took both her hands in his, his intent grey gaze
fixed on her face. "I know it! But I had to see you!
You know that he has refused my suit, but we cannot
let that make us part! Come away with me, my love!
If you will trust yourself to me—"

But Polly had taken a hasty step back, freeing her
hands from his grasp. She had paled visibly, her
cheeks as white as the pristine foulard at her throat.
"Run away with you? But—"

"You must know that I love you! Say you'll marry
me!"

For a moment Polly wavered. He was taking her
by storm, so ardent, so impassioned that she was
tempted. But her feelings were barely awakened and
everything in her upbringing conspired against him.
His very ardour alienated her. He knew, a moment
before she recoiled, that she was going to refuse him.

"Oh, no, indeed I could not! My father…the scandal…only think—" Polly's eyes were huge with the
horror of it. She broke off at the expression on Lord
Henry's face, suddenly aware that she might have
been a little precipitate. Those grey eyes, so warm

and tender before, were now so stony and withdrawn that Polly bit her lip. It was like looking into the face of a complete stranger.

The tears came into her eyes. She had a sudden conviction that she had just carelessly thrown away something infinitely precious, without truly understanding exactly what it was. She put out a tentative hand, but Lord Henry was already turning away.

"Polly!" The awesome tones were those of Lady Seagrave, who stood in the shadows, furious fire kindling in her dark eyes. "Come here at once! I knew I could not trust you on your own! And as for you, sir—"

She turned on Lord Henry, but he was already leaving. He sketched an immaculately elegant bow, first to the Countess and then to Polly.

"You need have no fears for your daughter at my hands, ma'am," he said, his tone one of frigid courtesy. "I give you my word that I shall never approach her again." And he was gone, leaving Polly with the comfort of her familiar world and a totally unfamiliar feeling of desolation in her heart.

Chapter One

1817

Sir Godfrey Orbison did not understand women. Never having entered the bond of matrimony and being devoid of close female relatives to guide him, he was ill-equipped to deal with a goddaughter he considered to be both foolish and ungrateful.

"You refused him because you did not love him?" Sir Godfrey's black brows beetled together and he glared fiercely at Lady Polly Seagrave, his tone incredulous. "What is that to the purpose, pray? A fine situation if one had to *love* one's intended spouse! The material point is that he is heir to the Duke of Bellars, and as such must be a better prospect than life as a penniless spinster! Aye, and a spinster who is fast approaching her dotage!"

The Dowager Countess of Seagrave was fluttering her hands in distress, but Lady Polly allowed herself a small smile, her elusive dimples peeping for a moment. She knew her godfather's ill temper would not last long for he was incapable of bearing a grudge and was so fond of her that she could get away with most things. Turning down her fifth suitor of the Season and the nineteenth eligible proposal of her life was, however, testing his indulgence to the full. And he was her trustee, along with her elder brother, and as such could cut up rough about her allowance if he chose. In eighteen months she would be twenty-five and should be mistress of her own fortune, but if Sir Godfrey chose to make her a penniless spinster, it was within his legal powers to do so. Clearly some tact and charm was called for.

She dropped a small curtsy and smiled at her god-father beguilingly. "Dearest Sir Godfrey, you have been like a father to me since my own papa died, and I do thank you for all your guidance and advice! But I am persuaded that you could not really wish me to marry John Bellars! He is a pleasant enough man, if as dull as ditchwater, but it is old Lady Bellars who would be the rub! Why, she has him completely under her thumb and is the most mean-spirited woman—"

"Humph!" Sir Godfrey opined.

"And she is penny-pinching, too!" The Dowager Countess of Seagrave put in, hastily improving on her daughter's theme. "I hear she keeps young John on a tight rein, for all that she has no real control over his fortune! And," she added artfully, with a flash of her dark eyes, "was it not Augusta Bellars who tried to snare you in your salad days, Godfrey? She pursued you quite violently, as I recall! They were taking bets in the clubs that she would catch you!"

Sir Godfrey's choleric gaze kindled again. "Gussie Grantley! Yes, b'God, I'd forgotten that! Tiresome woman, forever wheedling herself into my company, telling everyone there was an understanding between us! Well...'' he sighed heavily, ''...can't be doing with that connection in the family, then. Why, she might view this as a second chance to catch me!''

''It is not to be contemplated!'' The Dowager declared, smiling as much with genuine amusement as relief. The thought of the widowed Duchess of Bellars pursuing the elderly Sir Godfrey afforded her much secret amusement. In her experience, men often had a much-inflated view of their own attractions.

Sir Godfrey's gaze had fallen on Polly again, demurely sitting with her chin in her hand smiling at him. Fond of her as he was, he was obliged to view her as another example of an unsatisfactory female.

''All the same, Poll, this won't do, you know! Nineteen suitors, all worthy men, and not one of them up to your expectations!'' Sir Godfrey cleared his throat, intent on delivering a homily. ''I thought that you would take Julian Morrish when he offered this Season—damned...harrumph! Dashed silly not to! No better man in the whole of London! And Seagrave took Morrish's rejection that badly, I know...''

The Dowager Lady Seagrave cleared her throat delicately. She had been quick to see her daughter's discomfort, for the colour had come rushing into Polly's ivory complexion, making her look suddenly more animated and much prettier. That was how she used to look, Lady Seagrave thought with a sudden pang of regret, remembering a time five years before, when her daughter had been a bright and vivacious debutante rather than a cool and withdrawn young lady with a reputation for pride. The young Lady Polly had been an appealing girl, drawing quite a following to her with her lustrous cloud of dark hair and expressive brown eyes. She had not lacked for offers, but none of them seemed to meet her exacting standards. No man in five years had been able to persuade her of the merit of his suit.

As for Julian Morrish, that had indeed been an unfortunate affair and one which had caused ill feeling within the family for several weeks until Lucille, the Dowager's daughter-in-law, had interceded with her husband to forgive Polly. Nick Seagrave had been furious that his close friend, Julian Morrish, had been rejected by his sister. Everyone knew Morrish to be a fine man and one to whom no possible objection could be made on the grounds of rank, consequence, fortune or reputation. Polly's behaviour had put a great strain on the friendship between Seagrave and Morrish, and an even greater strain on relationships within the family. Polly's other brother, Peter, had strolled into the breakfast-room one morning and remarked that he would rather face the French again at Waterloo than be the butt of his brother and sister's ill humour.

"I think, perhaps, that it would be wise for Polly to retire for a little now, Sir Godfrey," the Dowager Countess said hastily, seeing that her daughter's colour was still high. "We go to Lady Phillips's ridotto tonight, and you know how Polly tires easily these days! Polly, my love—"

In response to her mother's meaningful nod, Polly got up, pressed a kiss on Sir Godfrey's whiskery face, and slipped out of the room. Her spirits had taken a tumble. The mention of Julian Morrish had been an unfortunate one.

Once out in the deserted entrance hall, Polly leaned against a marble pillar and rested one hot cheek against its coolness. She had known that Sir Godfrey would be angry at Bellars's dismissal, especially as it followed on so swiftly from the fiasco of Julian Morrish. And she had been as upset as anyone at the necessity of rejecting Morrish, knowing it would cause difficulties for Nicholas Seagrave in particular. Yet, she could not have accepted Morrish, not whilst the spectre of Lord Henry Marchnight persisted in imposing itself between her and every eligible man she met. A tear slid from the corner of one of Polly's closed eyes and she swallowed what seemed to be a huge lump in her throat.

Immediately after her estrangement from Lord Henry five years previously, Polly had been in very low spirits. She had berated herself fiercely for the lack of courage and the lack of faith that had led her to refuse to elope with Lord Henry. She had a curious feeling of loss, as though she had thrown away something priceless, something that would never be recaptured. The expression on Lord Henry's face as he had left her that night, the stony withdrawal, the contempt for her weakness, had haunted her for a long time. It was only later, when she was older and understood her loss all the more, that she realised that his love for her had been far more mature than the girlish passion she had thought that she had felt for him. She had simply not been ready to accept the full responsibility of his love and all its implications, not ready to defy her family and run away with him.

The most acute elements of her misery wore off with time, particularly as Lord Henry was absent from Town much of the time and his path and Polly's did not cross much for several years. Whenever she heard news of him it would invariably involve some highly coloured account of his amatory adventures, for he appeared to have become a thorough-going rake and wastrel. Polly's heart ached when she heard the tales, as though some part of her could not relinquish Henry for good. And then, the previous summer, her dormant feelings had been stirred into life again.

Lord Henry had been in Suffolk that summer, at the same time that Polly was at Dillingham with her mother and brothers, and it was inevitable that they should be in each other's company. Each tried to avoid the other as much as possible, their meetings made awkward by the history that lay between them. To Polly's horror, she had discovered that her childish infatuation had somehow transformed itself over the years into a frighteningly strong attachment. She realised that Lord Henry had unconsciously influenced her refusal of every offer of marriage over the past five years, and that since she was unable to marry him now, she would marry no one.

The realisation made her even more self-conscious in his company and she cursed her inability to match Henry's smooth detachment. Her original refusal to elope with him was now an awesome barrier between them, making the re-establishment of cordial or at the least civil relations between them well-nigh impossible. When Lord Henry had said, that fateful night, that he would never approach Polly again, he had meant just that. They were obliged to exchange a few words when they met in public, but he seldom sought her out. Then, of course, there was his reputation as a rake, which made every chaperon blench. Although many of his escapades were probably exaggerated, there was no doubt that he had become very wild and would not be considered a suitable escort for any unmarried lady. And now, there was an even more potent and unexpected reason why she could never hope to re-attach his affections...

The sound of voices at the main door stirred Polly from her thoughts. She straightened up to see her sister-in-law Lucille taking her leave of a couple on the doorstep and hurrying into the hall, pulling off her gloves. As Lucille's eyes adjusted to the sudden shade, Polly came forward to greet her.

"Oh, Lucille, I am glad to see you back!" Then, as her sister-in-law fixed her with a rather too perceptive gaze, she said hastily, "Who were those people? They looked a little eccentric!"

Lucille laughed. "The lady was a Mrs Golightly, who is a friend of Miss Hannah More, and was telling me all about her work with the Bettering Society! They work to improve the condition of the poor, you know! And the gentleman is a poet, Mr Cleymore, who is accounted quite good, I believe, although I cannot understand his work! They are complete originals, but not people of fashion!"

"Who cares a button for that?" Polly said stoutly. One of the things she particularly liked about Lucille was her lack of interest in worldly concerns. She would befriend people because she liked them, support causes because she believed in them, and gently rebuke even the most high-ranking Dowager who ventured to criticise her for her quaint interests. Lucille had grown in poise and confidence since her marriage to Nicholas Seagrave, Polly thought now, but she retained the innocent interest she had in everyone and everything. It was a quality that added to her novelty value in the eyes of the *ton*, who were always seeking fresh amusement. Lucille, with her slightly eccentric ways, had been a gift to such jaded palates. And the final titillation, of course, was the dreadful, brassy Cyprian who was Lucille's twin and had done her utmost to embarrass her sister, seeking her out at public events and trying to hang on her coattails. Lucille had dealt with all the pitfalls most admirably, Polly thought with a smile, taking her sister-in-law's arm and steering her towards the green drawing-room and away from Sir Godfrey and the Dowager Countess.

"Do you have time to take tea with me?" she asked hopefully, and Lucille's observant blue eyes scanned her face once more.

"Of course! Medlyn, tea for two in the Green Room, if you please!" She turned back to Polly. "But what has happened, Polly? You look quite blue-devilled! Oh, I know—" She wrinkled up her nose. "John Bellars has made you an offer and you have refused him! And..." she cast a glance towards the closed door of the blue drawing-room "...your mother and Sir Godfrey are on the high ropes over your behaviour!"

"Sir Godfrey has rung a peal over me," Polly admitted ruefully, as they went into the Green Room. "How did you know that Bellars was about to make me a declaration, Lucille?"

"I guessed," Lucille said serenely. "And I suspected you would refuse him. The only one I thought you might have accepted was Julian Morrish..."

Polly sighed. "I did think of accepting," she said reluctantly, "for I like Julian very well, and had I wanted a marriage based on mutual respect and liking, it might have served. But—" she shook her head "—I could not do it, for—"

"For you are still in love with Harry Marchnight," Lucille finished for her, disposing herself elegantly in a wing chair and looking at her sister-in-law with a rueful amusement.

Feeling a prickle of envy at the casual way Lucille mentioned Lord Henry, Polly sought to defend herself. "It is not that I am in love with him, precisely—"

The door opened to admit Medlyn with the tea. Lucille poured neatly and passed Polly a cup.

Once she had thanked him and the door had closed again, Lucille turned back to Polly.

"Come now, Polly, do you think you can cozen me? It may be that you originally suffered from a schoolroom infatuation for Lord Henry, but I am sure you have discovered that this has turned to something far more profound."

"You have not forgotten what I told you at Dillingham in the autumn," Polly said sadly. "I was being foolishly self-pitying! It was simply that your own wedding made me feel sorry for myself and I regretted the opportunity I threw away! But that was all over a long time ago! It is of no consequence!''

Lucille studied her sister-in-law over the rim of her teacup. ''But I am concerned for your happiness, Polly! All these gentlemen you refuse are so very eligible and do not take their rejection lightly! You know that you are getting a reputation for pride! And what are you to do if you do not marry?''

Polly shrugged, a gesture which her mother deplored. ''Oh, I shall devote myself to studying and good works! And if I miss the excitement of the Season in years to come, I shall set myself up as a chaperon for daughters of rich cits wishing to marry well!''

Lucille sensibly chose to disregard most of this. ''Do you think,'' she said carefully, ''that there is any likelihood of yourself and Lord Henry making a match of it? He has told me that he still holds you in the greatest esteem—''

But Polly was shaking her head violently. ''Oh, no, Lucille, that is impossible! Why, I am sure he had nothing but contempt for my poor-spiritness in refusing to elope with him five years ago and now I imagine he scarce thinks of me at all!''

She broke off, evading Lucille's eyes. Impossible to explain to her sister-in-law that the most potent reason that Lord Henry could no longer have any interest in her was because he had quite obviously formed a romantic attachment to Lucille herself. Polly wondered just how innocent Lucille could be. She had no doubt that the attachment was one-sided and entirely emotional rather than physical. But how could Lucille not have noticed that Lord Henry was forever in her company, seeking her views and advice, valuing her opinion? Why, even Seagrave himself had commented humorously what a lapdog Harry Marchnight was becoming, forever following his wife about.

Polly searched rather desperately for a change of subject. "Do you think that you shall be joining the Bettering Society, Lucille?"

"Probably not," her sister-in-law answered. "Nicholas has suggested that we travel a little at the end of the Season, and since I am still awaiting my wedding trip, I thought to encourage him! But—" she returned to the previous subject with an obstinacy for which she was well known "—we were speaking of you, Polly, not of myself! If you truly feel that any awkwardness with Lord Henry must be in the past now, why do the two of you spend all your time skulking behind trees or pillars in an effort to avoid each other? It makes matters very difficult for the rest of us! Why, Nicholas was saying only the other day that he wished to ask Harry's advice on those greys he was thinking of buying, but he hesitated in case you accidently bumped into him! Could you not speak to Lord Henry and put an end to this, Polly?"

Polly stared in disbelief.

"Speak to him," she echoed faintly. "Whatever can you mean, Lucille? Oh, I could not!"

Lucille's brows rose at this missish response. She knew that Lady Appollonia Grace Seagrave was a well-brought-up and entirely orthodox daughter of the nobility, but had not thought her merely a pretty ninnyhammer.

"Well, upon my word, I only meant that you

should discuss matters with him—clear the air!'' she repeated patiently. ''After all, you are both adults and cannot be forever behaving in this foolish manner! You yourself have said that it is all in the past! I apologise if I have offended your sensibility, but I should think that one slightly embarrassing encounter must be a small price to pay to be comfortable together in the future! If you truly believe that there is no hope for the two of you and you do not wish to try to re-engage his feelings, explain to Lord Henry that you have no wish to continue in this absurd way and that you should both regard the past as over! That way you may start afresh as friends!''

Polly sighed, reaching for the teapot. It was hopeless to try to explain to Lucille that gently bred ladies simply did not seek a gentleman out in order to engage him in a conversation of an intimate and personal nature. Disagreements such as the one Polly had with Lord Henry were simply to be ignored or endured. Lucille, who had earned a living as a schoolteacher before her marriage to the Earl, had no time for what she saw as the pointless prevarications of polite society, but Polly could no more approach Lord Henry than fly to the moon.

''*You* are great friends with Harry Marchnight,'' Polly said lightly, trying not to let her envy show. ''I doubt I could achieve your familiarity with him!''

''No, but I am a married lady—'' Lucille broke off at Polly's irrepressible burst of laughter, arching her eyebrows enquiringly. ''Why, whatever have I said?''

''Married ladies are precisely the type Lord Henry prefers, so I hear,'' Polly said drily.

"Oh, but—" For a moment Lucille looked confused, before regaining her poise. "Oh, no, it is not in the least like *that*! I am glad to have Harry's esteem, but that is all there is to it! Why, to suggest anything else would be pure folly!"

Polly smiled, unconvinced. It was true that not even the *ton*, with its penchant for intrigue, had suggested anything improper in the relationship between the two, but that did not mean that Lord Henry might not wish it so. Lucille, totally absorbed in her husband, would be the last person to realise. Polly, thinking now of the consuming passion between Lucille and Nick Seagrave, shifted slightly in her chair. They were always perfectly proper in their behaviour in company, but it only needed one look... Polly sometimes thought that if any man ever looked at her with that explicit mixture of warmth and sensual demand she would faint dead away. But perhaps Lucille was lucky. Perhaps she was the unlucky one, hidebound by a conventional upbringing in a house where preserving the surface calm had always been all important.

The problem of Lord Henry Marchnight twitched at the corner of her mind again. Lucille was right, of course. Polly did not delude herself that there was any chance of re-establishing a rapport with Lord Henry, and under the circumstances, it was both foolish and pointless to be forever dwelling on the past. Perhaps she could at least try to put matters to rights. If she could find the right words to convey a genteel acceptance that they had both been young and foolish... It might suffice and put an end to awkwardness.

"I will try to speak to Lord Henry if I have an opportunity," Polly agreed hesitantly. "I understand what you mean, Lucille. It is just so difficult..." She despised herself for her lack of spirit, even as her mind shrank from the thought of broaching such a personal subject with someone who was, to all intents and purposes, a stranger. Yet Lucille was also right that their social circle was relatively small: to try to avoid someone was always difficult. Friends always seemed to have other mutual friends or acquaintances and an invitation or chance meeting could prove awkward.

Lucille took a biscuit and poured a second cup of tea. "I own it will be a relief to have the matter settled," she said with a candid smile. "Then I may stop worrying about you and turn my attention to Peter and Hetty! They are causing me great concern!"

"It must have been a great blow for Hetty when Mrs Markham's ill health led to the postponment of the wedding," Polly commented, secretly glad that Lucille had turned the subject. "But what do you mean, Lucille? How can Peter be giving you cause for concern?"

Lucille frowned. Polly's brother and her own foster sister had been intending to wed that spring, but the marriage had been delayed indefinitely since Hetty's mother had succumbed to the dropsy.

"You know how silly Hetty became at the start of the Season," Lucille said, a little crossly. "Of course, she is very young and I think her head was turned by all the attention she received, but I thought that once she had returned to the country she might regain some of her natural sense! But only today I have had a letter from her telling me that Lord Grantley is in Essex and paying her lavish attentions! And your brother is as bad, Polly, for instead of posting down to Kingsmarton to see Hetty and untangle matters he persists in staying in Town, and last night at Lady Coombes's ball he was paying the most outrageous attentions to Maria Leverstoke…''

''But I thought she was Lord Henry's flirt,'' Polly said, studiously picking an imaginary thread off Fanchon's latest confection, and politely avoiding a description of Lady Leverstoke that might have been more appropriate but less discreet.

Lucille made an airy gesture. ''That may be so, but she seemed smitten enough with Peter last night! He is become the most dreadful philanderer! You are for Lady Phillips's ridotto tonight, are you not? Only watch, and you will see just what I mean!''

Chapter Two

Lady Phillips's ridotto was one of the major social events of the Season, but already the June weather had turned hot, prompting some of the *ton* to leave London for their country estates or the cooling breezes of the seaside. Nevertheless, there was a great crush at the house in Berkeley Square and, even with the french windows flung wide open the temperature in the ballroom was enough to make the guests perspire unbecomingly.

Almost the first person Polly saw on entering the crowded reception room was Lord Henry Marchnight, lavishing his attentions in a thoroughly improper way on a lady in bright scarlet satin. Polly, trying to ignore the pang of misery that assailed her, considered that the colour of the lady's outfit was an all-too-appropriate choice.

"Lady Melton," hissed the Dowager Countess of Seagrave to her daughter, "married to his lordship but a twelvemonth ago and already driving him to his grave with her extravagance and her *affaires*! So Lady Phillips is letting the *demi-monde* patronise her ball! I should have expected her to exercise more judgement!''

Polly raised her brows. The Dowager Countess was very high in the instep and would never countenance such guests at one of her own events, but not all *ton* hostesses were as discerning. A moment later, Polly heard her mother give a stifled groan, halfway between a shriek and a moan, almost as though she were in pain. The Dowager Countess had stopped dead in the middle of the marbled floor.

Polly stopped too and turned enquiringly to her mother. ''Mama, are you quite well?''

''Yes, only look! No, not over there...over by that pillar! The strumpet!''

Startled, Polly turned to scan the room. There were plenty of faces she recognised, but none surely to give rise to such vehemence in the Dowager Countess's breast. Why, her mother had gone quite pale, though whether with shock, anger or illness it was impossible to tell. Then, she saw the reason.

''Good Lord—'' The exclamation had escaped before she could help herself.

''Polly, you will not take the name of the Lord in vain!'' the Dowager Countess said energetically. She seemed slightly restored by her daughter's inadvertent slip into blasphemy.

''Yes, Mama, I am sorry, but it is Peter and—''

''I am as capable as the next person of recognising your brother,'' the Dowager snapped. ''We cannot acknowledge him, however! Come this way! Thank God that Nicholas and Lucille are not present tonight! That brass-faced trollop is always trying to embarrass us!'' She took Polly's arm in a tight grip and positively pulled her towards the ballroom.

"I thought that Peter had taken up with Lady Leverstoke,'' Polly said, obediently allowing herself to be steered away with only one backward glance.

"Humph! I never thought to consider Maria Leverstoke as the lesser of two evils—'' The Dowager broke off to give a tight-lipped smile to one of her acquaintance. "On no account must you allow your brother to approach you,'' she continued, as they squeezed past the orchestra to appropriate two rout chairs in an inconspicuous corner. "It would be quite unacceptable!''

"Perhaps it would be easier for us to go home,'' Polly said, a little dispiritedly. It was bad enough to be confronted by the prospect of Lord Henry flirting all evening with some fast-looking matron, but the thought of avoiding her own brother seemed quite ridiculous. Here, however, she ran up against the Dowager Countess's stubborn streak.

"Go home! And have everyone say that that trollop has ousted us? Certainly not! Besides...'' the Dowager looked around surreptitiously "...I most particularly wish to see Agatha Calvert tonight! She has not been up in Town this age and we have so much to catch up on!''

"Surely Lady Calvert can call on you tomorrow—''

The Dowager Countess looked disgusted. "Have you no pride, Polly? I assure you that the Cyprian will not drive me away!''

Polly smiled slightly. She could see her brother Peter coming into the ballroom at that very moment, threatening to put his mother's resolution to the test. Lucille had mentioned Peter's sudden descent into questionable company, but even she had apparently been unaware of this latest disaster. For with Peter Seagrave was none other than Lucille's sister, the notorious Cyprian Susanna Bolt, in a dress of the most outrageous plunging black silk and ostrich feathers.

"Peter, what *can* you be doing!"

"Why, I'm talkin' to my own sister!" Lord Peter Seagrave said, with pardonable indignation. "What could be more suitable?"

"You know that is not what I meant!" Polly looked up at him with asperity, feeling her annoyance begin to melt at the limpid innocence in those dark Seagrave eyes. It was so very difficult to be angry with Peter for long. Whilst Polly and Nicholas had inherited something of their father's gravity, Peter had a gaiety and insouciance that was almost irresistible. "Oh, Peter, how could you squire Susanna Bolt about and embarrass Mama so?"

Peter looked affronted. "Mama ain't embarrassed by me! Why, she's nose to nose with Agatha Calvert and has barely noticed me!"

"Only because she has not seen Lady Calvert for an age!" Polly looked across to where the two matrons were chatting nineteen to the dozen. "I assure you, she would not have allowed me to even speak with you else! Supposing Lady Bolt approaches us?"

"Lady Bolt is almost one of the family," Peter added virtuously, but unable to repress a slight twinkle, "and I am sure Mama would not slight a relative!"

"Fustian!" Polly was also trying not to smile. "Oh, this is too bad of you, Peter! I dare swear it is not for the family connection that you have sought her company!"

"Careful, Poll!"

"Well, if you are setting Lady Bolt up as your *inamorata*—"

"Polly!"

"Oh, I collect that it is acceptable for a gentleman to have such a thing, but not for ladies to refer to her?" Polly frowned at her brother. "And if you try to tell me that Lady Bolt has become respectable since her marriage I will count you a greater fool than I already do! What of Hetty, Peter?"

The amusement went out of Peter Seagrave's face like a candle blown out. He studied the dancers with sudden intentness. "Miss Markham and I are no longer... That is, we have agreed that we would not suit."

"Oh, Peter!" Polly looked up at him, genuinely shocked. Peter swung gently back on his rout chair, feigning nonchalance.

"It was only last summer that you were bowled over by her," Polly added reproachfully.

"Miss Markham was a different girl last summer." Peter was looking both annoyed and upset now. "Unspoilt, sweet-natured... It took only six weeks in Town to turn her into the type of silly simpering debutante that I detest! Besides," he added bitterly, "she is after bigger game than me now!"

Polly was silent. She could hardly deny that Hetty

had behaved very foolishly, flirting with any titled
and personable man who had shown her attention
and treating Peter in a most offhand way. She put
her hand on her brother's arm.

"It is only that her head was turned a little," she
pleaded. "Please will you reconsider—"

"Peter, darling!"

Peter rose to his feet, a schoolboy blush in his
cheeks as Susanna Bolt put a gloved hand caressingly
on his shoulder. The Cyprian gave Polly an appraising look and her feline smile. "Lady Polly..."

"Lady Bolt," Polly said coldly. She marvelled at
how different two sisters could be. There was a clear
innocence about Lucille Seagrave which contrasted
starkly with the predatory sexuality of her twin. Lady
Bolt might have achieved a fragile respectability
through her recent marriage, Polly thought, but her
previous activities continued much as before, encouraged, some said, by Sir Edwin Bolt himself. Susanna's blue gaze, as hard as the diamonds she preferred, raked Polly and dismissed her as an unworthy
rival.

"Peter..." this time she trailed her fingers gently
down his shirtfront "...you promised me you would
play deep this evening..." The phrase was loaded
with so much innuendo that Peter Seagrave looked
acutely uncomfortable and his sister almost surprised
herself by giggling. Doubtless she should have felt
shocked, but Lady Bolt was so superlatively over-
dramatic that it was almost impossible to take her
seriously.

"Do not let me keep you from your entertainments, Peter," she said sweetly, and watched Su-

sanna steer her sheepish brother away towards the cardroom.

There was a quadrille in progress, but Polly had refused a number of requests to dance because it was so hot and she had felt disinclined to become even more heated and flustered. The Dowager Lady Seagrave had moved away temporarily to chat with Lady Calvert and a number of other senior matrons, and when she had seen Peter approach his sister she had not troubled herself to disturb them despite her earlier words. The Dowager knew that Polly had so much Town bronze that she need not trouble herself to chaperon her too closely. After all, apart from one regrettable incident five years ago, her daughter had never given her cause to worry. Nevertheless, she kept her firmly within eyesight.

Peter's rout chair was only vacant for a moment, then a voice said ingratiatingly, "Lady Polly! Vision of loveliness! I bring succour!"

Polly stifled a sigh.

"Sir Marmaduke. How do you do, sir?"

Sir Marmaduke Shipley gazed languishingly at her. An ageing roué, he was a gazetted fortune-hunter who liked to think that he was dangerous. A certain indulgent smile on the face of the Dowager Countess as she looked across at her daughter gave the lie to this. Sir Marmaduke handed Polly a glass and took the seat beside her with an ostentatious flick of his coattails.

The room was getting more and more humid and the drink was very welcome. Polly, who had been intending to be very chilly towards the lecherous Sir

Marmaduke, found herself smiling gratefully at him instead.

"What exquisite looks you are in tonight, my lady," Sir Marmaduke murmured, his breath hot against Polly's neck. "Dare I hope that you will smile on me?"

"I doubt it, sir!" Polly said smartly, taking a mouthful of the drink. It was certainly not lemonade, but it tasted rather pleasantly fruity and quite innocuous, light and refreshing for a summer night. She took another sip.

"Still so cruel, divine one?" Sir Marmaduke's dissolute gaze roved over her familiarly. Lady Polly Seagrave had never been an accredited beauty, but there was nevertheless something very alluring about her, he thought. Tonight, in the deep aquamarine which was rather daring for an unmarried lady, albeit one of more mature years than the debutantes, she looked particularly attractive. Her dark hair was upswept and restrained with a diamond studded slide but she wore no jewels other than a string of pearls that had the same translucent glow as her skin. She did not need adornment. Sir Marmaduke's eyes lingered in lascivious appreciation. Whilst the dragonish Dowager was fully occupied, he intended to take full advantage of this unexpected tête-à-tête.

Polly sighed again. She had far too much assurance to feel threatened by Sir Marmaduke's slimy overtures. In a crowded ballroom she was in no danger from him, other than of being bored to death by his unwelcome compliments.

"So your young brother has fallen for the lure," Sir Marmaduke said, abandoning flattery and pursu-

ing a more scandalous line. "Never did a lamb go
more happily to the slaughter! The *on-dit* is that the
lovely Susanna had a mind to take him away from
her foster sister, and what chance did Miss Markham's untried charms have against such a wealth of
experience?"

Polly was shocked, but tried not to show it. It had
not occurred to her that Peter's flirtation with Susanna Bolt was anything more than a coincidence.
She knew a little of Lady Bolt's activities, far more
in fact than her mother would have thought proper,
and now that she thought about it she remembered
hearing of more than one occasion when Susanna had
set out to destroy a couple's happiness. But her own
foster sister? It argued a particularly harsh and jeal-
ous nature.

"Indeed?" Polly murmured, refusing to rise to Sir
Marmaduke's bait. "I do not care for this conversation, sir."

"No?" Sir Marmaduke's gaze moved thoughtfully
to her empty glass and he summoned another full one
from a passing flunkey. "Your pardon, I was only
wishing to warn you of Lady Bolt's vicious nature."

"I should hope that her ladyship's diversions
would not affect me, sir."

"No?" Sir Marmaduke said again. There was a
look of malicious amusement in his eyes which made
Polly profoundly uncomfortable. "Perhaps not. You
will not be interested in the most piquant part of the
tale, then, which is that young Peter is her ladyship's
second choice, for she first set her sights on Lord
Henry Marchnight…"

For a moment Polly's dark gaze met Sir Marmaduke's, then she looked away. She took another mouthful of fruit punch without noticing. It was so easy to take refuge in her glass to avoid difficult subjects. And the drink was so refreshing and unusual. Normally she was only allowed lemonade, which, now she considered it, was ridiculous for one of her age and experience. The Dowager Countess was such a high stickler, Polly thought. Perhaps it was time she asserted her independence.

"Your squalid gossip is of no interest to me, sir," she said distantly, wishing that more congenial company would present itself. Unfortunately, Lady Seagrave was still chatting, glancing across at her daughter with unusual and misplaced satisfaction. It would take a brave soul to interrupt Sir Marmaduke now that he was so entrenched, Polly thought resignedly. As if to underline the point, the elderly baronet stretched his arm along the back of Polly's chair and leaned closer. His breath was stale with wine.

"Can I not please you?" Sir Marmaduke murmured. "When my sole intention is your delight, beauteous lady—"

"Your servant, Lady Polly. Shipley…"

Polly almost jumped. She felt a quiver of awareness along her nerves even before her hand was taken by Lord Henry Marchnight himself. Perhaps it was the drink, which she was now regarding suspiciously, or perhaps the effect of Lord Henry's presence, but she felt suddenly light-headed.

"I am persuaded," Lord Henry said gently, "that you would do so much better dancing with me, Lady Polly. Will you do me the honour?"

For a moment, as Polly's startled dark eyes met

Lord Henry's narrowed, lazy gaze, she had the oddest feeling that he knew she had been thinking of him. Various thoughts jostled for dominance in her mind. Her first was that Lord Henry never asked her to dance. How could he, when he seldom even spoke to her? The second thought was that this was a waltz and the Dowager Countess would not approve. The third was that she was feeling ever so slightly odd—not unpleasantly odd, but definitely a little adrift... Which no doubt explained how she came to be waltzing in Lord Henry's arms before she even had chance to think about it properly.

The lilt of the music was very seductive and Lord Henry was an exceptionally good dancer. After one circuit of the floor, Polly realized with some incredulity that she felt rather delightfully abandoned, like thistledown floating on air. Lord Henry was holding her at an entirely respectable distance from his body, but nevertheless the strength of his arm about her, the unfamiliar brush of his thigh against the slippery material of her dress, was peculiarly exciting. Polly blinked slightly, aware that she was not feeling quite normal, but the thought slid away, out of reach. Normal? She felt marvellous.

"You are keeping dangerous company tonight, Lady Polly," Lord Henry said in her ear. The thought of his lips so close to the sensitive skin of her neck sent a delicious shiver through Polly. She tried to pull herself together. What on earth was wrong with her this evening?

"Are all the Seagraves courting scandal?" Lord Henry continued. "First your brother sets himself up as Lady Bolt's new..." he hesitated "...new flirt, then you grant Sir Marmaduke Shipley a tête-à-tête and compound your daring by dancing with me!''

Polly looked up fully into his face for the first time. His words crystallised the thought which had entered her head when first he had whisked her from under Sir Marmaduke's nose. Sir Marmaduke liked to consider himself a rake, but Lord Henry was the really dangerous one, a marauding tiger loose amongst the innocent flock of debutantes. Whatever was she about, to be dancing with him with such abandonment? Across the dance floor, she could see that the Dowager Countess had finally finished her conversation and was glaring at her most meaningfully. Polly felt exasperated. Why had her mother not objected to the unwelcome attentions of the odious Sir Marmaduke and yet had immediately perceived Lord Henry's arrival? It was most unfair. She deliberately looked the other way.

Lucille had once said, without an iota of partiality, that Lord Henry Marchnight was the best-looking man that she had ever seen. Polly could certainly understand what she meant, for Lord Henry had the classical regularity of feature beloved of all sculptors and painters. His thick fair hair, immaculately ruffled in the Windswept style, made ladies long to run their fingers through it. The lazy appraisal of those grey eyes could, as one infatuated maiden declared, positively cause one to swoon, and his sporting pursuits had given him a physique envied by those less favoured.

''Are you really so dangerous then, sir?'' Polly heard herself say. Surely that could not be her voice, so light, so teasing? She never flirted!

"I am accounted dangerous, certainly." Lord Henry had given her a quizzical glance, no doubt as surprised by Polly's flirtatiousness as she was herself.

"A real tiger, then, not merely a pussycat?"

This time Lord Henry's look was rather more searching. "Have you been drinking the arrack punch, Lady Polly?"

"Certainly not." Polly said with dignified aplomb. "I had some delicious fruit cup, but what is that to the purpose, pray?"

"Ah, the fruit cup," Lord Henry murmured with a slight smile. "It is so refreshing, is it not? I see the Dowager Countess is looking daggers at us," he continued indolently. "I must shortly redeem myself in her eyes and return you to her unscathed!"

"Oh, no!" Polly had suddenly remembered that she had promised Lucille that she would speak to Lord Henry about a matter of importance. She frowned in concentration, trying to remember what exactly the issue had been. It was something potentially difficult…embarrassing…but she did not feel embarrassed at the moment, only marvellously liberated. Her mind was a little fuzzy at the edges, perhaps, but she had not felt this confident in a long time! It was a moment before she realised that Lord Henry was looking at her with amusement.

"I beg your pardon, Lady Polly?"

"No, do not take me back just yet, sir!" Polly tried to grasp the appropriate words. "I…there is a matter I need…*must* discuss with you!"

"Indeed!" A faint smile touched Lord Henry's firm mouth once more. "You intrigue me, madam! I am at your disposal, of course!"

The music was ending. Lord Henry gave her a mocking bow, taking her arm to escort her through the crowd and across to one of the silk-draped alcoves. It was sufficiently far from her mother to make Polly feel much more confident. She could deal with this matter without the Dowager Lady Seagrave even realising!

Lord Henry stood aside for her to sit down first, but she made no move to do so. He raised an eyebrow. "Well, Lady Polly? What is this urgent matter that demands our attention? Will you not sit down so that I may at least do the same?"

Polly discovered that her thought processes were suddenly beautifully clear.

"I meant," she said deliberately, "that I needed to speak to you in private. Not here. There are too many people about!"

This time, Lord Henry did not scruple to hide his surprise. "A somewhat equivocal remark, my lady!" he said, with an ironic inflection. "Are you sure that is what you mean? It seems most singular."

Polly frowned at him. She had no time for argument. All she was aware of was the single-minded need to fulfil her purpose.

"The terrace should suffice, my lord," she said briskly, turning towards the door and praying that he would follow. Out of the corner of her eye, she saw the Dowager Countess getting heavily to her feet. It was a long way around the dance floor and the room was crowded, but it would take a determined Mama seconds only to rescue her charge. Polly saw one of the Dowager Countess's acquaintance accost her and heaved a sigh of relief. Old Lady Odgers was notoriously chatty and would not be easy to shake off. She prayed that this would give her enough time.

The terrace was deeply shadowed and Polly purposefully made for the furthest corner, only turning back to Lord Henry when she had gained its seclusion. The cool evening air had helped to sober her a little, but she still felt remarkably buoyant and determined. Yet as soon as she opened her mouth the words seemed to desert her.

"I hoped...I wished...I wanted to say..." Suddenly it seemed incredibly difficult to frame the appropriate phrases. She had wanted to be so gracious, easily putting an end to five years' embarrassment. At this rate she would cause five years' more! And Lord Henry was not helping her, lounging against the parapet and watching her with the same thoughtful consideration he had already shown.

"Yes, ma'am? You have already implied that you had something of importance to impart to me. I should not be here else."

Polly's cheeks, already flushed with unaccustomed high colour from the punch, became even rosier. "Oh, you are the most odious man! I only wished to say that I wanted us to be friends!" Memory came to her aid. "I want us to be friends in future and I want us to be comfortable together!" she brought out, triumphantly. It had a reassuring sound, although comfortable was about the last thing Lord Henry made her feel. "And if you wish it too, then there is no bar—"

"Ah, but perhaps I do not." Lord Henry was smiling a little now, for he knew that certain suspicions he had harboured about Lady Polly's lack of sobriety had been confirmed. She was not drunk, precisely, he thought, but she was not perfectly sober. And she was evidently too innocent to have realised her state. Or her danger.

"Oh!" Polly had anticipated his compliance and there was no doubt that this refusal to conform had thrown her plans. Lord Henry watched in amusement as she tried to puzzle it out. With her tumbled curls, pink cheeks and bright eyes, she looked wholly enchanting. He felt a certain impulse stir in him and tried half-heartedly to stifle it. He straightened up and took a step closer to her. Polly did not appear to notice.

"Well, if you do not care to be comfortable with me—"

"No, ma'am." Lord Henry was still immaculately polite, even as he calculated, quite coldly, what he was about to do. "Comfortable is not a word I could ever apply to our situation."

"Then—" Polly was at a loss. "If you do not wish us to be friends, what...?"

Lord Henry made a slight, dismissive gesture. "What could a rake wish for from a lady on a providentially empty terrace?"

"Oh!"

Understanding came to Polly at the very last moment, but her head still felt as though it was stuffed with wool. Time seemed to pass very slowly. Indeed, she had time to reflect that she had never been kissed by a man, since she had always been exceptionally careful to avoid being alone with any gentleman who was not a relative. Then she remembered that when she had been in the throes of her infatuation, she had quite ached for Lord Henry to kiss her as long as it had been in a completely undemanding fashion. Some chaste but impassioned salutation had been the height of her aspirations.

This kiss might have been impassioned, but in no way could it be described as chaste. Lord Henry's arm slid about Polly's waist and brought her into sudden, shocking contact with his body. His mouth captured hers with the ruthless skill of the expert, parting her lips so that her gasp of outrage was lost. For several long, spellbinding seconds, Polly was swept up in a passion too complex and demanding for her even to begin to resist.

Lord Henry let her go very gently and Polly stared at him in silence. The combined effects of unaccustomed drink and strong emotion made her feel quite shaken and she put a hand onto the parapet to steady herself. The stone was cool beneath her fingers, already damp with the night's dew. Polly frowned a little, confused. How could this have happened when she had intended so different an outcome? Then, utterly unexpectedly, Lord Henry took her hand and pressed a kiss on the palm.

"Do not look at me so reproachfully, Lady Polly," he said quietly. "Remember that you took your part in making me what I am."

He turned to go and was confronted once again by the Dowager Countess of Seagrave, rushing precipitately to the rescue. He gave her a most flawless, ironic bow.

"Lady Seagrave! How do you do, ma'am? I remember once telling you that I would never approach your daughter again. Alas that I am forced to contradict myself, for I find I have a most urgent need to make her reacquaintance! Your servant, ma'am!''

And he left the outraged Dowager spluttering for words.

Chapter Three

Polly woke up with the conviction that something was terribly wrong. Her head ached with an unaccustomed thick throbbing and her tongue felt furry. She rolled on to her back. The sun was streaming through the curtains and she could hear the sound of wheels in the street outside. It was late.

Through the woolly feeling in her head, Polly remembered the fruit punch, so apparently innocuous and yet so dangerous. Oh, how could she have been such a fool, she who had been out for five years! Drinking spirits, becoming flirtatious, crowning her folly with a drunken encounter on the terrace with Lord Henry Marchnight! No doubt he thought her the most unutterable fool! She squirmed, turning her hot face into the cool linen pillow in an attempt to wipe out the vivid memories which were flooding back.

''I've tried to wake her once already, my lady,'' a voice was saying, and Polly shot bolt upright, suddenly terrified that her mother was at the door. But it was only Lucille, who came into the room and pulled back the bedcurtains with a resounding rasp that echoed through Polly's head.

"Oh! Do not!" Polly's groan was heartfelt. She slumped back on the pillows, feeling dizzy. Her sister-in-law paused in surprise.

"Polly? Are you ill? I thought that you were coming with me to Lady Routledge's picnic?"

The light was making Polly's eyes stream. She squinted at Lucille through the brightness. There was a rhythmic pounding in her ears although she had no recollection of any major building works currently taking place on the house. "Oh dear...I think I may be sick..."

"If I did not know better, I should say that you were foxed," Lucille was saying severely, eyeing her sister-in-law closely. "I had no idea that Lady Phillips's ridotto had been such a hotbed of iniquity! Or was it the prawn patties you ate, perhaps? Yes, so much better for it to be the prawns, I think... That is what I shall tell your Mama. I will come and see you later..."

Polly was beyond replying. She turned over and was asleep again at once.

It was the afternoon when she awoke again, feeling marginally better.

"Lady Seagrave said that I wasn't to disturb you on account of you being so sick, ma'am," Polly's maid said sympathetically, when summoned at last by the bell. "Can I fetch you anything, ma'am? Some food?"

A spasm of distaste crossed Polly's face. "I think not, Jessie. Just a very large glass of water, if you please. I have seldom been so thirsty! And I shall get up now, I think.''

Jessie looked dubious. "Well, ma'am, if you're sure you're ready! My brother usually takes a day to sleep off his excesses..." She caught Polly's outraged expression and dropped a submissive curtsy. A country girl from the Seagraves' Suffolk estate, Jessie had a kind heart but no tact. "As you wish, ma'am!" she finished hastily. "Shall you be going out?"

"Yes!" Polly snapped, suddenly anxious to refute the suggestion that she was a drunkard to rival Jessie's brother. "We shall go·to the circulating library! My lilac walking dress, please!"

Half an hour later, attired in the lilac and lace dress and with a very becoming black straw bonnet on her dark curls, Polly sallied forth into the fresh air with Jessie trotting along behind. Lucille and the Dowager Countess had not returned from the picnic, but Polly thought it unlikely her mother could object to so innocuous a plan as a trip to the library. After all, no possible harm could befall her there.

It was pleasantly cool within and Polly spent an enjoyable time browsing amongst the shelves and choosing her books. There was something very soothing about the shadowy quiet of the library, something tranquil when Polly still felt a little disordered in both body and spirit. An elderly gentleman was dozing in a seat in the corner and two ladies were whispering together over a copy of Louisa Sidney Stanhope's *The Confessional of Valombre*. There was nothing to disturb the peace. Polly leant forward to pull a book from the shelf and found herself looking into a pair of sleepy grey eyes as someone selected a book from the other side at precisely the same moment as she.

"Oh!" She dropped all her books and recoiled a step, causing the two ladies to break off their conversation and hush her noisily. The gentleman came around the end of the bookcase, bent down and gravely handed her back the books of her choice.

"Good afternoon, Lady Polly," Lord Henry Marchnight said.

"What are you doing here?" Polly hissed crossly, forgetful of the fact that only hours earlier she had privately resolved never to speak to him again. He was looking immaculate in a dove-grey jacket which echoed the colour of those disturbing grey eyes and Polly felt both annoyed and ill prepared to meet him. If only she had stayed at home! The scene on Lady Phillips's terrace flashed before her eyes once more, adding to her confusion. It was the greatest piece of bad luck to be obliged to face him again so soon.

Lord Henry gestured to the two slender volumes under his arm. "Like you, I am selecting some reading matter," he said calmly. "A gentleman may attend the circulating library if he wishes!"

"Yes, but I would hardly have considered reading to be amongst your favoured occupations—" Polly bit her lip, aware that her confusion had prompted her to sound less than civil. "I beg your pardon, I only meant that I imagined you had other interests—" Again she broke off. That sounded even worse!

Lord Henry smiled, showing her the books. "Allow me to astound you then, ma'am! I have here Coleridge's *Biographica Literaria* and some Homer, which I have not read since I was in short coats! I assure you, I am far more erudite than you think me!''

Polly blinked, unable to refute the evidence of her eyes. It seemed singular that a man whose self-proclaimed aim in life was enjoyment to the point of dissipation should sit in alone with only his books for company.

''I am so glad to see you restored to health,'' Lord Henry continued smoothly. ''I was at Lady Rout-ledge's picnic earlier and your sister-in-law intimated that you had been taken ill after the ball last night. Something you ate—or drank, perhaps?''

Polly could feel herself blushing with vexation. The last thing that she wanted was to be reminded of the previous evening and Lord Henry's scandalous behaviour.

''I am quite recovered now, I thank you,'' she said stiffly. ''Good day, sir. I must be on my way home for we are promised for the theatre this evening.''

''Perhaps I may escort you back to Brook Street?'' Lord Henry suggested politely.

He held the door for her as she went out into the sunny street. It was tempting to accept his offer, but since Polly was still smarting with mortification over her behaviour the night before, Lord Henry's contin-ued presence could only be a dangerous reminder. She gave him a smile behind which her regret was imperfectly hidden.

''Thank you, sir, but I think not. I have my maid with me for company and it is not far to home.''

"I am disappointed, ma'am," Lord Henry said, falling into step beside her as though she had not spoken. "Are we not pledged to a better understanding? How may that be achieved if you refuse my company?"

"Pledged to a better understanding?" Polly stopped and stared up at him. The summer breeze was ruffling his thick fair hair and she stifled a sudden urge to touch it. She realised that she was still staring. Hastily, she started walking again.

"Why, yes." Somehow Lord Henry had taken her arm without her noticing. It seemed churlish to draw away from him. "We are to be friends, remember? You suggested it last night!"

"Friends!" Polly almost tripped up with shock and his hand tightened momentarily on her arm, sending all sorts of strange but delicious sensations through her body.

"Yes, of course you must remember! We were on the terrace—"

"Yes!" Polly squeaked, convinced he was about to remind her of every searing detail. She took a deep breath. "Of course I remember our conversation, sir. I had the particular impression, however, that you did not care for my suggestion!"

Lord Henry turned to look at her. It was a distinctly speculative look. "You did not find my response to you...friendly?"

Polly blushed with indignation. "I did not, my lord! Presumptuous, outrageous, but scarcely friendly!"

Lord Henry's shoulders were shaking with suppressed laughter. "Come now, Lady Polly! You are severe! Was my company so repulsive to you?"

Polly was in a dilemma. Modesty required her to lie but she had been brought up to be exceptionally truthful.

"Your behaviour was not that of a gentleman, sir!"

"Ah, true!" Lord Henry smiled whimsically. "But I find myself rather taken by your proposal, Lady Polly. I have an ardent desire to promote our friendship. Our encounter last night whetted my appetite for it!"

They had reached Brook Street, which was fortunate since Polly was utterly unable to think of a suitable response. Lord Henry kissed her hand. "If you wish to be persuaded further of my erudition, perhaps you might wish to join me in St James's Square? I have an excellent art collection which you might like to view…" His glance was wicked. "Unless you are already convinced of my scholarship and good taste?"

"I will accept your word on it," Polly said, still trying to be severe though tempted to giggle. "Good day, sir!"

Art collection, indeed! Polly blushed a little as she considered the implications of his teasing invitation. He must consider her a green girl to be caught by that one! Lord Henry grinned and strolled off down the street, with just one provocative look back. Polly was annoyed that he had caught her looking after him.

"There's a likely gentleman," Jessie opined, looking over Polly's shoulder. "Aye, and a dangerous one, too! You be careful, madam!"

Polly, who had been thinking exactly the same thing, turned away with studied indifference. "Oh, nonsense, Jessie! Lord Henry is just a flirt!"

"A flirt!" Jessie was indignant. "A rake, more to the point! Aye, and you like it, madam!"

Polly did not deign to reply.

As she dressed for the theatre that evening, she repressed a little shiver of excitement and apprehension at the possibility of seeing Lord Henry again. It seemed that her behaviour the previous night had, entirely unexpectedly, caught his interest. But his attentions could never be anything other than dishonourable, and as a result of her own actions he was now pursuing her in a wholly improper way.

The play that night was the farce *The Devil to Pay*, and the company was a merry one. Nicholas and Lucille Seagrave, the Dowager Countess and Polly, made up a party with Sir Godfrey Orbison and his cousins the Dacres. There was a vast number of their acquaintance at Drury Lane that night and the Dowager Countess spent an entertaining time leaning over the side of their box and identifying members of the fashionable crowd. When she saw Lucille's twin sister Susanna Bolt on the arm of a distinguished-looking gentleman of military bearing, she dug Lady Dacre in the ribs.

"Do look, Marianne! There is the Duke of Garston making a fool of himself over the Cyprian! Only see how she preens and pouts! Lord, what is it about these worthy gentlemen that makes them such easy meat for her?''

Fortunately, Lucille was engrossed in conversation with Nicholas and Lord Dacre and did not hear, but Polly leant forward curiously. Susanna Bolt was looking very striking again, she thought, in her bold and flaunting style. There were jewels glittering in her hair and her mouth was a deep, curving red as she smiled triumphantly over her conquest. The sapphire blue eyes which appraised the crowd were the exact shade of Lucille's but there the resemblance finished, for the Countess of Seagrave had such a sweetness of character and bearing that it softened every feature that Susanna's avarice had turned hard.

Polly sighed, just a little envious of Susanna's bold beauty. She knew that her own looks were pleasant enough, although she had never been considered an Incomparable. The Seagrave colouring of chestnut hair and dark brown eyes flecked with gold seemed to suit her brothers better, although her creamy complexion was much admired. And her figure was trim rather than voluptuous, which the gentlemen seemed to prefer. Polly wondered idly whether Susanna's appearance on Garston's arm indicated that her brief interest in Peter was over or whether she was just being naïve to imagine the Cyprian confining herself to one man at a time.

''Polly!'' the Dowager Countess said sharply, as a young buck raised his quizzing glass to ogle her daughter. ''Kindly sit back! You do not wish to attract the attention of the *hoi polloi*!''

Polly's heart skipped a beat and she sat back slowly, for she had just seen Lord Henry Marchnight in a box across from them. He was in a lively group with Simon Verey, his wife Therese and some of their friends, all laughing animatedly at a remark Lady Verey had just made. Polly felt a quiver of envy and repressed it quickly. It was not that she was bored with her own party, for she always enjoyed Lucille's company and the Misses Dacre were pleasant enough, if henwitted. Just for once, however, it would be fun to be part of a racier crowd. She was forever being chaperoned about by her mother or some other elderly female relative, which was all very well for a new debutante but decidedly slow for a lady of twenty-three. She risked another look across at the box, to find that Lord Henry was studying her with a concentrated regard which made her pulse beat faster.

The play began, but Polly found it incredibly difficult to concentrate. Normally she became engrossed in a performance, for playgoing was one of her favourite entertainments, but tonight all she seemed able to think about was whether Lord Henry was serious in his pursuit and whether she should respond. On the one hand, he could not have any serious intention and since her feelings were already engaged—and had been so for five years—she would be only stirring up all the old emotions that she should be trying to forget. On the other hand, she could not deny that she derived immense enjoyment from his company. If she managed matters well, perhaps... But could she manage Lord Henry? It would be very dangerous...a challenge, then? No, a risk and a hazardous one at that. Foolish even to consider it, knowing his reputation. But... Polly shivered. A risk worth taking? She had found the Season dull, repetitious. She wanted some excitement... The prim side of her character, the orthodox side, was asking her what on earth she was thinking of, to encourage the attentions of so notorious a rake.

There was a burst of applause, and Polly realised to her horror that the entire first act had passed without her even noticing. The audience started to chatter, to mill around and stretch their legs before the second act. Lucille took Polly's arm as they strolled out with everyone else.

"What do you think of Venn's performance, Polly? Is he as accomplished as Edmund Keen, do you think?"

Polly floundered. "Well, perhaps so... Or perhaps not... I need more time to consider—" She broke off as Lord Henry and the Vereys approached, and was not sure whether to be glad or nervous at the interruption.

Lord Henry greeted Lucille very warmly, and once again Polly felt a stirring of jealousy when she considered their friendship. She was not unsophisticated enough to think that just because Lord Henry had suddenly paid some attention to her, he might not be pursuing other interests. But surely Lucille could not rank as one of those! There was an innocence about the Countess of Seagrave which made such a thought seem foolish. Besides, Lucille had now turned her attention to the Vereys, leaving Polly and Lord Henry standing together.

"Are you enjoying the play, Lady Polly?" Lord Henry asked conventionally enough as they strolled down the corridor.

"Yes, thank you, my lord." Polly was desperately hoping that he would not question her too closely about it.

"You always enjoyed the theatre, did you not?" Lord Henry said with a smile. "You are not one of those who come only to see and be seen! I remember when we came to see *As You Like It*, you were so enraptured that no one could get a word from you for a full half-hour afterwards!"

Polly blushed. She could remember the occasion to which he referred and the memory troubled her. It had been very early on in their acquaintance, when she was first out, and she had sat through the play in a dream. Although utterly engrossed in the story, she had still been fully aware of Lord Henry sitting slightly behind her, his attention as much on her as it was on the play. He had leant forward, smiling at her enthusiasm, and it had seemed to Polly that his enjoyment had derived as much from her pleasure as from the entertainment.

The bell rang for the second act, saving her the necessity of reply.

"A moment, Lady Polly," Lord Henry said, when she would have excused herself and returned to the box. "Will you drive with me in the park tomorrow?"

Polly stood still, jostled by those returning to their seats.

"Surely not an unusual request?" Lord Henry said gently, with a smile that made her heart race. "You must be inundated by gentlemen asking to escort you!"

"Yes, but not by you—" Polly stopped herself.

"I beg your pardon. What I meant was that you never take a lady up in your phaeton!"

"Not often," Lord Henry amended, with the same disconcerting smile. "I am, however, accomplished enough as a whip to make the offer!"

Polly knew he was being deliberately obtuse. It was not his skill that was in question but the fact that it would cause a storm of comment if he took her up. Lord Henry handed her back into the box as the lights went down.

"I will see you tomorrow at five," he murmured, taking her acquiescence for granted, and was gone. Polly saw him slide into his seat in the box opposite and incline his head as he saw her watching. She was annoyed that he had caught her looking at him yet again, rather than at the play.

Chapter Four

"Well, I think it is a famous thing that you and Harry are now such good friends," Lucille Seagrave declared at breakfast, when Polly shyly confided that Lord Henry was to take her driving that afternoon.

"I do not think Mama will view it in quite the same light, Lucille," Polly said gloomily. The Dowager Countess had been almost apoplectic on finding her only daughter alone on the terrace at Lady Phillips's with the most notorious rake in Town. Polly's repeated statement that she and Lord Henry had only been talking together had met with short shrift. Not only did the Dowager disbelieve her but she had some pungent words to say about young ladies who decided to *talk* alone with rakehells.

A moment later, the Dowager swished bad-temperedly into the breakfast room and eyed her daughter and daughter-in-law with disfavour.

"What are you two whispering about?" she demanded querulously. She asked for a plate of kedgeree then picked at it so disagreeably that Polly's heart sank. She could already tell that the Dowager

Countess had a headache, induced by her late night at the theatre, and would be in a bad mood.

"I was telling Lucille that Lord Henry Marchnight is to take me driving this afternooon," she said, rather defiantly. "He is to collect me at five."

The Dowager flushed an unbecoming puce.

"Driving? With Lord Henry Marchnight? Have you taken leave of your senses, miss? Why, the man's unsafe!"

"As a whip or as a man?" Nicholas Seagrave enquired lazily, rustling his newspaper. He had given no indication that he had been listening to the previous conversation, but now Polly saw the look of amusement in her brother's dark eyes and her heart sank still further. If Nicholas objected as well, the trip was as good as ruined. Lucille gave her husband a reproving glance.

"I am persuaded that nothing so very dreadful can happen in the park, ma'am," she said mildly to her mother-in-law. "There will be plenty of people about, after all."

The Dowager cast her a darkling look. "You have no idea of what that man is capable, Lucille! And it is not simply the risk to Polly's person, but the damage to her reputation! If she is seen in company with him, all claim to respectability would be lost—"

"Oh, come, Mama, you are making too much of this," Nicholas interrupted. "Harry Marchnight is a good enough fellow! He will not do anything to injure Polly's good name! I say she should go!"

He folded his paper up a little irritably, got up, bent to kiss his wife and murmured that he was taking refuge in his bookroom.

"Some honey in your tea, ma'am?" Lucille said hastily, seeing her mother-in-law glare at Seagrave's departing back. "You know that it is very soothing for the headache."

The Dowager Countess smiled reluctantly. She was very fond of her unconventional daughter-in-law.

"Thank you, Lucille. It is good to know that you have so much concern for my health when my own brood seem set on tormenting me! Now, will you be accompanying me to Mrs Manbury's this afternoon? I realise that Polly—" she glared again "—will be otherwise engaged!"

Polly was to remember Seagrave's unlikely championing and her mother's reluctant acquiescence later, when she was ensconced in Lord Henry's perch phaeton and they were bowling along under the trees. They were attracting a great deal of attention from the fashionable crowds who had come to take the air and Polly had begun to wish that she had taken her mother's advice. She felt uncomfortable as the focus of so much speculative interest. Nor did Lord Henry stop to greet his acquaintance, but concentrated his attention solely on her. Polly thought she should have been flattered. Instead, such single-minded attention was beginning to make her nervous. She was suddenly unsure where it was leading—or where it might end.

And yet Lord Henry's conversation was unexceptionable. Surely she had nothing to fear.

"Are you enjoying the Season?" he enquired, expertly avoiding an oncoming vehicle which was be-

ing driven with considerably less skill and more way-
wardness than his own. "Do you like London?"

Polly relaxed slightly. It was most enjoyable to be
out in the fresh air, for it was another sunny day with
a cool breeze and to be driven with such expertise
was a real pleasure.

"Are those not two entirely separate questions, my
lord?" she queried with a smile. "I have found the
Season a little flat this year, but yes, I like London
a great deal, for there are so many beautiful buildings
and interesting sights to observe. There, will that
do?"

Lord Henry took his eyes off the road for long
enough to give her an amused glance. "Most com-
prehensively answered, my lady, but with little real
information given! Why has the Season been so tedious for you?"

Polly shrugged a little uncomfortably, regretting
her flippancy. She had no desire to sound like a spoilt
Society miss. "Well, the round of parties and balls
and entertainments is much like it was last time. Perhaps I am becoming a little jaded after all these
years—"

Lord Henry burst out laughing. "Yes, you have a
great many years in your dish, ma'am!" He lowered
his voice. "Perhaps it is just that you need a change
of scene? Do you go to Brighton in the summer?"

Polly nodded without much enthusiasm. "We do.
But it is the same people and the same diversions!"
She brightened. "I love the sea though, and find the
air most refreshing. I don't know why I should not
be looking forward to it..." Her voice trailed away.
She was regretting telling him of her boredom with

the endless, superficial round of society events, for it sounded as though she were simply complaining.

"Perhaps you prefer the country?" Lord Henry was saying thoughtfully. "Suffolk is a beautiful place to be. You seemed very happy at Dillingham last year."

"Yes..." Polly smiled "...I love Dillingham. I can ride, and paint and walk and please myself..."

Lord Henry flashed her another smile. "So you are a rebel at heart, Lady Polly! You wish to please yourself rather than follow the fashion!"

It was an appealing concept. "Gentlemen are more fortunate when it comes to such matters," Polly observed judiciously. "You may do as you please, but we are watched over and instructed and restricted... And if we marry, the tyranny of our parents is exchanged for the tyranny of a husband!" Filled with a sudden sense of absurdity at her own words, she started to laugh.

"I wondered whether that was why you had never married," Lord Henry said quietly. "Is that the reason, ma'am? That you had no wish to exchange a circumscribed girlhood for an equally restrictive marriage?"

Polly's laughter faded and she fell silent. The only sound was the noise of the phaeton's wheels and the cooing of the doves in the shady trees.

"No," she said slowly, "that was not the reason that I have never married."

"Then will you tell me what it is?" They had reached a quiet stretch of the road and Lord Henry was allowing his team to slow down while he concentrated on her. Their eyes met for a split second of tension.

"No," Polly said again, half-lightly, half in earnest, "I shall not, sir! You have no right to ask so leading a question on so small an acquaintance!"

She saw Lord Henry smile as he accepted her refusal and allowed her to retreat.

"I protest," he said easily. "I have known you for years, ma'am, yet you insist we are as strangers!"

"We may have been acquainted for years," Polly agreed, equally casually, "but for most of that time you have been away, sir, travelling or entertaining yourself…" She frowned as it occurred to her that she did not actually know what it was that had taken Lord Henry away so often. Society whispered that it was scandal—women, gambling, racing—but no one actually knew…

"Very true, ma'am," Lord Henry agreed, clearly unprepared to enlighten her further. "Like you, I find Society stifling if I spend too long in its company! I have noticed a change in London lately. Oh, the *ton* enjoy themselves as much as before, with as many outrageous amusements as they can devise, but the rest of the populace is not as tolerant as it used to be!"

Polly knew what he meant. There were so many of the dispossessed on the streets, looking resentfully as the rich and fashionable passed by, so many men who had served their country at war and now had no occupation in peace time. There were many who preached against the accepted order and agitated for change and some who would be prepared to resort to violence to get it.

"There is a sort of anger about the city at times," Polly agreed, shivering in the cool air. "I sometimes wonder how long things can stay unchanged…"

"Melancholy thoughts for so bright a day," Lord Henry observed. "My apologies for striking a discordant note. Why, look, is that not your esteemed relative Lady Bolt, over there? Your brother will be desolate that she has found a richer man in the Duke of Garston!"

"Oh, dear!" Polly looked across to the approaching curricle, where Lady Bolt was arrayed in a dress of scarlet silk entirely unsuitable for an afternoon's drive. A hat adorned with curling ostrich plumes framed her face. Polly felt both dowdy and insignificant in comparison.

"Henry!" Lady Bolt was hailing them now, with more familiarity than Polly liked to see. "How delightful to see you! Why—" her eye fell on Polly in amused scorn "—hardly your usual taste, my dear? So sweet and tediously dull!"

Polly flushed with anger and mortification. It would have been impossible to miss Lady Bolt since the two carriages had to pass each other, and as she and Henry had slowed down to talk, the Cyprian had come upon them almost unawares. Nevertheless it was unfortunate. The Dowager Countess would have a fit if she heard of the meeting, and as for Lady Bolt's barbed insults, it strained Polly's natural courtesy to accept them without retaliation.

"How do you do, Lady Bolt." Lord Henry spoke very coldly. "I fear I was so engrossed in Lady Polly's delightful company that I missed your approach! Good day, ma'am!'' And he gave the horses the office to move off.

''Oh, dear,'' Polly said again, when the infuriated Cyprian had been left behind, ''it is so very difficult! Lucille is so charming and her sister so much her opposite! I would not for all the world cut her dead, but—''

''But you have little choice,'' Lord Henry said grimly. ''Society dictates that a lady such as yourself should not even know what Lady Bolt is, let alone speak to her—as well you know, ma'am!''

''Yes, but—'' Polly was a kind girl; although she detested Susanna Bolt's nature, she could not help but feel uncomfortable. ''Lucille once said that they were both obliged to find the means to support themselves, and Susanna chose one course and Lucille another! It is easy to judge when one has not had to make such a choice!''

''You are all generosity, Lady Polly!'' Polly knew Lord Henry was laughing at her, albeit somewhat ruefully. ''Console yourself with the fact that Susanna Bolt is a harpy and you will then feel no need to sympathize with her!''

''You seem to know her very well,'' Polly said unguardedly, piqued by his amusement.

''I know her type,'' Lord Henry conceded. They turned through the park gates and back towards Brook Street. ''I am happy to continue this entirely improper conversation,'' he added, ''but only if you are willing to admit to being its instigator! I will not take the blame for discussing matters unsuitable for a lady's ears!''

''Society can be very foolish,'' Polly said crossly,

"dictating what a lady may and may not do, or hear, or say! It puts me out of all patience!"

The phaeton stopped and Lord Henry jumped lightly down, holding out a hand to help Polly descend. He did not allow their bodies to touch as he swung her to the ground, nor did he hold on to her hand for longer than was strictly necessary. Polly found herself disappointed. For some reason the drive had ended on an unsatisfactory note. Polly was inclined to blame Lady Bolt's interruption, although honesty prompted her that this was not really true. It seemed that she was dissatisfied when Lord Henry behaved properly and nervous when he did not. Flirtation was clearly not a game she could play with anywhere near Lord Henry's aplomb.

The flower cart arrived early in Brook Street the following day, bringing a beautiful posy of pale pink roses for Polly and a card from Lord Henry saying that he had been called unexpectedly from Town, but hoped to see her again shortly. Polly did not even attempt to hide her pleasure in the gift, merely burying her face in the soft fragrant petals when Jessie made pointed comments about fine gentlemen and pretty gestures.

The days of Lord Henry's absence crept by. There were only a few weeks of the Season left to run and the weather had turned very hot. The Dowager Countess became quite peevish when her ankles swelled up in the heat. She declined to accompany Polly and the Dacres on a sightseeing trip to St Paul's Cathedral and when her daughter returned enervated and exhausted, told her that she had known the weather had been too inclement for a trip out. She fretted over Peter's absence and when he did call, upbraided him for his foolishness in still running after Susanna Bolt. The servants all became very bad-tempered as they went about their work, and the house in Brook Street became a somewhat uncomfortable place to live.

"Everyone is so cross at the moment," Polly sighed to Lucille, after Jessie had grumbled ceaselessly over her decision to change her chosen dress for a *soirée* one night. "Have you noticed how the heat makes people quicker-tempered? It's very strange. Thank goodness there is to be no dancing tonight! I feel sure we should all melt into a puddle!"

Lucille fanned herself vigorously. "I hear that there were riots in The Strand last night," she said, frowning. "Some windows were smashed and shops looted. I am sure that this weather can only add to people's grievances. I shall ask Nicholas to give all the servants a day off on Saturday, and perhaps we may all go out of Town to somewhere cooler. Hampstead Wells, perhaps? A walk on the Heath might be quite refreshing."

Even the Dowager Countess agreed to the proposed trip, feeling that the village air would be less noxious than that in London. The day was sunny but not too hot and they spent a most enjoyable few hours strolling on the Heath, playing bowls, and taking the waters at the spa. Polly declared the water so unpleasant that she needed a cup of tea to wash away the taste, so they retired to one of the honeysuckle-covered tea arbours for further refreshment.

"Oh, do let us stay a little longer," Lucille urged, catching sight of a sign which promised a concert in the pump-room that evening, followed by fireworks. "There are plenty more of the gardens and grottoes to explore and it would be such fun to stay for the evening's entertainments!"

The light was fading when the concert finished and they came out on to the Heath for the firework display. It was busy and many of the benches on the edge of the hill were already full.

"Heavens, what a crush!" The Dowager Countess exclaimed. "I had no idea that the whole of Town would have come out for this! Let us walk a little way along and see if we can find any seats!"

Polly was dawdling along behind the others, pulling her velvet cloak closer, for the evening was cool now that the sun had gone. A florid gentleman and large lady, amorously entwined, bumped into her and almost sent her flying without noticing. Polly stumbled. The first of the rockets soared into the sky above her and scattered a trail of bright stars. Suddenly it was very dark and she could not see the others at all. The crowd pressed about her; ladies, gentlemen, servants, tradesmen, cits and people of quite another sort.

A voice said: "All alone, lady? Let me take care of you!" He was young and attired as a gentleman, but Polly knew him to be no such thing. He was also drunk. And as she looked around wildly for her family, he took her arm.

"Your help will not be necessary, sir," a voice said smoothly, from behind her. "The lady is with me, but I am grateful to you for your consideration."

Polly recognised the voice even before she swung around to see Lord Henry Marchnight standing so protectively close to her. Something in his demeanour also communicated itself to the man who had accosted her, for he mumbled something about meaning no harm, and stumbled away. Lord Henry watched him go with a slight smile then turned his attention back to Polly.

"Tell me, Lady Polly," he said conversationally, steering her out of the crowd to the edge of the path, "is this part of your claim for independence, to wander alone on Hampstead Heath in the dark? It seems rather foolhardy!"

"Don't be absurd!" Polly snapped. Reaction was setting in now and she was horrified at what had almost happened to her. "I have become separated from my party, that is all! We were looking for seats for the fireworks—" Another rocket soared overhead as though to illustrate her point.

"Well, they could be anywhere now," Lord Henry said resignedly, looking at the crowds. "It will be best for me to escort you back to your carriage, I think. They should have no trouble in finding you there. Is Seagrave here with you?"

Polly nodded.

"Thank God. He at least will have the sense to keep the others calm and search for you in a sensible fashion! Now, if we go down this path it should take us to the Well Walk. Did you leave your carriage there?"

Polly nodded unhappily. She knew that the Dowager Countess would be beside herself with worry and could not but regret spoiling the end of such a lovely day.

"We were having such a nice time," she said regretfully. "I am sorry that it has had to end this way."

It was very dark down the steep little passage that led to the street where the carriages were waiting. The scent of honeysuckle still hung in the air and the stars arched above them. Polly, trying to find her way in the dark, suddenly remembered that she had not even thanked Lord Henry for rescuing her.

"I am sorry," she said in a small voice, "I should have thanked you. Your arrival was most timely, my lord. I hope that I have not taken you away from your friends?"

"I am here alone," Lord Henry said, sounding preoccupied. "It is comforting to think that you feel safer with me than with that ruffian!"

This was an aspect of the situation that had not occurred to Polly at all. She stopped in an arched doorway. It was not possible to see Lord Henry's face in the pale light. "Oh, I never even thought—" she said, uncertainly.

"Perhaps you should have done." Lord Henry sounded grim. "You were flatteringly quick to entrust yourself to me, but my reputation is scarce such that a young lady should consider taking a walk in the dark with me!"

"Well!" Polly had had time to become indignant. "I think it most unfair of you to ring a peal over me for trusting you, sir! I had little choice but to consider you the lesser of two evils!"

She heard Lord Henry laugh at that. "Better the

devil you know?'' His shoulder brushed a spray of honeysuckle and released fresh scent into the air. He was very close and Polly suddenly became intensely aware of his physical presence. Her throat felt constricted.

''Besides...'' she was clutching at straws now ''...on the last occasion that we met, sir, you behaved with perfect propriety! It led me to believe that what I had heard of you was grossly exaggerated—''

She had taken a cautious step forward as she spoke, missed her footing on a step, and felt Lord Henry's arms go around her to steady her.

''You misjudged me,'' Lord Henry said with satisfaction, ''and this, Lady Polly, is where I have been wanting you ever since I saw you this evening.''

The dark night was intimate and warm. Polly felt curiously anonymous, as though she could say anything, do anything, without it really mattering. She did not try to break away from him, but stood in the circle of his arms, their bodies touching lightly. In the silence she could hear him breathing.

She raised her mouth to Henry's, waiting in a fever of anticipation for the gentle persuasiveness of his first kiss to deepen into passion. She pressed herself against him, entwining her arms about his neck to hold him close. He was keeping his kisses frustratingly light, but when Polly slid her hands into his hair she heard him groan and his mouth returned to hers with more force and more demand. She parted her lips beneath the sensual pressure of his and leaned back against the doorway, drawing him with her. It was as though she had become a creature of sensation only. Her cloak had slid back and she could feel the warmth of his body against hers creating a delicious, seductive need within her. One of his hands brushed the cloak aside and moved to caress her breast very gently. His mouth was rough on hers now and she revelled in it, gasping his name against his lips. And then, suddenly, it was over and she was left shivering in the chill breeze.

"Enough, sweetheart! It seems I misjudged you, too. Such sweet responsiveness will be my undoing!"

There was an undertone of laughter in Henry's voice, but he still sounded shaken. "My innocent, wayward Lady Polly—have you any idea just what you are doing?"

With great deliberation he pulled her cloak close about her and turned her around.

Polly felt cold and bereft. She wanted to be back in his arms, wanted it quite dreadfully. And yet, all she had ever been taught suggested that this had to be wrong. It was desperately confusing.

"I'm sorry—" she began, in a small voice, but Henry took her arm in a comforting hold.

"Do not be. It was my fault. I thought I knew what I was doing, but you proved me wrong." She saw him grin. "You may have been smothered in propriety but it seems there may be a chance to redeem you!" He took Polly's face in his hands and kissed her again lightly. "Now, we must go down to the Well Walk before I forget myself even further."

He took her hand and drew Polly reluctantly down the remaining steps, taking care to let her go before they emerged into the lamplight. The carriages were all drawn up on the Walk and Lucille and the Dowager Countess were already there, turning hopefully at the sound of footsteps, their faces breaking into relief.

"Polly! Poor child! Whatever has happened to you? You're shaking!" Lucille enfolded her in a comforting hug. Over Polly's head she said to Henry, "Nicholas is scouring the Terrace, but he should be back directly! Oh, he will be so grateful, Henry! We were so worried!"

Polly shrank into the shadows whilst the Dowager Countess pressed her slightly more grudging thanks on Lord Henry. She was sure that she must look as bemused and dazed as she felt.

"Thank God she came to no harm," the Dowager was saying gruffly, eyeing her daughter's flustered face and fortunately attributing her confusion to the shock of being lost. "We are indebted to you, sir."

Lord Henry smiled. "By great good chance Lady Polly came to no lasting hurt this evening." His eyes met Polly's and she saw the wicked twinkle there. She hoped desperately that it was dark enough to hide her burning face. "Do not be too hard on her, ma'am! I have taken her to task enough for her behaviour!"

"Harry Marchnight playing the moralist!" the Dowager Countess said as the coach rumbled home. "Who would have thought it! Evidently he has an understanding of proper behaviour after all! I expect he was most uncompromising!"

Polly shivered, remembering the explosive heat of the encounter with Henry. There had certainly been little of compromise about it. "He was indeed,

Mama!'' she said, and only Lucille saw the shadow of a smile that touched her sister-in-law's mouth as she sat back in her corner of the carriage and dreamed.

It was much later that night when Lord Henry Marchnight strolled unobtrusively into the cardroom at White's and glanced around with apparent lack of interest at the games that were in progress. At one table an older gentleman of military bearing was winning steadily at whist, a shrewd look in his eye and a glass of water at his elbow.

''Fitzpatrick has the luck of the devil,'' Simon Verey said in Lord Henry's ear. ''How does he do it?''

''Easily,'' Lord Henry said laconically, without turning his head. ''He is sober—the others are drunk. It is an unequal contest.''

Verey grinned. ''You look as though you could do with a drink yourself, Harry! You're uncommon serious tonight! Is it love or business that prompts such severity?''

Lord Henry smiled reluctantly. ''A little of both, perhaps... Mr Ditton is losing heavily,'' he added with apparent irrelevance, nodding towards a table where a dandy clad entirely in yellow was slumped in his chair, scowling ferociously at the cards in his hand.

Verey was no fool and he knew more than most about Lord Henry's preoccupations.

''Ditton has always been intemperate in his habits,'' he observed quietly, ''but lately...''

''Yes, he plays too deep—'' Lord Henry broke off

to greet an acquaintance and turned away from the card tables, moving to a quieter corner.

"Another one for whom matters do not prosper," Verey said, watching Peter Seagrave weaving his way a little unsteadily between the tables. "Extraordinary, I always thought him the most straightforward of the family! Nick Seagrave was the very devil for gambling and women before his marriage and now he's as quiet as a lamb and it's Peter who has lost fifty thousand in one sitting!"

Lord Henry winced. "As bad as that?" he asked. "And in one of Lady Bolt's preferred gaming hells, I have no doubt!"

Verey shrugged. "She has her claws into him now, for all she's after Garston's fortune as well! He would have done better to settle for that sweet little Miss Markham!"

"In praise of marriage, Simon?" Lord Henry said mockingly. "You have become quite the old married man yourself these two years past!"

Verey grinned a little self-consciously. "I'll not deny that I count myself the most fortunate of men to have found Therese," he said, a little gruffly. "I am only here tonight because my sister Jane is up from the country and the two of them sent me out so that they could have a gossip in peace!"

"How does the Duchess?" Henry asked lightly, smiling as always to think of Jane Verey with so weighty a title. Her brother laughed.

"She does very well, I thank you! I shall pass on your regards! I doubt she will be in Town for long, for Delahaye returns from the continent shortly and will no doubt be in haste to claim his wife! Ah, these tales of married bliss! One might almost consider it fashionable to dote on one's spouse these days!''

Henry took a glass of wine proffered by a passing waiter. "Almost you convince me, Simon!"

"You? Parson's mousetrap?" Verey looked almost comically surprised. "Do I know the lady?"

"You should do," Henry murmured. "She is the only one I have ever evinced an interest in marrying!"

Verey spluttered into his wine. "But...I presume you mean... But that was five years ago, old fellow! Mean to say, I thought it was a thing of the past!"

"So it was, but not any more."

"Well!" Verey sat down a little heavily. "Am I to wish you happy, then?"

"Not yet." Lord Henry's gaze returned thoughtfully to the slouching figure of Tristan Ditton. "Certain business is getting in the way. When it concludes..."

There was a crash from across the room as Peter Seagrave tried to take his place at a faro table, clutched unsteadily at his chair and succeeded only in overturning it and drawing attention to himself.

"Hope she has more steadiness of character than her brother," Verey said gloomily.

Lord Henry grinned. "Oh, decidedly! And it may be unchivalrous in me to say so, but she holds her drink with a great deal more charm!"

Chapter Five

"It will not be long before Mama warns me," Polly said gloomily as she and Lucille strolled along Bond Street in search of items for Lucille's belated wedding trip. "Oh, look, Lucille, those satin dancing slippers are the most exquisite things! Why do you not take those with you?"

"I fear they will see little wear in the Lake District," Lucille observed mildly. "A pair of stout walking boots would be more the thing!"

"And a parasol to keep the sun off! Mama would consider it deplorable for you to return with a tan!"

Lucille laughed. "A fine figure I shall cut in boots and a parasol! Why do you not buy the slippers yourself?"

But Polly's gaze had alighted on an embroidered reticule which would look perfect with her striped walking dress. "I have only enough of my allowance left for one purchase," she said regretfully. "Oh, look at those beautiful silk gloves! Now I am in a quandary!"

Lucille laughed. "Do you need any of these things?"

"Oh, no! At least—" Polly wrinkled up her nose. "Not need, precisely, but it would be pleasant to have them! Am I monstrously extravagant?"

Lucille, who privately thought that her sister-in-law was surprisingly unspoilt for all her privileged upbringing, reassured her that this was not the case at all.

Once the reticule had been settled upon and bought, and they were walking on, Lucille said suddenly, "I was attending to you really! What is it that she will warn you about, Polly?"

Polly looked puzzled, then her face cleared. "Oh, about Lord Henry Marchnight! In fact, I am surprised that Mama has not spoken before now! It is unlike her to allow me so much licence!"

In the previous two weeks, Lord Henry had been much in evidence in Brook Street, calling on Polly, taking her riding or driving, accompanying her to routs, parties and picnics. Polly had tried to take his attentions lightly but it was becoming increasingly difficult not to think that he might have serious intentions and, oddly, Lucille's next words echoed this.

"I believe that your mama is in a dilemma, Polly," she said thoughtfully. "She feels that she should warn you against Lord Henry's advances, but she cannot quite disabuse herself of the hope that he is in earnest! Not even your mama is prepared to offend the Duke and Duchess of Marchnight by suggesting that one of their sons is not a suitable match for her daughter!"

Polly bit her lip. "Do you truly think... I try not

to let myself hope too much, but—'' She broke off. ''I dare say I should not set too much store by his behaviour. After all, he is a shocking flirt!''

''He has not flirted with anyone else since he started to pay serious court to you,'' Lucille pointed out quietly.

The colour flooded Polly's face, then receded to leave her very pale. ''No, that's true! I had not thought... But perhaps he is only flirting with *me*!''

''You may judge for yourself whether Lord Henry is sincere,'' Lucille said with a little smile, ''for I see him coming this way!''

It was true. Lord Henry Marchnight, in company with the Vereys and a young lady of schoolroom appearance, was sauntering along the pavement towards them. Polly saw him quicken his step as he caught sight of them and the two parties met and greeted each other with unaffected pleasure.

''Lady Seagrave! Lady Polly!'' Lord Henry was smiling at Polly in a way that made her feel suddenly rather hot. ''What good fortune!'' He turned to the very young lady by his side. ''May I make you known to my sister Laura?''

Laura Marchnight, simply but expensively clad in the demure apparel of the debutante, dropped a shy curtsy. She was a sweet-looking girl with the same corn-coloured hair and grey eyes as her brother. Polly remembered hearing that Lady Laura was delicate and had recently returned from a trip to Bath Spa with her mother, where the medicinal waters had apparently done wonders for her health.

''We were just planning an outing to Richmond,'' Henry was saying, his gaze still fixed rather disconcertingly on Polly. "Tomorrow, if the weather stays fair. We would be delighted if you were able to join us—" he turned courteously to Lucille "—and Lord Seagrave as well, of course, if he is free."

Lucille, who had been exchanging a few words with Therese and Simon Verey, looked rueful. "We are promised for a visit tomorrow and cannot cry off," she said apologetically, "but I am persuaded that Polly would be able to make up one of your party. What do you think, Polly? Are you already engaged for tomorrow?"

Polly shook herself out of the slight confusion which Lord Henry's presence always seemed to stir up in her. "Oh, no...yes...indeed! I have no other plans! I should be delighted!"

Therese Verey smiled. "I am sure your mama will let me stand as chaperon! Laura is to accompany us, and Simon's sister Jane Delahaye, and one or two others. It will be great fun!"

"We thought to ride," Lord Henry murmured. "I understand that you are a keen horsewoman, Lady Polly. Would such a plan meet with your approval?"

Polly turned her glowing face to his. "Oh, indeed, that would be most enjoyable! I have missed riding out since I have been up in Town!"

They parted in mutual accord, having agreed that Lord Henry would call for Polly in his phaeton and drive her to Richmond. The Vereys undertook to provide the horses from Simon's extensive stables and Polly started to look forward to the excursion very much. She hurried home to review her wardrobe, certain that she had absolutely nothing to wear that was worthy of a trip to Richmond with Lord Henry

Marchnight. After she had considered every dress she owned, draping them over the bed and holding them up in the mirror, a grumbling Jessie pointed out that she would be wearing a riding habit anyway. That meant a choice of green, red or navy blue and Polly chose the blue, then spent almost the entire evening at the *musicale* they were all attending, wondering whether she had made the correct choice. She was then struck by the awful thought that it might rain on the morrow even though it had not done so for several weeks. All in all, it was a wonder she had any sleep that night.

Fortunately, it proved to be the most perfect day for a ride. Polly had greatly enjoyed the drive to Richmond and the party had met up at the Roehampton Gate, taken a ride to Pen Ponds and were now turning back for a cold collation at the Star and Garter Inn.

"I had no idea that you were such an accomplished rider, ma'am," Henry Marchnight said to Polly as, out of breath and laughing with exhilaration, she slowed to a canter as the Gate came in sight once more. "I had heard that you were keen, but the two are not always synonymous! I should have suggested such an outing much sooner!"

His frank gaze admired the colour in her cheeks and the brightness of her eyes. "It is pleasant to escape the confines of the Town, is it not?"

Something in his tone reminded Polly of the night at Hampstead Wells, when Henry had told her that she was a rebel by nature. Certainly her unrestrained enjoyment of a gallop through the park seemed to prove his point. They had not approached the intimacy of that night at Hampstead again; indeed, Henry seemed very careful to avoid any behaviour that could be construed as questionable. He made sure that they were never alone together and he treated Polly with utmost propriety. She found his behaviour puzzling, to say the least. She sensed that it did not come naturally to him to keep himself on so tight a rein, and yet she was half-grateful that he did not attempt to shorten the distance between them. She was confused by her feelings for him. On the one hand she wanted more, far more, from him, but she was still held back by the constraints of her upbringing.

Now, to give herself time, she turned away and studied the sweep of the land towards the river, the charming little woods scattered about them and the herds of deer grazing peacefully in the distance.

"Have you seen John Boydell's aquatints of the river?" Lord Henry said casually, slowing his horse to a walk to allow the rest of the group to catch them up. "They are held to be very pretty, I believe."

"Yes," Polly smiled. "They are quite charming. And it is such fun to be able to match his pictures to all the places along the river, but I do believe that he gives a more rural feel to the prints than is truly accurate!"

"I must suppose that anyone brought up in Suffolk considers the area around London to be too close to the city to be truly rural," Lord Henry observed. "And no doubt I shall shortly be reminded of the difference for myself. Were you aware that we are to spend some time near Woodbridge this summer?

My mother has decided that it would be good for Laura's health to go to the seaside, but to avoid crowds and excitement.''

There was something dry in his tone which suggested to Polly that Henry had very similar views to her own on the Duchess of Marchnight's mollycoddling of her youngest daughter. Lady Laura was a little ahead of them now on her grey mare, her charming countenance turned towards young Lord Blakeney, who was evincing every sign of pleasure at being her chosen escort. Certainly Laura looked the picture of health and was revelling in the outing and the company.

''I am sorry that Lady Laura has been unwell,'' Polly said cautiously, ''but she seems much recovered now. The waters at Bath must have a remarkably curative effect! And I hope,'' she added hastily, seeing Henry's look of amusement, ''that she will find Suffolk similarly restorative and not too dull!''

''Alas, I am the one who is likely to find the country slow,'' Henry said humourously, ''especially as it will be devoid of your presence, Lady Polly, which is the only thing that might have made it tolerable for me!''

Polly could not help blushing. She was also regretting rather strongly the Dowager Countess's avowed intent of spending the summer in Brighton. Perhaps she could contrive a stay at Dillingham? But she did not want Lord Henry to feel too encouraged...

''Nonsense, Lord Henry,'' she said bracingly. ''You have told me many times that you consider

Suffolk a vastly pleasant county! I am sure you will find plenty to amuse you there!''

Lord Henry's lips twitched. ''It was such a pretty compliment too,'' he murmured. ''I am sorry it did not please you.''

Polly tried not to smile. ''It was very pretty,'' she agreed solemnly, ''but I was not sure how much it was worth!''

Lord Henry burst out laughing. ''I cannot put you out of countenance, can I, Lady Polly? You may take it as true—I should be very sorry to spend the summer months out of your company!''

Fortunately for Polly's composure, Therese Verey brought her horse alongside at that point and Henry fell back to talk to Simon. They clattered into the yard of the Star and Garter and were pleased to find themselves expected and a delicious cold collation laid out on trestles in the garden. Polly, drawn into conversation with Therese and Jane Delahaye over the meal, only noticed Lord Henry's absence as the party gathered itself to depart.

''Where is Henry?'' Lady Laura asked innocently, as they walked slowly through the arch into the inn courtyard. ''He was here a moment ago! I thought— Oh!''

''Rather showy,'' Polly heard Simon Verey say to Lord Blakeney, ''and too short of bone— Oh, I say!''

The scene in the courtyard appeared to have a similar effect on all members of the party. One moment, Polly thought, they had been chatting amongst themselves and the next they had all fallen into horrified silence.

There was a carriage drawn up in the yard, pulled by the four showy white horses which Lord Verey had just been disparaging. Lord Henry Marchnight was leaning against the side of the coach and chatting to its occupant, a smile of appreciation on his lips. As he saw the group emerge from the garden he straightened up and Polly saw a fleeting look of annoyance cross his face as though he had no wish to be interrupted. A moment later, the lady in the carriage had leaned out and, taking Henry by surprise, planted a lingering kiss on his mouth.

There was no doubt that Lady Bolt had staged the action for maximum effect. From within the carriage she would have seen Henry's companions emerge through the archway and her sense of malice had done the rest. And whilst Henry moved away from her as quickly as he could, the damage was done. All the witnesses had an image of Lady Bolt's hands resting lightly on Henry's shoulders as she lowered her smiling scarlet mouth to his for several long seconds. Polly winced at the sight.

After that, everything became a little confused. Lady Bolt's carriage rolled out of the yard, rather in the manner of the wicked fairy vanishing in a pantomime. Simon Verey had a quick word with Henry, who seemed to disappear as quickly as Lady Bolt had done.

"In front of his own sister too," Lord Blakeney was saying, outraged, as he shepherded a pink-faced Laura Marchnight protectively into the inn. "Lady Laura, please wait here whilst I have my phaeton brought round! You cannot drive back with Lord Henry after that—"

But here Laura Marchnight proved surprisingly obstinate. "I assure you, Lord Blakeney, I have no difficulty in accepting my brother's escort back to Berkeley Square. I should be *delighted* if he chose to take me up!"

It was a shame Lord Blakeney could not see that he was doing himself great disservice in Laura's eyes by criticising her brother, Polly thought. She was very loyal to Henry.

Polly saw the look of mingled regret and exasperation that passed between Therese Verey and Jane Delahaye, as Therese said to her, "Lady Polly, it would be best, perhaps, if both you and Lady Laura drive back with us. It will be a bit of a squeeze, but I am sure none of us will mind…"

And Simon Verey had hastened away to attend to the setting to of his carriage.

Polly felt dazed and a little sick. Whilst she had common sense enough to see that Lady Bolt had planned the whole encounter, the memory of it filled her with revulsion. And Henry was hardly blameless. He had been chatting to the Cyprian only a moment earlier and had obviously been enjoying her company. Perhaps he had even arranged to meet her there to arrange a tryst later that day! Polly's lost hopes mocked her. She had begun to believe Henry sincere, to trust him. Well, now she saw the error of her ways!

Polly spent the whole of the journey back to Brook Street in a numb silence and then went straight to her room, declining to tell even Lucille about the events of the day. Miserably she wondered why Lord

Henry had made no attempt to see or speak to her before they had left. He had disappeared with the speed of a man effecting a guilty exit. Had he approached her it would have been difficult to know how to deal with the situation, but she would have preferred to have had that opportunity. Evidently he had not cared sufficiently about her opinion to make an effort to explain to her.

Defiantly, Polly put on her favourite dress and prepared for the ball at Mrs Fleetwood's that evening. If she was going to have to face Lord Henry Marchnight and the attendant scandal, she was determined to look her best.

As Polly had anticipated and dreaded, the tale was all over Town.

"How foolish of Harry..." Lucille sighed, as she and Polly fended off the fifth curious gossip-monger "...and how unlike him!"

"I collect you mean he was foolish to be caught," Polly said tartly. She sat down rather heavily and rubbed a foot where her dainty dancing shoes were pinching. It did not add to her good humour.

Lucille looked reproachful. "I mean to have allowed himself to have been trapped by Susanna! She is forever up to these little tricks just to amuse herself!"

Polly thought that Lucille was probably right, but she did not have any sympathy for Henry.

"I am persuaded that Lady Bolt did not force him into any situation unwillingly," she said coldly. "I think you are too indulgent of his folly, Lucille!"

Lucille raised her eyebrows at this reproach.

"Well, upon my word, you are very harsh! Susanna has succeeded admirably!"

This caught Polly's attention. "Whatever can you mean, Lucille?"

"Why, simply that Susanna is currently engaged in an attempt to ruin the future for yourself and Henry! She has already succeeded in improving on the estrangement between Peter and Hetty. I think…" Lucille smiled serenely "…I *hope* that she will not accomplish a break between Nicholas and myself! I think that beyond even her charms!"

Polly was staring at her sister-in-law in horror. "You think that this is all a plot of Lady Bolt's?"

"Assuredly! She will engineer any chance to cause trouble! You should know that by now, Polly—" Lucille broke off with a little gasp and, turning her head, Polly saw that the object of their discussions had just come into the ballroom. As if to underline Lucille's words, Susanna Bolt was hanging heavily on the arm of Peter Seagrave.

"Oh, truly," Lucille said, sounding more vexed than Polly had ever heard her, "this is the outside of enough!"

It had been an unenjoyable evening. Polly danced a few desultory dances, chatted half-heartedly and waited in vain for Lord Henry Marchnight to make an appearance. They retired early, leaving Lady Bolt in triumphant possession of the floor and of Peter Seagrave, and the Dowager Countess railed ceaselessly against her all the way home. Polly slept fitfully and woke with a headache.

* * *

"Do you come with me to the Royal Humane Society lecture this afternoon?" Lucille asked, finding her sister-in-law sitting quietly in the drawing-room that lunchtime. Her eye fell on the improving book which Polly had been reading earlier. "Or perhaps you are so enthralled in that righteous tome that you have no wish to go out! Etiquette for young ladies! Upon my word!"

Polly laughed, despite herself. Etiquette and deportment might be very uplifting and suitable for a young lady, but it was also tedious. Somehow the disastrous scene at Richmond had prompted her to revert to all that was proper and conventional. She entertained no more hopes of reforming a rake, particularly as the rake in question clearly cared so little for her opinion of him that he had not troubled to seek her out.

The Royal Humane Society sounded to be a very suitable place for a lady of charity to spend some time and at least she would not be bothered by Lord Henry's presence there! Feeling pleasantly virtuous, she agreed to join Lucille on the outing.

The marble entrance hall of the Royal Humane Society was cool and shadowy after the brightness of the day outside. The ladies furled their parasols and hurried to join the group of people going into the lecture room. Polly was astonished to see a number of their acquaintance there. She had thought that this latest interest of Lucille's was yet another slightly eccentric and obscure hobby, but now found that the Society was a magnet for the fashionable.

"I had no idea that such a lecture would be so popular," she murmured in Lucille's ear as they slid into their seats and a gentleman nearby raised his hat and murmured a greeting. The room was filling rapidly. Across the aisle, Polly could see the Huntlys and Lady Havisham, and returned the wave of Miss Ditton, a neighbour of the Seagraves from Suffolk.

"The Society has become a popular means of exercising benevolence," Lucille replied quietly. "You remember that I told you it was originally established by two doctors to promote resuscitation? It now hands out medals and rewards to those people who have helped save lives. I believe that a small group of members are researching means of reviving the drowned and the hanged..."

Polly shuddered. "How very unpleasant! I am all in favour of exercising benevolence, and indeed I suppose that genuine scientific research should never be discouraged, but what can be the attraction for some of these people? Why, it is positively ghoulish!"

She touched Lucille's arm.

"Look at Mr Ditton, for instance! He is almost slavering as he talks to that gentleman over there and his eyes are gleaming with unholy excitement! Ugh, unwholesome man! And you cannot tell me that Mr and Miss Ditton are here because they like to involve themselves in charitable causes! A less benevolent pair would be difficult to find!"

Lucille laughed. "I have to agree! It is a sad fact that the more macabre aspects of the Society do attract those people who have a fascination with the gruesome!"

Fortunately, the lecture that afternoon was on the charitable aspects of the Society's work, Lucille herself having no interest in its more grim activities. A number of projects were explained to the listeners, many of whom were happy to offer financial support. After the lecture there was a sumptuous luncheon at which the guests could mingle and chat, and meet some of the people helped by the Society's work. Lucille and Polly soon found themselves effusively greeted by the Dittons, and were obliged to stop to exchange pleasantries.

Polly had known Miss Thalia Ditton and her brother Tristan all her life. Unfortunately, familiarity had not bred affection. She found both the Dittons bordering on the vulgar with their preoccupation with rank and fortune. Beside Miss Ditton lounged the young gentleman who had the misfortune to be her betrothed: Mr Bunlon was a gentleman of considerable estate, even though he had no title, and his blank, good-natured face wore the perpetually surprised look of one who was not at all certain how he came to be betrothed to Miss Ditton in the first place.

After a few moments they managed to excuse themselves and were moving towards the door when Polly clutched her sister-in-law's arm.

"Lucille! Look! It's Henry Marchnight, of all people! Now whatever can he be doing here? I am sure Lord Henry does not trouble himself to exercise benevolence!"

As soon as the words left Polly's lips she regretted them, for it occurred to her that Lucille herself might have arranged to meet Lord Henry there. A moment later she chided herself for even thinking such a thing. She knew that her unhappy feelings for Lord Henry were warping her judgement and making her prone to jealousy. It was a new and uncomfortable experience for her.

Lucille followed Polly's look to see Lord Henry, deep in conversation with one of the Society's members over by a marble pillar.

"Good gracious, you are right, Polly!" A frown furrowed her smooth brow. "It does seem a little out of character, but I must suppose we do not know Lord Henry well enough to judge him!"

"Well, let us not distract him from his conversation!" Polly said hastily, suddenly anxious not to have to confront Lord Henry after the débâcle of Richmond. Yesterday she had wanted an explanation; now, to be allowed to withdraw quietly from his company was the best that she could hope for. It was now clear that he did not intend to approach her and she thought dully that she should perhaps credit him with proper feeling for sparing her that embarrassment.

Lucille was looking at her quizzically. "You seem very anxious to avoid him, Polly! You will have to speak to him again one day, you know! Perhaps you might even give him the chance to explain himself!"

Polly blushed. "I am embarrassed by what happened yesterday," she admitted, "and I wish to give myself a little time to recover. You must know that I had started to cherish some hopes for Lord Henry and myself, but now I see that I was mistaken. I was prepared to hear him out, but he has not given me that opportunity, Lucille! Clearly it is not important to him! Best to let the matter pass, I think!"

Lucille looked as though she would have liked to have argued, but as the Dittons were approaching them again they beat a hasty retreat out into the sunshine and the matter was dropped.

"I do see that the Society serves a worthy cause," Polly said, in answer to Lucille's enquiry as to whether she had enjoyed herself at the lecture, "but I fear I cannot appreciate its more gruesome aspects. Oh, I am sure it serves a worthy medical purpose," she added hastily, "but I do feel it encourages people like Mr Ditton to *gloat* over unpleasantness! As for the benevolent aspects—do you not feel uncomfortable about the way some people congratulate themselves on their generosity? Why, some of them were positively glowing with self-worth! Maybe I am unkind—" She saw Lucille smile and added defensively, "Well, do you not agree, Lucille? You are always so discreet in your charitable activities, and never expect fulsome thanks!"

Lucille laughed. "Yes, Polly, I do agree with you, as a matter of fact. I am not at all certain that I shall be returning to the Royal Humane Society! And at all costs we must avoid your mama discovering our trip to investigate the Society's activities! One mention of resuscitating the dying and she will very likely have a fit of the vapours!"

Chapter Six

The ball at Mrs Ellery's that night could hardly have been further removed from the Royal Humane Society lecture, but a number of the same fashionable crowd graced the occasion.

It was another hot night, too hot for dancing and humid enough to worry Mrs Ellery that she had not ordered enough champagne to quench the thirst and would be deemed penny-pinching by the *ton*. Polly, vigourously fanning herself after attempting the boulanger with Simon Verey, could only be grateful that this was the very last ball of the Season and they would shortly be leaving Town.

The Dowager Countess was chaperoning her daughter to the ball and was keeping a closer eye on her than she had done at Lady Phillips's. Polly returned punctilliously to her mother's side after each dance, as anxious as the Dowager to avoid any encounter with Lord Henry Marchnight. It was not possible to ignore him completely, for Lord Henry was escorting his sister to the ball, but it was entirely possible to avoid any opportunity for direct conversation and Polly was bent on proving this. Her heart was sore. He had only been amusing himself with her, after all.

At the end of the following set of country dances, Polly found the Dowager Countess seated next to the fearsome Dowager Duchess of Broxbourne, with the Dittons and a few others in sycophantic attendance. Simon Verey had been dancing with Lady Laura Marchnight and as Polly rejoined her mother she saw Lord Henry at close quarters for the first time that night, casually bending over his sister's chair to exchange a few words. Polly felt the blood come up into her cheeks as his grey gaze drifted thoughtfully over her. She avoided his eye and turned her shoulder so that he was not in her line of vision. Disconcertingly, she felt as though he was still watching her and that his gaze contained amusement. She hated being so aware of his presence.

"We were talking of the Chapman case," the Dowager Duchess of Broxbourne said, looking at Lord Henry through her lorgnette and permitting a faint, wintry smile to touch her thin lips. He was a reluctant favourite of hers. "Mr Ditton was just saying that the desperado has escaped!"

A soft gasp escaped from the lips of those ladies who found themselves overset at this piece of news.

"Escaped on the way to the gallows, what!" Mr Ditton confirmed excitedly. "A whole gang of the felons set upon the cart and overpowered the guards! There was rioting in Skinner Street and St John Street, and Chapman disappeared into the crowds and was never seen again!"

The Dowager Duchess's large bulk shuddered.

"None of us are safe in our beds! Why, the man is a robber and murderer!"

The group looked around as though expecting Captain Chapman and his murderous brigands to burst in through the ballroom windows. And, indeed, it did seem for a moment that the chandeliers grew dim and a cold wind blew through the room.

The Chapman case had become something of a *cause célèbre* in recent weeks, its topicality fanned into flames by the radical press. Chapman had been arrested during a theft on a gunsmith's and the claim had been that he was stealing arms for an insurrection. Further investigations into Chapman's activities suggested that he had also been behind a number of robberies of violence perpetuated on members of the *ton*, whilst his actions as a rabble-rouser were well known. The very name could send a shiver down the spine. It was as though he had become a figurehead for the poor, hungry and oppressed, who threatened the established order.

"They say," Mr Ditton put in with the same eager ghoulishness Polly had recognised in him earlier in the day, "that the man has a powerful protector, a nobleman who is bored with his own easy existence and seeks excitement. They say that he has spirited Chapman away!"

A murmur of appalled protest ran round the group. "Surely not one of us!" Miss Ditton said, looking about to faint dead away.

"*I* had not heard that rumour," the Dowager Duchess said, a little irritably. "Is it certain?"

Mr Ditton shrugged elegantly. "Dear madam, who can say? But it would give a great deal of help to

Chapman and his cronies to have a wealthy supporter! And not just that, but a man who has the entrée to *ton* functions—why, such a person could advise on the subject for a robbery with violence, he could—''

''You're frightening the ladies, Ditton,'' Lord Henry said gently.

Polly looked at him. He was wearing the same, languid look of boredom that was his habitual expression in general company and yet for a second she could have sworn that there had been keen interest in his face, as though he were absorbing all that Tristan Ditton was saying.

''But are you not concerned, Marchnight?'' the Dowager Duchess demanded. ''Do you not fear for your life?''

Lord Henry smiled. ''Alas, no, ma'am. I have no energy to waste worrying about criminals and agitators. The set of my coat, the quality of my linen—those are the matters that preoccupy me! Excuse me!''

And he strolled away into the cardroom.

''Well!'' the Duchess said explosively. ''Was there ever such a man-milliner! I am thankful we do not have to depend on the likes of Henry Marchnight to defend us from the common people!''

''Of course,'' Mr Ditton said, a sly look on his equine face, ''it may all be a façade, ma'am! What if—'' he leaned forward avidly ''—Lord Henry is our man? The pose of dandy would be a fine way to dispel suspicion!''

This time there was a shocked gasp from his audience. Even the Duchess seemed uncertain how to react. Polly stood up. The candlelight seemed suddenly to make her head ache and she was aware of a constriction in her throat. Everyone seemed to have forgotten the presence of Lady Laura Marchnight, who was looking so pale she looked in danger of fainting.

"Perhaps you will be so kind as to accompany me to the refreshment room, Lady Laura," Polly said firmly, taking the younger girl's unresisting arm. "I feel in need of some lemonade. No, thank you, Mr Ditton," she said sharply, as Tristan Ditton leaped to his feet, "Lady Laura and I will do very well on our own!"

"Lord Henry is far too lazy to put himself to the trouble of planning insurrection!" the Dowager Duchess said, meaning well, but almost undoing all of Polly's good work.

Mr Ditton's eyes gleamed. "You may be correct, your Grace," he said smoothly, "but how can we know? I tell you, I shall be regarding Henry Marchnight with the greatest suspicion from now on!"

Laura gave a faint moan.

"Poppycock, Ditton!" the Duchess said, pinning her colours to the mast. "You should have more care, slandering a man like that! Lucky for you Marchnight's too idle to call you out!"

Polly did not wait for matters to get worse. She practically dragged Lady Laura along the edge of the ballroom towards the door. In the background the music continued to tinkle and a few couples were attempting the cotillion in desultory fashion.

Polly found that she was very upset and chided herself for her foolishness. She could hardly blame others for dismissing Henry Marchnight as light-weight when he himself encouraged precisely that impression. It puzzled her, for the man she knew was in no way superficial, and yet in general company he appeared to change character and become as shallow as any other pleasure-seeker in the *ton*. For a moment she remembered that lightning change in Henry's expression from acute intelligence to amiable blandness, then a stifled sob from Lady Laura recalled her to the person who had been most injured by Mr Ditton's malicious remarks and the Duchess's clumsy attempts to smooth matters over.

"It isn't *fair*," Lady Laura said passionately, biting her lip to stop herself from crying. "Everyone is so unkind about Henry when he is the sweetest person imaginable! Oh, I could hardly bear to hear them! I nearly said something I regretted, Duchess or no!"

She looked at Polly, half-mutinous and half-ashamed. Polly smiled at her encouragingly.

"Mr Ditton is unpardonable," she said quietly, "and her Grace of Broxbourne scarcely less so!" She put out a hand on the other girl's arm. "Please do not regard it, Lady Laura! I am sure you are right—you must know your brother better than any of us!"

"He is not at all as everyone imagines," Lady Laura said earnestly, gratefully taking the glass of lemonade that Polly passed her. "People think him stupid, or frivolous, but they do not at all appreciate his qualities! Why, I know that he is currently involved in work which—"

"Laura?"

It was difficult to tell whether it was Polly or Laura who jumped more. Laura had been engrossed in her attempts to exonerate her brother and Polly was fascinated by whatever it was she had been about to reveal. When Lord Henry himself paused beside them they both looked up, flushed and disconcerted. He raised an eyebrow.

"Whatever can the two of you be plotting? Why, you look the picture of guilt!"

It was too much for Laura. Her eyes filled with tears again and with a murmured word of apology to Polly, she positively ran out of the refreshment room.

Henry watched her go with a heavy frown on his brow. He touched Polly's hand briefly.

"I had no idea that Laura was so upset, Lady Polly. I apologise for interrupting your conversation when she evidently wished to confide in you." His searching gaze rested on Polly's face for a moment. "I had better make sure that she is all right. Our mother has not accompanied Laura tonight and I promised to keep an eye on her. Excuse me..."

Polly had no inclination to return to the ballroom. She watched Lord Henry's tall figure skirt the floor and cross urgently to Lady Laura's chaperon, saw the lady point and Lord Henry set off in that direction. Polly sighed. It was unforgivable of Mr Ditton to make such ill-bred remarks about Lord Henry Marchnight in front of his sister and hardly surprising that Laura had been deeply distressed. Nor did she doubt Laura's whole-hearted defence of her brother. For a moment Polly wondered what Laura had been about to say to her, and she remembered the incisive look in Lord Henry's eyes as he had listened to Mr

Ditton. There was no doubt that Lord Henry was an enigma, assuming a superficial and indolent air when he chose, but using it to disguise something deeper... Surely she could not be the only one to have noticed? And yet, it seemed she was.

Mr Ditton, his sister and Mr Bunlon came into the refreshment room, laughing and chatting, and Polly went out into the ballroom to avoid them. It was almost the last dance of the evening; the orchestra was tuning up again and Polly felt oddly flat. The Season was trailing away in rather insipid fashion now that the excitement of her false flirtation with Lord Henry had ended. She wished...

"Lady Polly, may I speak with you?"

She had not seen Lord Henry approaching her, for he had come along the edge of the dancing floor, where a line of pillars cast a dark shadow. What Polly *could* see, however, was Lady Seagrave advancing purposefully once more from the other side of the room. Lord Henry saw it too and his lips tightened.

"Come and dance with me," he said a little abruptly. "Your mother will scarcely pursue us on to the floor!"

It was the waltz which was playing, all too reminiscent of their previous encounter at Lady Phillips's rout. Now, however, there was a definite constraint between them. There was a heavy frown on Lord Henry's brow and for a moment Polly wondered whether he was going to broach the subject of the scene at Richmond. Her heart beat a little faster.

"I must thank you, Lady Polly, for your kindness to my sister just now. Clearly you removed her from a distressing situation before matters could get worse. I am most grateful.''

Polly felt obscurely disappointed. So they were to continue as though nothing had happened, and yet the barriers between them were now reinforced. She had little choice but to follow his lead. Normally so open and amiable, his expression now was preoccupied and almost severe. There was still a frown between those dark brows and an angry set to Lord Henry's mouth.

''Lady Laura told you what was said, then.'' Polly spoke a little hesitantly. ''I am sorry that she should have been so distressed. Even if Mr Ditton spoke in jest it was in bad taste and ill conceived—''

''Would that I could call him to account for it,'' Lord Henry said furiously, ''but just at the moment I can ill afford—'' He broke off suddenly, refocusing on Polly, and some of the latent anger went out of him.

''Oh, well,'' the nonchalance had eased back into his voice and was well-feigned, almost convincing ''—Ditton is an unpleasant fellow, when all is said and done, but not worth disturbing oneself over. Such matters never are worth the trouble...''

Had Polly not been so aware of Lord Henry she might well have been taken in by his assumption of good humour, but with her own feelings in turmoil she found she could contain herself no longer. The words popped out of her mouth before she even had time to consider them.

''Why do you pretend to be of no account, interested in nothing but foolish, frippery things, my lord? I am not taken in by your pretence that you do not care about Ditton's words! It does not cozen me, though I confess I find other aspects of your behaviour rather more puzzling!''

For a moment, she saw the surprised speculation in Lord Henry's eyes, before the bland amiability that so frustrated her returned.

''I collect that you refer to my other exploits, Lady Polly? You do not consider high play and the pursuit of the fair sex to be serious occupations for a gentleman, ma'am?''

Polly almost stamped her foot.

''I am well aware that you might find them so! But I know you are seeking to distract me, my lord, funning me about something when I know you consider it a serious matter... I *saw* you when Mr Ditton made his remarks about Chapman's protector—''

She broke off as his hand tightened warningly on hers. Her voice had risen as her feelings spilled over, and other couples had turned curiously to see what was going on. Lord Henry bent close to her ear.

''Yes, you can read me better than most, Lady Polly, because I have chosen to show my true self to you. And it is also true that I do not choose to behave in company as I do with my closest friends. But just for now, I must beg you to forget what you know of me and accept that I am nothing more than a foolish, frippery fellow who cares only for the set of his neckcloth...'' His mouth twisted into a smile at her look of amazement. They were very close. This time there was no attempt to distract her from the topic. There was a compelling force in his eyes that silenced her, demanded her compliance.

Polly's thoughts tumbled over themselves. Why

the pretence at boredom and dandyism? What was he hiding? Perhaps Tristan Ditton had been right: a man playing a part; a nobleman, bored with his easy lifestyle, craving excitement... But it was not possible! Lord Henry had integrity, honour... Surely, he would never become embroiled in criminal activities simply to amuse himself...

Polly's troubled gaze searched Lord Henry's face. "But why are you playing a part? What—"

"Forgive me." Lord Henry's tone had softened as he saw her look. "I cannot tell you that now. And forgive my abruptness. I should not have spoken so, but it is of the greatest importance that you should keep your suspicions to yourself, Lady Polly. One day I will tell you why..."

Polly shook her head slightly, retreating into pride. "It is of no consequence if you do not wish to explain yourself—"

"Yes, it is of consequence! I do not give a rush for what others think of me, but I do care for your good opinion." He was still frowning. "When I can, I shall explain all to you, including those aspects of my behaviour which have appeared most questionable!" A smile lit his eyes briefly. "For now, I can only ask you to trust me..."

The music finished with a final flourish but Polly scarcely noticed as Henry led her back to the Dowager Countess, who had returned to gossip with the Duchess of Broxbourne. He excused himself immediately.

"My sister and her chaperon have already left and I must make haste to my next engagement. Good evening, Lady Polly.'' He bowed to the Dowager Countess, ''Good evening, ma'am...''

Polly watched him go. She was even more confused than she had been before she challenged him over his odd behaviour. It seemed that there were more mysteries to Henry Marchnight than met the eye, and none would be explained to her in the near future.

Polly's mouth drooped. She felt tired and bad-tempered with the onset of a headache. Nor did the Dowager Countess seem much inclined to linger. She was suffering from an unusual reticence resulting from her part in the unfortunate scene with Lady Laura.

''For it was very *bad ton* of Tristan Ditton to speak as he did,'' she commented, once she and Polly were in the seclusion of their carriage, ''and though Lady Laura is a little mouse and I had quite forgotten her presence, I feel badly that I did not give him the setdown he deserved...''

Polly murmured something in agreement, leaning her head against the seat and closing her eyes. Although the day had been fresh, the wind had now died and the night was almost unbearably humid. Thunder rumbled faintly in the distance and Polly could see the flicker of lightning away across the river. She shivered within her cloak, wishing they were already home. There seemed to be something malevolent in the air.

They had gone perhaps two-thirds of the way back to Brook Street when there were sudden violent shouts outside the carriage, making Polly open her eyes and the Dowager Countess, who had been lulled into a doze by the rumble of the wheels, jump out of her skin.

Torches flared outside the window, and by their flickering light, Polly could see a huge mass of figures, jostling and shouting, their faces twisted and malignant. There was a sound of breaking glass and the snap of firecrackers, sudden and shocking, and a growl of excitement rose from the crowd. The carriage lurched, slowing to a crawl.

''What on earth—'' the Dowager began, leaning forward to peer out of the window, and then the carriage door was flung open without warning and the nightmare came in.

Filthy hands caught Polly and the Dowager Countess, and dragged them forcibly into the street. The smell of unwashed bodies and the sweet stench of spirits was in Polly's nostrils. The howl of the mob was all around them. Hands plucked at their clothes, ripping them, and snatching at their jewellery. Lady Seagrave was screaming; Polly felt a sharp pain as her pearl necklace was wrenched from about her throat. She was blinded by the glare of the torches and by the tangle of her hair as her jewelled headband was pulled off. All about her was the swell of menacing power as the mob tested its strength— Polly could feel it and it terrified her.

The coachman was shouting and swearing horribly, his arm raised to defend himself against the blows raining down. In all the noise and confusion, he had not even noticed that Polly and the Dowager Countess needed his aid, and he would have been unable to defend them anyway. The footman had been pulled from the box and was hanging on to the door of the carriage for dear life as the rabble tried to drag him into the gutter. And then, for a moment, the crowd thinned and the coachman, seizing his chance, whipped the horses into a gallop. The carriage lumbered off down the street with the mob jeering and stoning it.

"All alone, now," a voice breathed in Polly's ear, but she scarcely noticed, for before her was a scene from hell that was beyond her worst fantasy.

There had been another carriage behind theirs in the road, and this one had been set on fire. Flames roared from the roof and the open door. A man was kneeling in the gutter, his evening dress smouldering, his hands horribly burned and disfigured. Beside him, a woman was scrabbling about amongst the cobbles, sobbing hysterically. Polly caught her breath as the firelight caught the glitter of something amongst the cobblestones. The woman leant forward, but a hundred hands were quicker than hers, snatching up the coins and precious stones and laughing in scorn. The woman sobbed all the louder.

"She's crying for her money," Polly whispered, horrified.

The Dowager Countess screamed again, pummelled and jostled by the mob. A ragged cheer went up from the crowd as the fire spurted upwards. Polly shrank back, trying to evade the grasping hands, but there was nowhere to run.

"And now, my little dove..." the leary, whisky-sodden voice murmured again. "My, you're a pretty one, ain't ye?"

The frenzied scene began to fade as Polly felt herself slipping into a faint. Her mother was crying and sobbing, but Polly found she could not cry. Nor could she fight this inexorable tide that had swept them up and carried them on a wave of exultant power. The noise was terrifying and the darkness, with the flames illuminating those freakish, evil faces, only added to her fear.

She hardly noticed when a change came over the crowd, so far was she gone in terror and revulsion. There was a whisper running through the mob like wind through corn, and the edges of the crowd began to fray and break away.

"Don't try... Not worth it... He has a pistol... Two pistols... Let's go..."

An arm slid about Polly's waist, hard and strong, and she was too tired to fight. Let them carry me off and do what they must, she thought tiredly. I cannot do any more...

"This is no time for swooning, Lady Polly," Lord Henry Marchnight's voice said, very calm and very resolute. "I must ask you to show some mettle."

Polly opened her eyes to find that he was real and holding her very close. Those brilliant grey eyes were blazing into hers. The nausea receded a little. He gave her a slight shake.

"I need you to be strong now, Polly. Don't disappoint me."

Polly's chin came up. Though utterly unprepared for the horrors that had happened to her, she responded instinctively to the authority in his tone. Besides, there was her mother to consider. The Dowager Countess was stumbling to her feet, her clothes in tatters, filthy and stained. The mob was falling back, hesitant and sullen, slipping away in ones and twos down the dark alleys and lanes, melting into the darkness as they had come. Lord Henry was bending to help the Dowager Countess to her feet and as he did so, his black cloak swung back and Polly saw the pistols at his belt.

"The militia are coming…" The whisper caught and ran round the remains of the rabble. The madness was dying. "Let's go…"

"Can you walk, ma'am?" Lord Henry was solicitous, his voice betraying neither fear nor panic. "If not, I will carry you home. It is not far, but I think we should be moving."

The Dowager, like her daughter, had a strong streak of courage in her. She straightened up and pushed her tumbled hair away from her face.

"I can walk, sir, if you give me your arm. But the other lady and gentleman…? I thought, I was sure…Lord and Lady Ballantyne?"

"They have gone," Lord Henry was saying, already shepherding them away from the smouldering hulk of the carriage, "and we can only hope that they managed to escape the mob. We must concentrate on getting you home safely, ma'am."

The dark streets were empty, littered with broken glass and smouldering wreckage. It seemed to Polly, summoning the last of her strength to get herself safely back to Brook Street, that the journey could have taken two minutes or two hours. The Dowager Countess limped along, huddled within the tattered remains of her cloak, leaning heavily on Lord Henry's arm. His other arm remained, most improperly, about Polly's waist. But she did not care for propriety or convention. Polly needed the reassur-

ance and strength Lord Henry's presence conveyed,
and would have clung to him if all the mobs from
hell had erupted about them.

Lights flared from the house in Brook Street and
the front door stood open. Lord Henry helped the
Dowager Countess up the steps and into the hall. The
whole place was in uproar. Nicholas Seagrave, his
face tense and white, was supporting a man Polly
recognised with relief as John, the coachman. There
was a huge, livid bruise on his temple and dried
blood caked to his face. His eyes were wild as he
clutched at the Earl's arm. The butler, looking almost
as shaken as Seagrave himself, was firing orders at
a host of servants who appeared to be running aim-
lessly in all directions.

As they came in at the door, there was a moment
of complete silence. Then the Dowager tottered over
to the staircase, clutched at the bannisters and sat
down rather heavily on the bottom step. And Lord
Henry Marchnight, with the casual aplomb that
would not have been out of place at the most exclu-
sive of social gatherings, said, "Your servant, Seagrave. I am happy to be able to restore the Dowager
Countess and Lady Polly to you."

Much later, the Dowager Countess had been cos-
seted and exhorted into bed by her daughter-in-law,
and Polly was propped up against her pillows, sip-
ping a cup of hot, sweet tea. She felt light-headed
with exhaustion, but the shock had prevented her
from sleeping. Nicholas and Lucille, horrified and
distressed, had heard the whole story, and were now
sitting at the end of the bed.

Lord Henry Marchnight had slipped away before anyone had had the chance to thank him properly.

"…and the strangest thing," Polly was saying, stifling a yawn, "was that Lord Henry appeared to come from nowhere. And when he did, the rabble turned tail and fled. It was most extraordinary. He is a most mysterious man…"

Her eyelids were closing. Lucille gently took the cup from her grasp and set it down on the washstand. She tucked up Polly's covers.

Polly could feel herself slipping into sleep at last. She tried to rouse herself.

"Lady Laura Marchnight told me that Henry was not as everyone imagined…" she said drowsily. "And now I see it is true. A man who takes a brace of pistols to a ball is quite unusual…"

Lucille's eyes met those of her husband. Nick raised an eyebrow but did not speak. Polly slid further down into the bed. It was warm and safe, and suddenly she was not afraid any more. But there was something else she had to tell them. It was worrying at the edges of her mind and would not let her rest. With an enormous effort, she managed to get the words out.

"I love him so much, you see," Polly said, quite as though it explained everything. "I always have." And then she slept.

It was early the following morning that Nick Seagrave called in at St James's. The discreet and deferential manservant who answered the door could not confirm that Lord Henry Marchnight was yet out of bed, a statement which elicited a look of amused disbelief from Seagrave, if nothing more. He was not surprised when Lord Henry joined him within five minutes, fully dressed and showing no signs that he had recently arisen.

"I am here to offer my thanks on behalf of all of us for your timely actions last night, Marchnight," Seagrave said, accepting a chair and the offer of a cup of coffee. "My mother could barely be restrained from coming around here to thank you herself! Indeed, she will be singing your praises to all and sundry from now on!"

A smile twitched Lord Henry's lips. "How very uncomfortable! I will have to think of a way of dissuading her!"

"No doubt you'll come up with something," Seagrave said, also smiling. He allowed his gaze to travel around the room, appreciating its elegant style and tasteful furnishing. There were a number of books on the shelves which he recognised but had not touched for years and some very fine pictures. Seagrave was not surprised.

"How fortunate for my mother and Polly that you happened to be passing at the moment the mob turned on them," Seagrave continued blandly. "Much in the same way that you were passing on Hampstead Heath the other night!"

Lord Henry picked up the coffee pot, avoiding his guest's penetrating gaze.

"It was fortunate, indeed."

"No doubt," Seagrave pursued, "you had taken a pair of pistols to Mrs Ellery's ball just to be prepared. One cannot be too careful these days!"

Lord Henry, pouring the coffee into large china

cups, checked slightly. His grey eyes met Seagrave's inscrutable dark ones.

"Ah, the pistols. I assume...Lady Polly?"

"She's an observant girl," Seagrave agreed, "but I expect you have already realised that."

"Your sister sees a little too much," Lord Henry agreed, with grim feeling. He passed the cup across and Seagrave sat back in the chair, savouring the strong aroma of the coffee.

"I hope," Lord Henry said, "that neither the Dowager Countess nor Lady Polly will have taken any lasting hurt. That was a hellish scene last night, Seagrave. They were both unconscionably brave."

Seagrave's mouth tightened into uncompromising lines. "Chapman, was it?" he said grimly. "It was a bad day when he escaped. How close are you to retaking him?"

Lord Henry was looking just as implacable. "Close enough," he said. "Maybe it would have been last night if I hadn't been diverted on to other matters!"

"And at Hampstead?"

Henry shrugged. "A rumour...a suggestion that he had been seen. You know how it is, Seagrave—the rumours have him everywhere from Clerkenwell to Chelsea! But yesterday I was closing in. I had found out where he had been hiding."

"At the Royal Humane Society?" Seagrave asked, with a smile. "Polly mentioned that she and Lucille had seen you there! They were most impressed by your interest in charitable work, old chap!"

Lord Henry laughed reluctantly. "The only act of benevolence I would like to commit at present is ridding the earth of scum like Chapman! It was a masterstroke on his part to use the Society as cover. They are so tied up with their own generosity that they do not even press a fellow for his name. And what is one unkempt and ragged fugitive amongst so many dispossessed, looking for a few nights' shelter?''

''And the tale of a rich protector?'' Seagraves asked, putting down his empty coffee cup.

Lord Henry hesitated. ''I have my suspicions…''

Seagrave nodded. ''Well, I had better be going. But I do thank you, Harry. If you had not intervened… I hope it has not damaged your chances of taking your man.''

Lord Henry gave him a rueful smile and shook Seagrave's proffered hand. At the door the Earl paused.

''If you ever need any help, just let me know. Oh, and Harry—'' The younger man looked at him enquiringly, ''Be careful,'' Seagrave said. ''I realise why you intervened last night and I would not wish anything to prevent you from eventually making your declaration!''

And he raised his cane in mocking salute and left a startled Lord Henry staring at the door.

Chapter Seven

London wilted in the heat of a blazing July. Polly, made lethargic with the combination of heat and the shock of the riot, kept largely to her room, whiling the time away reading or playing patience until Jessie told her sharply that she was turning into a recluse. She hardly cared. Each night her sleep was broken by snatches of nightmare in which grasping hands captured her and dragged her away to unspeakable places. She would wake in tears, gasping for breath, comforted only when she realised that she was safe in her bed. During the day she had no energy or inclination to go out and gradually the invitations decreased, although plenty of callers still came to see the Dowager Countess and sympathise with her over her ordeal. Polly had not seen Lord Henry since the night that he had rescued them and rumour had it that he had left London on some of the mysterious, unspecified business that seemed to take him away sometimes. Polly's heart ached. She had needed to see Henry again, wanted to thank him, and now she felt dissatisfied that matters had somehow ended in an unsatisfactory way.

Whilst Polly played patience and the Dowager Countess languished artistically, Lucille had persuaded Nicholas to make good his promise of a belated wedding trip to Scotland and the Lake District. Meanwhile, Peter Seagrave announced with bravado that he would be spending the summer at a very racy houseparty in Buckinghamshire at the seat of Lord Wellerden. The Wellerden carousals were almost legendary for their deep play and libidinous entertainments. The Dowager Countess's mouth turned down in a line of decided disapproval when she heard his plans, but she said nothing and Nicholas just commented that since Peter had evidently chosen to go to hell, he might as well do it in fine style. Remembering Nicholas's own hellraising some years before his marriage, Polly thought that he had probably been wise in leaving Peter to follow his own course.

The Dowager Countess's intention to spend the summer in Brighton had been quite overset by the shock of being caught up in the riot and she had decided to go instead to the Seagrave estates in Suffolk, where the country peace might help calm her shattered nerves.

"Are you sure that you wish to accompany me to Dillingham, Polly?" Lady Seagrave asked, a little dubiously, when Polly had said that she preferred to visit Suffolk rather than go to the south coast. "The country is very slow and we could easily arrange for you to go to Brighton. The Bells are taking a house on the Steyne and I am sure they would be pleased to have your company, or perhaps the Dacres, but it must be your choice…''

She looked at her daughter with concern. Polly had been pale and listless since that horrible night, and her unwillingness to go out and shyness in company worried her mother. Surely the girl needed entertainment and companionship rather than to hide herself away? She would never get over her experiences if she became a hermit!

Polly looked out at the dusty street and thought of the jostling, raffish Brighton crowds. The world and his wife would be at the seaside and there would be company and balls and *soirées*… And at Dillingham there would be the sun on the cornfields and the river tumbling to the cold sea and the call of the plovers… And, of course, there was the chance that Lord Henry Marchnight might be in Woodbridge if his plans had not changed since that momentous day at Richmond.

''Most singular,'' Sir Godfrey Orbison observed with disapproval, when acquainted with the Dowager Countess's plan and the fact that his goddaughter proposed to immure herself in the middle of nowhere for the summer. ''Tell you what, Cecilia, you'll never get that girl married off if she persists in this eccentric behaviour! Why, I wash my hands of her! She'll die an old maid!''

He warmed to his theme, sticking out his ample stomach in its embroidered waistcoat.

''And as for that foolish young puppy, Peter, I've heard he's going to Wellerden's place at Wycombe,'' he growled. ''Damned fool of a boy, wasting his substance on women and gambling. Don't know what this family is coming to, Cecilia! Dashed bad form!''

In the event, Suffolk proved nowhere near as dull as Sir Godfrey might have imagined. The arrival of the Seagraves and the Dittons from London amplified the existing gentry families such as the Farrants and Fitzgeralds, and there were plenty of parties, outings and entertainments. Indeed, it sometimes seemed that the whole of the Town had made its way to Suffolk that summer, and four weeks later, when Nicholas and Lucille returned early from their wedding trip, Dillingham Court really came to life.

"Lucille is in a Delicate Condition,'' the Dowager Countess said coyly to Polly, the evening after her son and daughter-in-law had arrived back. "She needs to rest, and what better place than here in the good country air? And though I am desolated to be so soon a grandmother, I am delighted that she is *enceinte*. It is wonderful news!''

Polly had been visiting the Fitzgeralds when Lord and Lady Seagrave had returned and so was not able to see her sister-in-law until the next morning. Lucille did indeed look a wan sight, propped up on her lacy pillows, her face a creamish white and her huge blue eyes shadowed with purple.

"I feel wretched,'' Lucille admitted in response to Polly's anxious enquiry. "We were having such a nice time as well—the scenery was so beautiful— then suddenly I began to feel hideously unwell and could hardly bear to be cooped up in the carriage all those hours!'' She shrugged. "Well, if this is marriage, I shall go and live alone in a cottage with a cat and my books!''

Polly laughed.

''I am so sorry you feel so miserable, Lucille! But think how many people you have made happy! Why, Mama is in seventh heaven, despite what she says about the ageing effect of being a grandmother, and as for Nicholas, he looks like the cat that got the cream!''

''Well, it's all right for him!'' the Earl's ungrateful wife said crossly. ''He just had the enjoyable part to play! But I shall have my revenge by being a very difficult patient!''

''Have you had any breakfast?'' Polly asked practically, looking round the bedroom and espying a plate of toast on the table.

Lucille shuddered. ''Your mama sent me some plain toast and dry biscuits—she said it was the best thing for the sickness, but the sight of it made me feel even worse! Monstrous! And yesterday all I wanted was a pickled egg!''

Polly giggled. ''You will feel better soon, Lucille. Mama said so and you know how she is always right! Now, can I bring you anything before I go out? We are visiting the Dittons this morning, so you may count that as my punishment and not think yourself the only one suffering!''

Lucille managed a pallid smile. ''Perhaps there are some benefits to being confined to bed, after all! Come in and talk to me when you get back. In the meantime, I am determined to have Nicholas at my beck and call!''

* * *

Lucille's interesting condition was the main topic of conversation amongst the ladies visiting the Dittons, but when the gentlemen came in from the stables, the gossip turned to news of the Dowager Duchess of Broxbourne, who had had all her jewellery stolen in an audacious midnight raid on her London home the very night before the Dittons left London.

"The Dowager Duchess slept through it all apparently," Mr Ditton reported, with an excited laugh, "but now her Grace is refusing to leave London at all, for fear her entire house will be ransacked! The *on-dit* is that she sits up all night with the butler beside her armed with a blunderbuss!"

Lady Seagrave shuddered. "What in the world are things coming to when one is not safe in one's own home? Why, I for one shall be staying here in the country until that felon Chapman is captured! At least I may take the air in Woodbridge without being set upon by a gang of ruffians!"

Mr Ditton leant forward, almost impaling himself on his ridiculously high shirtpoints. "Can you be sure that the country is so safe, ma'am? They do say that there is a gang of smugglers who still work the coast near here, so take care if you choose to step out at dark of the moon!"

"Enough, Tristan," Mrs Ditton said, quite sharply for her. She had seen the Dowager Countess shudder and cast her son a look of profound dislike, and Mrs Ditton had no intention of finding her invitations to Dillingham Court rescinded. She cast about swiftly for a new piece of gossip to distract attention.

"I have heard a far more riveting piece of news," she said, brown eyes sparkling and her turban atwitch. "Mrs Cozens told Maria Wilcox, who told me that the Marchnights are coming to Woodbridge!"

There was a sudden silence, but for the muted clink of china. All conversations seemed to have been suspended as everyone turned to Mrs Ditton for further information.

Lady Seagrave raised her brows. "How extraordinary! Are you sure, Eustacia?"

"Well…" Mrs Ditton had the grace to retract a little "…it is only the Duchess and Lady Laura. I understand that they have been in Bath these four weeks past…" again her brown eyes twinkled with gleeful malice "…but Laura is being pursued by a *most* unsuitable young man and the Duchess is at pains to remove her from his company!"

There was a gasp of speculative interest from the assembled ladies. Lady Laura, only eighteen and the sweetest of debutantes, was the perfect target for scandal.

"How delicious," Miss Ditton breathed in excitement. "Lord Blakeney was paying her particular attention in Town—I wonder if he followed her to Bath—"

"*I* had heard," Lady Seagrave said a little tartly, "that Lady Laura is delicate and that Sarah Marchnight was thinking of a sea break even before they left Town, for the good of Laura's health. But why they have chosen Woodbridge…?" and she frowned at the thought of her hegemony of Suffolk society being under threat.

"But the most piquant part," Mrs Ditton finished triumphantly, "is that they are to be escorted here by

Lord Henry. Lord Henry Marchnight is coming to Woodbridge!''

This time the gasp contained a *frisson* of excitement as well as interest. Almost every one of the ladies present had a deep interest in discussing and deploring the activities of so notorious a rake. That he might be about to create a stir in their little backwater was almost too stimulating to consider. Lord Henry might be condemned as being quite beyond the social pale, but he remained one of the most eligible and unobtainable prizes on the marriage mart.

Polly, despite having had foreknowledge of Mrs Ditton's words, jumped and spilt a little tea on her lilac silk dress. Miss Ditton's sharp brown eyes, so like her mother's, noted Polly's pallor.

''Lud, Lady Polly, the news has quite overset you!'' she said, with spurious sympathy. ''I do so sympathise. How can you face the strong rescuer who saved you from the mob? How can you look him in the eye after what you have been through? I know I should be quite overcome!''

''*I* shall face him with gratitude,'' Lady Seagrave said trenchantly, wading in before her daughter could even speak. ''Regardless of my previous opinion of Lord Henry, I cannot but be profoundly grateful that he was passing that night. Such good fortune! And he was truly courageous in facing down that mob and risking his life to help us! I shall not hear another word against him!''

Polly raised her eyebrows at such a staunch defence of a man her mother had previously dismissed as a dissolute wastrel.

''I vow,'' Miss Ditton said archly, ''Lord Henry

has achieved a champion in you, has he not, ma'am! But I would wager all my pin money that it will not be long before he does something truly *dreadful*," her eyes sparkled at the thought of it "—and we are all deploring him for a villain!" She cast a spiteful sideways look at Polly. "After all, remember the incident at Richmond! I am sure that Lady Polly will never forget it!"

Someone tittered behind their hand. Polly felt the familiar fury rising at this denouncement of Lord Henry, mixed with the pain that the memory of that day could still occasion her.

"Lord Henry would no doubt be flattered to think that his activities could command such interest, Thalia," she said coolly.

Miss Ditton, reddening, sought to sharpen her claws.

"It must be very pleasant to have your brother and sister-in-law back at Dillingham," she said, smiling at Polly. "And I hear that your brother Peter has been intent on getting to know Lady Bolt much better! Such interesting family connections the Seagraves have!"

Polly knew better than to rise to that. Miss Ditton derived all her pleasure from the little pin-pricks and sharp words that could discommode her listeners. She yawned, as though somewhat bored with the topic of conversation.

"Oh, as to that, Peter has always been a most sociable creature! I am blessed with two very amiable brothers, Miss Ditton. No doubt I am the envy of all about me!" Polly's gaze lingered just long enough on Tristan Ditton to make her point. In no way could Mr Ditton be coveted as a brother.

A tiny frown of annoyance marred Miss Ditton's narrow forehead and Polly was grateful when Mrs Fitzgerald came across to join them and dilute the conversation. She was afraid that she was about to be very rude to Miss Ditton.

The Dowager Countess and her daughter left soon after, with the Dittons coming out on to the front steps to wave them off in state.

''Do give dearest Lucille our best wishes and tell her that we shall be over to Dillingham soon to see how she goes on!'' Mrs Ditton gushed.

The Countess and Polly exchanged a look, in total accord.

''Poor Lucille,'' the Countess murmured *sotto voce*. ''Just when she was beginning to feel a little better as well!''

The unrelenting summer heat continued. The Dowager Countess had taken to dozing the afternoon hours away, and with Lucille also confined to bed and Nicholas out about estate business, Polly would wander in the shade of the gardens or curl up with a book in the pergola beside the lake. It was too hot for riding. Her mind was preoccupied with thoughts of Lord Henry Marchnight. Part of her longed to see him when he came to Woodbridge, but her practical side told her that this was unlikely. Whilst Lord Henry might well escort his mother and sister on the journey, he would hardly stay long in a provincial backwater which could hold no interest for one used to far more sophisticated pleasures. It seemed even less likely that Henry would choose to seek her out. Since he had not called in London after the ordeal, he would be unlikely to do so now.

Polly frowned, putting her book down on the painted seat of the pagoda and looking out across the dazzling water of the lake. There was no doubt that Lord Henry Marchnight was an enigma. She had guessed he was not the foolish dandy he pretended to be, though his reputation as a rake was perhaps another matter. But there was something suspicious in his behaviour. Mr Ditton's words at the ball, half-forgotten, came back to give her a slight shock. A gentleman who was bored with his aristocratic life-style might well become involved in criminal activities for excitement. He might well be lurking during a riot—could even be an instigator of the discontent that had led the mob to turn on them. Polly shivered. Surely she was being foolish, particularly when she cared for him as she did. She could not equate her feelings for him with such doubts about his integrity. Yet something did not quite fit...

She got up, intending to walk off her fit of the dismals. She took the path which skirted the lake, enjoying the play of light on its surface and considering whether it would make a suitable subject for her painting. Polly had not picked up her paintbrush since returning to Suffolk, but it was an activity which she thoroughly enjoyed and she had some skill. It was a beautiful day to be outside, although a little too hot for comfort, but Polly's parasol kept the direct sunlight off her face.

The Dillingham lake drained, by way of a small stream and a sluice gate, into the River Deben, and

Polly slipped through the little gate and took the riverside path. Strictly speaking, this was not Seagrave land and belonged to Charles Farrant, but Polly knew he would not mind her trespassing. The Farrants and the Seagraves had grown up together.

There was a small fishing-house a little way further down the bank. With a smile, Polly remembered that this had been the scene of various childhood expeditions in the hot summers of years that had gone by; they had sat on the balcony of the fishing-house, dangling their lines in the river and losing patience before they had caught anything. The boys had been allowed to swim, but her governess had scolded Polly for asking to join in too, and had only reluctantly allowed her to dangle her bare feet in the water of the pool inside the fishing-house. Polly smiled at the memory. The pool, lined with coloured tiles and marble imported specially by Charles Farrant's father, had always fascinated her. The water had been so clear and deep, shadowed and secret. She was minded to peek inside just to see if the reality was anything like her childhood memories.

Polly pushed open the fishing-house door and, in the split second that followed, her startled gaze took in everything before her. The interior was smaller than she remembered, but the tiles of a swirling green and blue were just the same. Light filtered down from the balcony above, dappling the water and illuminating the statues of mermaids and merman, which, in varying states of tasteful undress, lined the walls. Polly certainly did not remember them. Her gaze lingered, half-shocked, half-intrigued at the sensuous display. Then she looked again at the pool and experienced a sensuous shock of an entirely more physical nature.

The pool was occupied. Polly, her hand still on the latch, took a hasty step backwards. And at that moment Lord Henry Marchnight, his wet, fair hair as sleek as an otter's pelt, hauled himself out of the pool, the water running down his bronzed torso, shimmering droplets glistening on his naked body.

Polly gave a strangled squeak. She clapped her hand over her mouth, then wondered foolishly if it would be better to shield her eyes, since she seemed incapable of tearing her gaze away from Lord Henry's body.

His nakedness was a shocking echo of the classical poses of the statues. But they were inanimate, whilst he was all too vividly alive. The strong, graceful lines of his body were utterly compelling. Somehow, Polly managed to raise her gaze to Lord Henry's bare, broad chest, where it appeared to become fixed once again. He had an excellent physique, she thought dazedly, without an ounce of fat, the powerful shoulders and chest tapering to the narrow waist and down to strong thighs, all too clearly displayed to her view.

Lord Henry turned aside in leisurely fashion to reach for the towel which lay across a wicker chair and Polly's fascinated gaze followed. Then, as he finally draped the towel about his waist, she was released from the spell and met his eyes, full of speculative amusement.

"Have you seen enough, Lady Polly?" Lord Henry asked, scrupulously polite, his hand hovering suggestively over the knot at his waist.

Polly could not answer. A huge wave of heat washed over her, compounded of sheer sensual awareness and burning embarrassment. Even as her mortification struggled for mastery, she was aware of other, more demanding and disturbing feelings, feelings she could not control or understand. She turned on her heel, bumping clumsily against the door in her attempt to get out of the fishing-house more quickly. The path was rough beneath the flimsy soles of her shoes as she ran from him. The sun suddenly seemed blindingly hot, the grasses threshing against her skirt, the colours spinning in a whirling kaleidoscope. Behind her, she thought she heard Lord Henry shout, "Polly! Wait!"

She did not turn. Branded on her mind was the vision of Lord Henry's naked perfection, overlaid with the conventional gloss of how utterly she had humiliated herself and that she would never be able to face him again as long as she lived.

She did not see the rabbit hole, did not realise her danger until she had tripped headlong into the grass and nettles to lie still, winded, with tears of pain and embarrassment stinging her eyes and the sound of Lord Henry's footsteps drawing ever closer.

Chapter Eight

Polly brushed the tumbled hair out of her eyes and hastily attempted to sit up. A sharp pain shot through her ankle as she tried to put her weight on it. At the same time, tiny stinging patches of nettle rash seemed to rise on every exposed bit of skin. With a groan she lay back in the grass.

The blue sky was abruptly blotted out.

"What the hell do you think you're doing?" Lord Henry Marchnight demanded, with something less than his customary aplomb.

Even through her pain and misery, Polly was aware of relief that he had taken time to dress before he had followed her. He was not, perhaps, as immaculately turned out as usual, but there was something powerfully attractive about the sight of such casual dishevelment. Polly turned her head away with another groan. To be able to think of nothing but Henry Marchnight's attractions at a time like this argued a disordered intellect.

Henry's gaze took in her tumbled hair and the

lines of pain on her white face, and his tone changed abruptly.

"You're hurt!" He stretched out a hand and Polly flinched back, trying to scramble to her feet. She saw the angry colour come into his face at her reaction, though his voice remained level.

"I assure you that you can trust me, Lady Polly. I am not so far gone in debauchery as to take advantage of a defenceless woman! Besides, what were you intending to do—get up and hop away from me? Attack me with your parasol, perhaps?"

He had gone down on one knee beside her in the grass now. "This is no time to be missish." He had taken her ankle in his hand now and was exploring it with gentle fingers warm against the silkiness of her stockinged foot. Polly closed her eyes in an agony of confusion and mortification. Still shocked and aroused by their confrontation in the fishing-house, she found his touch almost unendurable.

But there was nothing remotely suggestive in Lord Henry's behaviour.

"You have sprained your ankle," he said in matter-of-fact tones. "I doubt that you could walk on it even if you wanted to! I will take you back to the Court. It is not far." He scooped her up in arms that made nothing of her weight.

Polly had started to feel very unwell. The heat and the pain were making her head swim and the colours all seemed too bright and blurred. She turned her head against Lord Henry's shoulder, forgetting for a moment her earlier discomfort in his presence.

"Oh, no, you cannot! I cannot allow—" Her qualms surfaced again before they had gone more than twenty steps. Lord Henry did not even slow his pace.

"Indeed? Can I not?" He sounded grimly amused. "And how do you intend to stop me?" He settled her more comfortably in his arms. "Close your eyes, if you cannot bear to think of being in my arms!"

After the bright glare of the sun, the cool entrance hall at Dillingham Court was blissfully shaded. Polly, who had been lulled into comparative peace by the gentleness with which Henry had carried her, opened her eyes with reluctance. Medlyn was hurrying across the hall towards them, his brows almost disappearing into his hair at the sight of Polly clasped close to Lord Henry yet again. It was beginning to look like a habit.

"Lady Polly! Lord Henry! Whatever has happened, sir?"

"Lady Polly has fallen and hurt her ankle," Lord Henry said tersely. "Send someone for the doctor please, Medlyn, and if you could show me to Lady Polly's room—"

"Put me down!" Polly hissed in a mortified whisper.

"Certainly not," Lord Henry said, in exactly the same terse tone. "Do not be so foolish! You cannot stand!"

"I can try!" Polly said obstinately, her mouth set in a tight line.

Lord Henry looked as though he would have liked to have slapped her if he had had a hand free. "Pray do not martyr yourself—"

Fortunately, the drawing-room door opened at that moment and the Dowager Countess and Nicholas

Seagrave came out into the hall, stopping dead at the sight in front of them.

"Polly!" the Dowager Countess said faintly. "What on earth—"

"Lady Polly has sprained her ankle," Lord Henry said again, with commendable patience. "If someone could show me to her room?"

"Of course." Nicholas Seagrave had recovered himself and now appeared to be trying to suppress some amusement as he considered his sister's flushed face and her unwilling rescuer. "Bring her this way, Marchnight! Has Medlyn sent for the doctor? Oh, good... Here..."

Polly's pillows were soft beneath her head. She could feel her mother fussing around her as Seagrave steered Lord Henry out of the room.

"Wait..." It came out as a croak. She opened her eyes. Despite her mortification, there really was something she had to say.

"Thank you, sir," Polly said, reluctantly looking at Lord Henry, and for a moment she saw the expression in those dazzling grey eyes soften as he smiled at her. It made her feel quite weak, and not from sickness.

"At your service, Lady Polly. I hope that you will be feeling better shortly..."

"We're indebted to you for your help yet again, Marchnight," Seagrave was saying pleasantly, shaking his hand. "A glass of something before you go, perhaps? If you come down to my book room..." The door closed behind them.

There was a moment of silence, then, "Polly," the

Dowager Countess said imperiously, "I *demand* that you tell me what is going on!"

Polly's lashes flickered. For a moment she hesitated, but it really was easier to pretend that she had fainted. She gave a little sigh, turned her head on the pillow, and lay still. She heard the Dowager Countess sigh with exasperation.

"Polly Seagrave! I vow and declare that you are the most trying child sometimes!"

Polly vouchsafed no reply.

"So," Lucille said, patting the bed beside her to encourage her sister-in-law to sit down, "you may now tell me precisely what happened between yourself and Harry Marchnight!"

It was a week since Polly's accident and she had proved a poor patient. She had kept to her room for the first day or two, resting her ankle as the doctor had instructed, but the enforced inactivity had begun to bore her and she had begged Seagrave to carry her down to the drawing-room, where she could at least have some company. And on this particular morning, she had hopped into Lucille's bedroom as her sister-in-law was taking her morning chocolate.

Lucille was much better. The morning sickness that had brought her low whilst travelling had now receded and she looked radiant. She fixed Polly with a wicked look over the rim of her chocolate cup.

"Do not seek to cozen me! Oh, I know the story you have told your mama! But it stretches *my* credulity too far to believe that you happened to be strolling by the river and tripped, and Henry Marchnight was just passing and was able to rescue you when you fell! So?''

Polly hesitated. She could not deny that it was heaven to have Lucille back to confide in. The Dowager Countess was very kind under her starchy exterior, but it would have been impossible to tell her mother the story of what had really happened. And since Lucille had been shrewd enough to guess at the fabrication...

''Well,'' she said cautiously, ''it was true that I was walking by the river. Mr Farrant has a fishing-house down there—just beyond the edge of our land—and for some reason I felt compelled to go and explore it. I don't know why.'' The memory of Lord Henry's magnificent physique came back to Polly, as it had done countless times in the past week. ''I wish—oh, how I wish I had not gone in there!''

Lucille's lips twitched. ''Come, now, it cannot be so tragic! Was Lord Henry in the fishing-house?''

''Yes!'' Polly raised stricken brown eyes to Lucille's blue ones. ''But he was not fishing! That would have been quite innocuous! Oh, Lucille—''

Lucille raised her eyebrows. ''I see! I have not been in the house, but Nicholas mentioned it had a plunge pool below the balcony. They used to swim in the river in the hot summers, he said, but...'' Her eyes widened. ''Oh, glory, Polly, do you mean to say that Lord Henry was in the pool?''

Polly nodded. ''Yes, but—''

''But?''

''He was getting out of the pool—''

Lucille clapped her hand to her mouth, her eyes

enormous. "Oh, Polly! Was he— Did he— Was he *undressed*?"

"Completely!" Polly admitted. She saw Lucille's appalled gaze and added miserably, "I know! And what did I do but stare in the most shameless manner imaginable! I do not know what came over me precisely! But, Lucille, I could not tear my gaze away!"

Lucille, with her superior experience and understanding of such matters, rather thought that she could understand how Polly had become so transfixed. Despite her years, Polly was rather an innocent, as no doubt she ought to be. It seemed to Lucille that the Earl and Countess of Seagrave had gone to great lengths to protect their only daughter, with the result that Polly seemed like Sleeping Beauty, quite lacking the innate, age-old understanding of the games played between the sexes. Polly seldom flirted or practised her charms on any of her admirers. She seemed quite unawakened, and yet there was something about Lord Henry Marchnight which obviously stirred her, and it clearly both intrigued and frightened her.

Lucille's sense of humour began to get the better of her, despite Polly's tragic expression.

"I imagine Lord Henry must have been well worth looking at!" Lucille said, trying not to laugh.

"Lucille!"

"Well?" Lucille's blue gaze was amused. "There is no harm in admitting it, Polly! Leastways, not to me, though I dare say your mama would not approve! Come, it is not a tragedy! Lord Henry is a very attractive man, and you have a *tendre* for him... It would be more worrying if the sight of him had left you unmoved! But whatever happened next?''

''I ran away,'' Polly said baldly. ''Which was how I came to trip and fall, and Lord Henry came after me—''

''Fully dressed by now, I hope!''

''Yes, indeed! But when he offered to help me I was all missish, for I was so embarrassed to have stared so, and so confused... I have never felt that way before, at least not with anyone else...'' Polly's voice trailed off hopelessly. There was a moment's silence, then Lucille patted her hand.

''Listen, Polly, there is nothing to be ashamed of in your behaviour. Such matters are not discussed, I know, but your reaction to Lord Henry was entirely natural!'' She looked at Polly's woebegone face and smiled encouragingly. ''You have nothing to reproach yourself for.''

''No,'' Polly said wretchedly, ''but Lord Henry already has a low enough opinion of me, Lucille! He will be thinking me the veriest lightskirt! I did not tell you before, but do you remember the morning you went on the picnic, and how poorly I was feeling?'' At Lucille's nod she rushed on. ''I became intoxicated with the fruit punch at Lady Phillips's Ball the night before, and then I tried to tell Lord Henry that I wished us to be friends, but I got it all wrong and he ended up kissing me on the terrace and it was dreadful—''

Lucille was looking thunderstruck. ''Wait, wait! What on earth were you doing drinking the punch?''

''I thought it was fruit cup,'' Polly said, suddenly and unaccountably wanting to giggle. ''It was a very

hot night, you see, and the drink was so refreshing…
Anyway, such a peagoose as I was, I did not realise
that I was intoxicated! So when I had the chance to
speak to Lord Henry I felt marvellously brave, but
he did not interpret my words in quite the way I
wished and before I knew it he was kissing me—''

Suddenly she felt the laughter welling up again,
and once she had started she could not stop. Lucille
put her cup down and sat in amused bewilderment.

''Polly, Polly! Whatever happened?''

''I told you,'' Polly said, between giggles, ''he
kissed me!''

''And you said it was dreadful.'' Lucille finished.

''Well, no…'' Polly's giggles started to subside at
last. She wiped her eyes. ''The kiss itself was not
dreadful, it was quite delightful…'' Again, her voice
faded away as she remembered the stirring of her
senses, so intriguing and yet so frightening. ''I
wanted him to go on kissing me for ever,'' she finished naïvely.

''Well, what is so wrong with that?''

Polly's eyes were enormous. ''But, Lucille, a lady
does not kiss a gentleman before they are married!''
She frowned. ''And then, when he rescued me at
Hampstead Wells…'' again she found herself re-
pressing a giggle at Lucille's rapt expression
''…why, I positively threw myself at his head! He
must think me very fast!''

''I doubt it,'' Lucille said drily. ''It all sounds
highly comical to me and hardly the stuff of which
loose women are made!''

Polly, to her own surprise, started to laugh again,
''Yes, I do see what you mean! Although I have to

say that there were certain similarities between my conduct and that of Lady Bolt at Richmond!''

''No, truly? I have underestimated you, Polly!''

''That is what Lord Henry said!'' Polly admitted with a giggle, provoking a look of speculative amazement from her sister-in-law.

''Now, Richmond…'' Lucille tried to look severe. ''I assume that you have not discussed it with Lord Henry?''

Polly sobered slightly. ''No, and I cannot see that we shall ever do so. I am still resigned to the fact that there is no future for me with Lord Henry, for he is clearly unable to abandon his rakish habits.'' A shade of colour crept into her face. ''Indeed, it is one of the reasons why I feel particularly badly about my behaviour.'' She struggled a little for the words. ''It is not as if…that is…were we betrothed…''

But Lucille was smiling again. ''It does not do to worry too much about such things, Polly! I have the strangest feeling that all will turn out for the best. Lord Henry, I am persuaded, thinks no less of you for your conduct.'' Her eyes twinkled. ''Your folly in becoming foxed, however, is a different matter!''

Polly found herself laughing again in spite of herself. ''Yes, it was unforgivable in me and really very unpleasant to boot! I am sure Lord Henry thinks me a complete fool, which is dreadful! And now this business at the fishing-house… Oh, Lord, I really have made a complete cake of myself!''

And she collapsed into fresh giggles.

Lucille was also laughing. ''And you think this a calamity? It's the funniest thing I have heard this age!''

"Yes!" Polly raised eyes brimming with tears of laughter. "I see now that it is! Oh, thank you, Lucille! I feel so much better!"

"Our encounters seem to be becoming ever more dramatic, Lady Polly," Lord Henry Marchnight murmured, taking the seat next to hers in Mrs Fitzgerald's drawing-room a week later. "Is it possible for us to converse in a seemly fashion, do you think, or will something untoward occur simply through our proximity?" There was a blend of mockery and amusement in the low tones which Polly found infinitely disturbing, but she was not going to allow him to put her out of countenance.

He had not called to see her during her convalescence and that alone was enough to make her treat him coolly. Although she would never have admitted it, Polly had waited in vain through the hot summer days, hoping that each peal of the doorbell might be Lord Henry, or that each floral tribute might be his. She should have known better—it was all of a piece with his behaviour in London—but it made it no easier to bear.

She gave him a cool smile. "Provided that you are able to behave yourself we may do tolerably well, sir," she said lightly. "And now that I am so much better, I shall at least be able to make my escape! But—" her smile gained a shade of warmth "—I have not yet had the opportunity to thank you for the service rendered to us in London that night—"

Lord Henry touched her hand so briefly, so quickly that no one noticed; Polly thought she might have imagined it were it not for the sensation of warmth his touch aroused. She looked away, confused.

"Do not speak of it. I am just glad that no real harm came of the occasion."

Polly reflected that Lord Henry's attractions lay not only in his undeniable physical attributes but also in his charm of manner. She had hardened her heart against him and yet she could feel herself weakening already. He spoke as though she were the only person of importance in the room and the intent look in those cool grey eyes was for her alone. And yet it had to be an illusion, for Polly had seen him charming a dozen other women with that mixture of concentrated attention and lazy grace.

In the days of Henry's absence, Polly had taught herself to be sensible. She had accepted Lucille's dictum that the feelings aroused in her by Lord Henry were perfectly natural, but she was not at all sure that she wished to experience them again. Lord Henry was a rake who understood such matters; Polly was aware of her own inexperience and timidity and she had no intention of letting Lord Henry, whose intentions could only be dishonourable, complete her education. But avoiding him would be difficult in the small social circle of Woodbridge, and remaining impervious to his charm was even more of a problem.

To distract herself, she turned her brightest smile upon him. "And what do you find to amuse you in Woodbridge, sir? It must be intolerably dull for one accustomed to more sophisticated amusements!"

Lord Henry raised his eyebrows. "And what other pursuits do you imagine me preferring, Lady Polly?"

Polly blushed. "Now, sir, I warned you—"

"I assure you it was a genuine question," Lord Henry said idly. "People have the most extraordinary preconceptions about my behaviour, you see!"

"No doubt completely without foundation," Polly said with asperity, meeting his bright, guileless gaze. She smiled. "Tell, me then, sir, to avoid misunderstandings, what it is you find of interest in this part of the country."

"Well…" Lord Henry looked thoughtful "…for a start, my father has commissioned me to oversee the making of his new yacht down at the boatyard, so that keeps me busy for part of the time. Charles Farrant, over at Leetwood, is a good friend of mine, so I have spent some time there. Then there is the society to be had here and the entertainments in the Town. But above all, Suffolk is so pretty a county I feel I could walk and ride and swim—" he cast Polly a wicked sideways look "—for as much time as I have available to me. So you see, I do not lack amusement."

Polly had been feeling quite in charity with him, until the mention of the swimming, for she found Suffolk the prettiest and most tranquil place on earth. Now, however, the vision of Lord Henry emerging from the pool was before her eyes again and she knew she had turned bright red. Worse, she knew that he knew what she was thinking of, for he said, very softly, "It was a most stimulating encounter, Lady Polly."

"I would call it shocking, sir."

"No, not at all…enjoyable, provocative…"

She knew he was teasing her, pushing her to see

how much licence she would allow him. And indeed, it was most difficult, Polly thought, for he made her feel so much less prudishly conventional than normal. There was a quickening in her blood in response to this banter and he could read the signs, knew she was responding to him even against her better judgement.

"Enough, Lord Henry!" But Polly could not prevent herself smiling and she saw him incline his head, though his eyes were still bright with challenge, as if to say: "I will accept your decision this time but I know that you are weakening…"

"You will be wishing me away, then, ma'am," he said politely.

"You must consult your own inclination, sir."

A faint smile touched Lord Henry's eyes. "Oh, as for myself, ma'am, I could sit here all day! But I promised my sister I would ask you a favour." He nodded in the direction of Lady Laura, who was sitting under the watchful eye of the Duchess. "Laura feels a little isolated out at Fenchurch alone and I know she longs for a change of company! You have been good enough to show her some kindness in the past. May I beg the pleasure of bringing her to you now?"

Lady Laura had caught his eye and was looking hopeful. Polly smiled. "By all means, Lord Henry. I should be delighted."

The arrangement was soon effected. Lady Laura took the seat beside Polly and they chatted pleasantly for ten minutes, with Lord Henry adding the odd, laconic comment every so often. Laura expressed herself very taken with Suffolk, although a little lonely in the house out towards the sea on the Orford road. She explained that the Duchess had taken it with the thought that the bracing sea air would do Laura good, although she had not felt herself pulled down by her weeks in London. Polly's poor opinion of the Duchess's domineering ways grew. It seemed that she wanted to keep her daughter in what almost amounted to seclusion. Laura admitted to liking the house and its situation near the beach, but regretted the lack of companionship close by. She was about to venture some further comment when Charles Farrant, who had been conversing with Miss Ditton, drew up a chair and asked if he might join them. Laura blushed and fell unaccountably silent.

Polly observed this development with amusement and not a little surprise. Mr Farrant was hardly so romantic a figure that a young girl would develop a *tendre* for him. He was in his late thirties, pleasant and slightly earnest, and he had a look of complete doglike devotion in his kindly eyes as they rested on Laura. She in turn, seemed unable to look directly at him, but with shy smiles and sideways looks indicated that she was not indifferent to his presence. Polly, catching Lord Henry's speculative gaze as he assimilated this unlikely attraction, shared a look of conspiratorial indulgence with him. A moment later, he suggested that they go and admire Mrs Fitzgerald's gardens together, leaving the smitten couple to progress their surprising romance.

"Who would have thought it?" Lord Henry said pensively, helping Polly descend the wide, shallow stone steps which led from the drawing-room to the chamomile lawn. "I have the greatest regard for Farrant, but I never imagined he would set the world on fire! Yet Laura seems to find him agreeable enough, and has done so from the moment they first clapped eyes on each other at Fenchurch!'' He slanted a look down at Polly's serene face. ''I am further in his debt, for I imagine you would not have consented to step outside with me were you not tempted to play matchmaker! Shall we take a seat beneath that oak tree? You should not walk far until your ankle is fully mended.''

They were still in full view of the house and it seemed perfectly proper. The tree cast a cool shade and Polly sank on to the seat with some gratitude.

''Thank goodness! It really is too hot in the full sun!''

''Are we really mere acquaintances, to be discussing the weather?'' Lord Henry asked lazily. ''I can think of far more interesting topics!''

It occurred to Polly that the proximity of the house and the fact that anyone could see them from the window would not deter Lord Henry from his customary outrageous behaviour. His hand was lying along the back of the wooden seat behind her and she was almost certain that he was touching her hair. A moment later he had entwined one of her ringlets about his fingers, just brushing the sensitive skin of her neck as he did so. Polly moved her head sharply away.

''Will your parents look with kindness on an attachment between Lady Laura and Mr Farrant?'' Polly asked, both to distract Lord Henry and also because she had a genuine interest in Laura's future.

Henry sighed. ''I doubt it. They intend her for

John Bellars—'' He stopped as he saw Polly's face.
''I know Bellars made you an offer and you refused
him, and no doubt you share my opinion of him! But
rank and consequence will always be in demand...''
He shrugged, as though the thought made him a little
uncomfortable.

''Is Lady Laura receptive to his suit?'' Polly asked
hesitantly. She did not wish to be thought prying, but
she could not believe that a girl who was showing
all the symptoms of love, as Laura was, could be
easily persuaded to look at another man.

''She was indifferent to all the plans made for
her,'' Henry said bluntly, ''until she met Farrant. I
observed her partiality from the start and wondered
at it! But it will make matters devilishly difficult.
Well—'' he shrugged again ''—we will see...'' He
smiled at Polly. ''A little while ago we were discussing my interests here in Suffolk. What do you
find to do with your time in this delightful backwater?''

Polly accepted that he wished to change the subject. ''Oh, I go riding when it is not too hot, and I
walk and read and paint. I have a fondness for watercolours, although I would say my talent is small.
And as you have seen, there is much company to be
had.''

''Yes, though not all of it congenial,'' Lord Henry
observed. ''I find myself becoming ever less tolerant
of poor company these days. I rate intelligent conversation and good company above all other claims
of rank and importance!''

''Outrageous!'' Polly said, trying not to laugh.
''You were not always so selective, sir!''

Henry raised an eyebrow. "Can you be taking me to task, Lady Polly?"

There was a martial light in Polly's eye. "Your attentions are bestowed somewhat indiscriminately, my lord!"

"I protest! There is no truth in those rumours!"

Polly looked sceptical. "How can you deny it, sir? I suppose that at the least I should commend your taste in admiring my sister-in-law!"

Lord Henry raised a lazy eyebrow. "I collect that you refer to Lady Seagrave?"

"How many other sisters-in-law do I have, sir?" Polly snapped, wishing she had not started on this line of conversation. "Can you deny that you hold her in great esteem?"

"Certainly not!" Henry said promptly. "She is a woman of great good sense and I admire her extremely! But that is all there is to it!"

Polly noted how relieved she felt and perversely wished to punish him.

"That at least could be understood I suppose! But as for Lady Bolt! Do you forget that I saw you with my own eyes at Richmond?"

"Ah." Lord Henry stretched his long legs and admired the polish on his boots. "I wondered whether you would ever have the courage to challenge me with that particular incident!"

"Courage!" Polly was really annoyed now. "It does not require courage, sir, only a little less regard for convention than you would usually find in me! I certainly have the fortitude to accuse you of trifling with my feelings and of falling prey to Lady Bolt's blowsy charms!"

Henry was laughing now, which only added to Polly's anger. Normally she would never have spoken thus. To challenge a gentleman about his behaviour was simply not done, particularly if that behaviour involved a member of the demi-monde.

"How unladylike in you to disparage a rival! I would never have thought it of you, Lady Polly!"

Polly was incensed. "Lady Bolt is no rival of mine! She is welcome to you, sir!"

She tried to rise, but Henry caught her wrist and held her still. "You think, then, that I had arranged to meet Lady Bolt at Richmond?"

Polly tried to sound scornful. "I had assumed that to be the case! Or perhaps I misjudge you! Perhaps you simply seized an opportunity that presented itself to you?"

Henry was still looking amused but there was now a grim edge to his smile. "Oh, no, you are quite correct! I did arrange to meet Lady Bolt, but perhaps not for the reason that you suspect!"

"I am sure we were all able to guess what that reason was, sir!" Polly was smarting now from having her suspicions confirmed, and in so apparently unconcerned a way. Evidently Lord Henry was dead to all sense of propriety!

"And if I were to say that I was more sinned against than sinning? More kissed against than kissing, perhaps—would you like to know how that feels, Lady Polly?"

Their gazes locked for a heated moment, then Polly glanced instinctively towards the house, a bare twenty yards away.

"You would not dare!"

"A dangerous assumption!"

Afterwards, Polly was never quite sure how much had been duress and how far she had moved of her own volition. Certainly Henry had kissed her and when he had stopped she had been in his arms, with no indication of how she had got there or how long she had been there. Indeed, she had no memory of anything other than the delicious pleasure of being kissed by him, a pleasure it would have been foolish to deny since her body was betraying her enjoyment by pressing closer to him.

"Oh, dear, Lady Polly," Henry said with regret, "it seems that the experience was not so repulsive for you as it was for me with Lady Bolt!"

He gave her a mocking smile that made Polly want to slap him and with an unforgivable breach of good manners, abandoned her on the garden seat and strode off indoors.

"Oh!"

Polly only realised that she had spoken aloud when she saw the Dowager Countess hurrying across the lawn towards her.

"Are you unwell, my love?" her mother asked, her face creased with concern. "You sounded quite as though you were suffering from the indigestion! And Lord Henry implied that you are not feeling in quite plump currant. He said that the sun had gone to your head!"

"Oh!" Polly thought that she would explode with indignation and outrage. "Conceited, intolerable man!"

The Dowager looked concerned. "Really, my

love, I do think you might show a little more gratitude! Lord Henry has done us more than one great
service! If you find you cannot like him, at least you
could pretend!''

Chapter Nine

Polly was mortified when Lord Henry chose to escort his mother and sister to Dillingham the following day. She had spent a restless night tossing and turning, reproaching herself for her hasty words to him and for giving him the opportunity to humiliate her further. It was only when she had become calmer that Polly had wondered what Lord Henry had meant by saying that his reason for arranging to meet Lady Bolt had perhaps not been what people might think. Though she puzzled over it, Polly could think of no explanation other than the obvious. It was another mystery to add to all the other riddles surrounding Henry Marchnight.

Fortunately Polly was not required to sit in the drawing-room and make polite conversation with him. Nick Seagrave offered to show Henry the stables and the two of them went off, leaving the ladies alone.

The Duchess and the Dowager Countess Seagrave had never been close friends, but they quickly found common ground in mutual acquaintants and experiences, and when they were comfortably established, Laura turned to Polly with a shy smile and asked if she might see the orangery.

"I have heard that it dates from the seventeenth century and is very fine," she confided, as they strolled along the covered colonnade that connected the main part of the house to the conservatories. "Mr Farrant, who was telling me something of the history of the house and the village, said that lemons were grown here as early as 1690 and that your family had wanted to carry on the tradition! Only fancy! He is a very agreeable gentleman, is he not?"

Polly, who had allowed her thoughts to drift in the inevitable direction of Lord Henry, was amused and a little surprised at the determined manner in which Laura had already steered the conversation on to what interested her. She smiled.

"Indeed, he is! We have known Charles Farrant for an age and always found him a most pleasant and congenial man."

"I was surprised," Laura said a little hesitantly, avoiding Polly's gaze, "that such an amiable man was as yet unmarried. But perhaps he has some understanding with…that is, perhaps there is a lady…" Her voice trailed away and she fixed Polly with a hopeful look from her grey eyes.

Polly pushed open the orangery doors and they entered the humid interior, heavy with the scent of citrus.

"Oh, no, I think it is simply that Mr Farrant has not yet met a lady who made him wish to give up his bachelor state! He was a great admirer of Lucille—Lady Seagrave—before her marriage, but I believe he has never sought to enter the state of marriage himself!''

Laura was listening with attention. Polly was diverted by the concentration the younger girl was devoting to the topic. Clearly it mattered to her a great deal.

''And his family?'' Lady Laura pursued, pretending to admire the orange trees in their ornamental tubs. ''It is perfectly respectable, is it not?''

Polly's lips twitched. ''Oh, entirely unexceptionable! But...'' she hesitated, thinking it only fair to sound a word of caution ''...forgive me, I have no wish to pry, but I am not entirely sure that Mr Farrant would be smiled upon as a suitor for the daughter of a Duke! His estate is relatively small and although the family name is an old one—'' She broke off, shocked, as Laura burst into tears and sat down rather heavily on one of the painted wooden benches.

''Oh, my dear!'' Polly, both taken aback and touched, sat down beside her. ''I am so sorry! I had no wish to upset you—''

''No,'' Laura said, groping for a handkerchief, ''it is entirely my fault, Lady Polly! Oh, thank you—'' as Polly pressed her own handkerchief into her hand ''—it is just that I love him so much and I do not think that I can bear it!''

Polly was silenced by this frank admission. Evidently the Marchnight household was not one in which feelings were repressed—or else Laura simply felt so strongly that in her youth and inexperience she could not conceal it.

''It is as you say,'' Laura was continuing desperately, dabbing at her reddened eyes. ''I believe that

Henry had no objection for Mr Farrant is a friend of his, but Mama spoke to me this morning—she said that Mr Farrant, whilst being a perfectly pleasant man, was not a suitable match for me. She felt that his attentions were becoming too marked and that I should discourage him. But I don't want to discourage him!'' Her voice rose. ''I am sure Mama will warn him off! Or I shall be sent away! Oh, what shall I do?''

Polly reflected that she was not necessarily the best person to advise Laura on the wisdom or otherwise of going against her family's wishes. Laura was the same age as she had been when she had been persuaded to refuse Henry's proposal, although Laura could not know that. For all her gentleness, Laura Marchnight seemed to have more certitude and determination than Polly had ever felt. She was certain of her love for Charles Farrant and would not scruple to admit it. Polly, remembering her own doubts and indecision, felt curiously unqualified to advise her.

Fortunately Laura seemed to feel better simply as a result of pouring her heart out, and was now drying her eyes and tidying herself.

''I expect I look a shocking fright,'' she said, with a brave attempt at a smile. ''I do apologise, Lady Polly—''

Polly touched her hand. ''Do not! Believe me, I can understand how you feel! And that is why my advice is that you can only follow your heart. But make no hasty decisions! It may be that your parents may relent when they see how steadfast is your affection.''

The bright light of determination was suddenly in Laura's eyes. "Oh, I will! Thank you!"

"You had better come up to my room to tidy up," Polly said, getting to her feet. "It is unconscionably hot in here, anyway! And it is fortunate that it is such a sunny day! We may tell your mama that the sun has made your eyes water!"

It was unlucky that they came down the staircase at the moment the gentlemen were crossing the hall from the stables. Henry gave his sister a searching glance and followed it up with a no less penetrating look at Polly, which she tried to meet with equanimity. Laura's eyes were still a little pink and puffy, and her hastily proffered excuse that she had been out in the sun met with Henry's look of blandest disbelief. He made no demur, however, when Polly suggested that they join the others.

"I supppose Laura has been telling you of the scene about Charles Farrant," he said *sotto voce* in Polly's ear as he held the drawing-room door for her. "It is to be hoped that you were suitably unencouraging!"

Polly's eyes flashed. "I seem to remember that you professed friendship for Mr Farrant yesterday!" she hissed, under cover of ringing the bell for more refreshments.

It was impossible to pursue any further conversation, but Polly's heart sank when she considered the implications of Henry's words. If he was not prepared to support his sister, her case looked unhappy indeed.

Fortunately, the Duchess did believe Laura's pretence where her son had been more discerning.

Scolding Laura for going out in the sun without a parasol, she also scrutinised Polly's complexion for blemishes and gave a small nod when she failed to spot any freckle.

"Perhaps Lady Polly might like to accompany me out into the garden—with a parasol, of course," Henry suggested wickedly.

His mother frowned. "A splendid idea, my boy, but not today! Had you forgotten that we are promised to the Fitzgeralds shortly?" She lumbered to her feet and gave a gracious farewell. Polly wondered fleetingly whether Laura would ever be as fat as her mama.

"Charming," said the Duchess, pinching Polly's cheek painfully on her way out. "Quite delightful. You are to be congratulated on your daughter, ma'am! We shall see you again soon, I hope!"

Nicholas Seagrave was trying unsuccessfully to repress his laughter as they watched the coach rumble off. "I believe you have just been given the maternal seal of approval, Poll," he observed. "What an accolade! The Duchess of Marchnight favours you as a daughter-in-law!"

Polly, examining her mixed feelings, was obliged to acknowledge that one would have to love Henry very much to willingly accept such a mother-in-law.

"Well," the Dowager Countess said fairly, "Laura Marchnight is also a charming child, dutiful and well behaved! Sarah Marchnight was only saying just now that Laura had never given them a moment's trouble! Why, Polly—" she looked at her daughter with concern "—you look quite pale all of a sudden! Too much sun, I suppose! Oh, the evils of a hot summer!''

Polly was in fact dwelling more on the twin evils of leading the innocent Lady Laura astray and being considered as a potential bride for Lord Henry. If her mother only knew the advice she had dispensed to Laura but fifteen minutes ago! And the irony of suggesting that Lord Henry should marry anyone when he was so obviously incapable of a necessary steadiness of character!

Polly wandered slowly back up the steps as her mother forged on ahead, instructing Medlyn to have the drains checked, ''For this heat is causing all kinds of noxious vapours!''

The sound of horses' hooves on the gravel gave Polly pause just as she was about to go inside. A lone horseman was galloping up the drive, sliding from the saddle in front of her and flinging his reins carelessly to a grinning groom with a familiarity that suggested that he was happy to be home.

''Peter!''

Peter Seagrave picked his sister up and twirled her about.

''Hello, Poll! Who was that visiting just now? Pretty little piece, ain't she!''

''Peter,'' Polly said with asperity, ''that was Lady Laura Marchnight and she has come to the country precisely to avoid rakes such as yourself! Besides,'' she added with a little smile, ''you will have to fight Charles Farrant for the privilege—he only met her a se'nnight ago but he is already smitten!''

''Oh, well…'' Peter let her go and gave her a smile that seemed a little frayed at the edges ''…I'll secede graciously to Farrant's prior claim! I daresay I am not very welcome here, am I? But I had nowhere else to go!''

Polly slipped her hand through his arm. ''You are not in Mama's good books, certainly, but you know she is always glad to see you at heart! What has happened, Peter?''

''Pockets to let,'' her brother admitted reluctantly. ''I haven't a feather to fly! Oh, God, Poll, I've been an unmitigated fool! I heard that Hetty had become betrothed to Edmund Grantley and I got blind drunk and let Wellerden's cronies fleece me. So I've come to throw myself on Mama's mercy!''

''It's not just Mama,'' Polly said, bluntly. ''Nicholas is here too. He and Lucille returned early from their tour, for Lucille is increasing. You have missed all the news, Peter!''

''So it seems,'' Peter said, clearly torn between pleasure at the news of an impending niece or nephew and concern at finding his brother unexpectedly in residence.

Polly squeezed his arm. ''It will be all right. But how did you hear about Hetty's betrothal?''

''Lady Bolt told me,'' Peter said bitterly. ''She was at Wellerden's place. Said she'd had a letter from Hetty herself! Straight from the horse's mouth!''

Polly reflected that there were plenty of things one might call Lady Bolt, of which a horse was the most flattering.

''I scarcely think Mrs Markham likely to allow Hetty to correspond with Lady Bolt,'' she said carefully, "foster sister or no! I think you may have been duped, Peter!"

Her brother seemed much taken by this idea. "Lord, I never thought of that!" He paused in the entrance hall. "The scheming harpy!"

"I thought you were much struck by Lady Bolt," Polly said, suppressing a giggle. "I remember that you admired her exceedingly and were most cast down when she favoured Garston over you! You do not sound so complimentary now!"

Peter shot his sister a darkling look. "Dashed improper of you to say so, Poll, though you may be right!" He grinned suddenly. "The truth is the woman's a dishonest doxy! And anyway, I couldn't afford her!"

Polly, enchanted by this graphically unflattering description of Lady Bolt, nevertheless tried to get back to matters which were more important.

"But what do you intend to do about Hetty?" she asked demurely. "This news of a betrothal may all be a hum, Peter, and you do still care about Hetty, don't you?"

"Of course I do," Peter said crossly. "The silly chit is supposed to be marrying me, not Edmund Grantley! I tell you, Poll, it goes against the grain with me to sit here and do nothing, but what *can* I do? Can't rush to Kingsmarton and call the fellow out, can I?"

"At least you could go to Kingsmarton and find out what is going on," Polly suggested hopefully.

Her brother looked unconvinced.

"Suppose I'd better go and beard Nick in his lair before I decide what else to do," he said glumly.

"He's bound to cut up rough at me losing so heavily to Wellerden. Still, I'm not the only pigeon his lordship is intent on plucking! I heard that Marchnight was due to arrive in a couple of days' time and you know what a gamester he is! Lady Bolt was *aux anges* to hear that he was joining them!"

"Lord Henry?" Polly was amazed and, she discovered, annoyed. "But he has been here in Woodbridge these four days past! He has just been here now!"

"Well, he's expected at Wellerden's place shortly," Peter asserted incontrovertibly. "Heard about it from Wellerden himself! Like I said, Lady Bolt is waiting for him in an agony of impatience! She don't let her bed go cold!" And with this final, scandalous sally he strolled off to Seagrave's bookroom, unaware of the variety of emotions, all of them unpleasant, which he had aroused in his sister's breast.

Peter stayed only a day at Dillingham, much to his mother's dismay. He had an uncomfortable interview with his elder brother, emerging silent and tight-lipped from Seagrave's room after half an hour.

The next morning Peter left for Kingsmarton at first light.

"I do hope that matters will sort themselves out," Lucille sighed, sitting with her sister-in-law under a huge tented pavilion which had been erected on Dillingham Court's green lawns. "Perhaps I was wrong to encourage Hetty to accept Peter last year. She is very young, after all, and marriage is a very serious business. She has shown a sad unsteadiness of character these months past—''

''So has Peter,'' Polly said frankly. ''This outrageous business of Lady Bolt, for example! He and Hetty deserve each other!''

Polly knew she sounded bad-tempered even before Lucille gave her a look of amused concern. Peter's intelligence that Lord Henry was taking up with Lady Bolt again should not have surprised her, but it had certainly made her very crabby. To have to console the Dowager Countess over Peter's abrupt arrival and departure had been almost too much to bear, when his advent had brought her such unwelcome news.

''Upon my word, you sound very severe!'' Lucille said calmly. ''Quite as though you are suffering the gout! Perhaps your own affairs are not prospering either?''

''You are very acute, Lucille,'' Polly admitted with a half-smile, feeling some of her good humour start to return. ''The truth is that I seem to have been dispensing advice liberally these past few days, yet I can only seem to make a mull of my own business!'' She sighed and got to the point. ''I understand from Peter that Lord Henry Marchnight was taking his place at Wellerden's houseparty—in more ways than one!''

Lucille put her book down. ''Here's a tangle! You mean to imply that Lord Henry has taken up with Lady Bolt? Surely Peter is mistaken?''

Polly shrugged pettishly. ''Is it so surprising after that flagrant public display at Richmond? Oh, Lord Henry denied it to me, but I did not believe him! What an extraordinary woman! Peter, Lord Henry and the Duke of Garston all in the space of a few short weeks! Anyway—'' she shrugged again ''—I neither know nor care! I am done with Lord Henry! He is forever flitting hither and thither like some will o' wisp! It tries my patience!''

''He certainly seems very busy for a man who has no purpose in life,'' Lucille agreed, straight-faced, remembering certain secret information Nicholas had imparted to her about Lord Henry's activities.

''No purpose!'' Polly's indignation was well established again now. Like many people who were seldom disagreeable, once she really lost her temper she had to give it full rein.

''He seems to have purpose enough in gambling and debauchery! And to take up with Lady Bolt, who has been bought and sold by half of London! Well, I will not take her leavings!''

''Oh, dear,'' Lucille said, lips twitching into a smile, ''you are hopelessly in love with him still!''

''In love! I have a mind to marry the next man who asks me!''

Polly caught Lucille's eye and her anger simmered into reluctant amusement. ''Well, no doubt I am a fool to want a man to be other than he is…''

''Not at all!'' Lucille stretched like a cat in the warmth of the sun. ''Rather, you would be a fool to settle for second best! But I am still not entirely sure that Lord Henry has succumbed to Susanna's rather overblown charms!'' She yawned. ''And let us hope Hetty does not feel as you do, or Peter may return home without her! She certainly has a great deal to forgive in his behaviour!''

Polly sighed. Despite the bright promise of the day, she felt strangely discontented.

"Love!" she said crossly.

"'Most loving mere folly,'" Lucille quoted lightly, "Lord, why do I feel so tired all the time?" And she fell asleep where she sat.

The interview with Peter had obviously made Nicholas Seagrave as out of sorts as his brother. He was curt almost to the point of rudeness at lunchtime, announced that he had a number of visits to make about the estate and asked Polly, somewhat surprisingly, whether she would like to join him on the ride. As the day was fine and cooler than of late, Polly agreed with alacrity. They called at a couple of the tenant farms, had tea and cakes at each since Polly was too kind-hearted to refuse the offer, and finished with a gallop along the springy turf at the edge of the sea before turning for home.

The fresh air and exercise had quite restored Polly's spirits and it was unfortunate that as they entered the lime avenue that led up to Dillingham Court, the cause of her ill-humour should appear before her eyes and undo all the good work of the afternoon.

Lord Henry Marchnight, on an elegant bay, was just trotting down the drive and reined in hastily at the sight of them.

"Lord Seagrave! Lady Polly! This is good fortune indeed! I am just come from the house, where I was told you were out about the estate. I came to take my leave, for I shall be departing Suffolk on the morrow."

Coming so quickly after Peter's assertions, this could only confirm Polly's suspicion that Lord Henry was for the Wellerden houseparty. Her chestnut mare jibbed slightly as her hands tightened involuntarily on the reins.

"Is this a permanent departure, Lord Henry?" she enquired sweetly. "You seem to be forever travelling hither and thither! Such a busy life!"

Out of the corner of her eyes she thought she saw a flicker of a grin cross her brother's face, but Lord Henry remained impassive.

"A temporary separation only, Lady Polly," he said, very courteously. "As you know, I am as fond of Suffolk as anywhere on earth! I shall be back as soon as I am able."

Polly made a great show of examining her riding gloves. "And where is your present destination?" she enquired, as though it was of no great moment. "I have heard that Buckinghamshire is proving very popular this summer!"

Lord Henry raised his eyebrows. He was looking so lazily amused that Polly felt herself go hot with annoyance. So he thought it a diversion to trifle with her feelings and then go after other game as the fancy took him!

"Good luck and godspeed then, Harry," Nick Seagrave said, leaning over to shake his hand. Polly, watching this display of masculine complicity with irritation, nevertheless noticed the significant look which passed between the two men. She frowned a little as Lord Henry turned his horse and cantered away. It was almost as though Seagrave knew something, and yet what was there to know? Lord Henry was, by his own admission, a man whose prime concern was to seek after pleasure, and if there were other, more mysterious, aspects to his character, what could Nick Seagrave know of those?

"I collect that you were wishing him good luck in his gambling," she said crossly.

"In all his ventures," Seagrave agreed smoothly.

Lady Laura Marchnight was becoming a regular visitor to Dillingham Court, where she and Polly would walk together in the gardens or set their easels up with some idyllic aspect before them, in the hope of capturing it in watercolours or charcoal. Laura made no further reference to her burgeoning relationship with Mr Farrant, and at the evening *soirées* and parties in Woodbridge, under the watchful eye of the Duchess, she appeared to be avoiding him. Polly was sad but not surprised that rank and consequence had won the day. In the face of the Duchess's powerful disapproval, it was difficult to see how the romance could have prospered. She asked no questions but simply enjoyed Laura's company, which was certainly a welcome change from that of the Dittons.

The Dittons were relentlessly sociable, especially with those they sought to cultivate, and it was difficult to avoid all their invitations. Polly, having managed to excuse herself from a trip to the theatre in Woodbridge in their company, found that good manners forced her to accept the next pressing invitation, which was to make up a party to visit Myrmingham Abbey, a former Franciscan priory whose ruins were particularly romantic and picturesque. The scenery

was indeed very fine but the company a sad trial with
Mr Ditton uncertain whether to bestow his dubious
compliments on Polly or Laura, and Miss Ditton
sulking at not being the centre of attention.

"Lady Polly is becoming quite tanned," Mrs Ditton observed to the Dowager Countess, with a hint
of malice, as they returned to the carriages at the end
of the day. "I should not encourage my Thalia to
wander about in the sun without a parasol!"

Lady Seagrave looked hard at her daughter but
could observe no more than a healthy colour. "Polly
looks very well," she said coldly. "And she always
wears a hat with a very wide brim!"

They all returned from the outing in a scratchy
mood that the romantic ruins had done nothing to
soothe and Polly was sorely tempted to reject the
suggestion that they all go to the Fair at Cold Hollow
two days hence. Rather to her surprise, however,
Laura Marchnight seemed very eager to attend and
almost begged Polly to go with her.

"The Fair is accounted to be great fun, Lady
Polly," Laura said, looking hopeful. "I am persuaded that you would enjoy it a great deal!"

Her anxious face relaxed into a smile at Polly's
reluctant acquiescence.

In the event, Polly rather enjoyed the spectacle.
Cold Hollow was only a small town, but its Fair was
famous for miles around. The proceedings were
opened by the Town Crier ringing the revels in as
the Mayor processed down the street, accompanied
by four civic dignitaries. They seemed very full of
their own importance and Polly and Laura could not

help but laugh at their rather tattered livery of gold and blue.

Once the ceremonial part was over, the traders and stallholders were free to start peddling their goods. The visitors strolled between the booths, admiring the variety of entertainments, from livestock to a small circus. Tristan Ditton was persuaded to show his prowess in the boxing booth, despite Mrs Ditton's protests that it was not suitable in front of the ladies. He took a heavy fall almost immediately against the Suffolk Champion, Mal Marcombe.

"Oh, dear," Lady Laura whispered in Polly's ear, "I believe Mr Ditton's pride has taken the heaviest tumble! He looks quite furious! Do let us stroll on ahead, Lady Polly, and avoid his ill temper!"

The day was fine with a light breeze, and it was fun to meander through the crowd, eyeing the attractions. Lady Laura caught Polly's arm.

"Oh, look, a gypsy fortune-teller! I am minded to go in and discover my destiny!"

Polly hesitated, for she was not at all sure that this was the sort of entertainment of which the Duchess of Marchnight would approve. Turning around, Polly saw that Mrs Ditton, their chaperon for the day, was a considerable distance behind and appeared to be involved in some kind of altercation with both her children and an angry stallholder. Polly's heart sank. She had no wish to rejoin them and become embroiled in the dispute, and Lady Laura was already at the tent entrance, ready to pull aside the flap and go in.

"Very well," Polly said weakly. "I shall wait here for you, Laura. And do not let them cozen you!"

But it was too late. Lady Laura had already disappeared into the tent's dusky, sweet-scented interior
and with a sigh, Polly sat down on the grass to wait.

It was very warm in the sun and Polly was almost
convinced that she had nodded off to sleep, although
when she opened her eyes again everything looked
much the same. She could not see the Dittons, for
which she was profoundly grateful, but as she
blinked against the bright sunlight, she was almost
certain that she saw Lady Laura, arm in arm with Mr
Farrant, just passing out of sight behind the round-
abouts. She scrambled to her feet, pulling aside the
tent flap and peering into the gypsy's den.

Dark, inquisitive eyes surveyed her from top to
toe.

"Fortune, lady?" the old woman asked, holding
out a hand to encourage Polly forward. "I can tell
you all about the handsome gentleman waiting to
steal your heart—"

"No, thank you," Polly said hastily, backing out
of the tent. So Laura had slipped away! Polly hurried
past the stalls that lay between her and the fun fair.
Where had they gone? Polly could not spot Laura's
slender figure anywhere. Bells for sheep, leather gai-
ters, linen gaberdine for labourers, Birmingham jewellery…Polly's head spun. She hurried around a corner, convinced she could see Laura in the distance,
and found herself back in front of the fortune-teller's
tent. Nor was she alone there.

"Good afternoon, Lady Polly," Lord Henry
Marchnight said politely.

Shock at his sudden appearance and the recollection that she had failed in her duty to keep an eye

on his sister held Polly silent for a moment. Henry was smiling very slightly.

"Have you lost your party again, perhaps?"

"No, of course not," Polly snapped, brushing the grass from her skirt and feeling foolish at having been caught in such a situation. "I saw the Dittons but a moment ago and I have been waiting for Lady Laura, who—"

"Who has tricked you into thinking she was having her fortune told whilst in fact she is making secret assignations," Lord Henry finished a little grimly. "I take it that that is why I find you outside Madame Rose's tent, Lady Polly? You were not thinking of parting with your money in return for the assurance that a tall, fair gentleman would presently sweep you off your feet?"

"Oh!" A variety of emotions, mostly uncomfortable, warred for ascendancy within Polly. She was not going to give him the satisfaction of a reply. She accepted Lord Henry's arm and they started to walk slowly between the booths.

"It is too bad of Laura to take advantage of your good nature," he said, after a moment, seeing that Polly's innate good manners made it impossible for her to criticise his sister. "In mitigation I can only say that she is very young and very much in love, and has not yet realised that true friendship should not be abused."

"If only she had confided in me—" Polly broke off, not wishing to suggest that she would have helped Lady Laura deceive her family. Lord Henry's sudden appearance in search of Laura and his grimness in the face of his sister's behaviour suggested that she certainly did not have his support.

"Is it certain?" she asked carefully. "Do you know that she has arranged to meet Mr Farrant? I did think that I had seen them a moment ago."

"Indeed you did." Henry sounded rather grim. "I saw them myself, walking past the gunsmith's stall. In fairness to Laura, I do not think that they mean to do more than meet and enjoy each other's company, but she should know better... Of course, she had no notion that I should be here today and see through her deception."

This brought Polly's mind back to other matters, equally disagreeable. "I understood you to be at Wellerden," she said, a little crossly. "You are forever coming and going, are you not, sir?"

Henry laughed softly as he noted the martial light in her eyes. "Ah, the gossips have been busy again! Indeed, I spent a few days there—"

"In most entertaining company, I understand," Polly said, despite herself.

"Oh, the best! Can you doubt it?"

Polly almost stamped her foot, but knew he was only trying to provoke her.

"Well, I dare say our tastes differ there, my lord."

"I should hope so!" Henry laughed again as he saw her look of fury. "Come, you know that I travel widely and have many interests, Lady Polly! I am only teasing you!"

It was in some ways fortunate that they came across Mr Farrant and Lady Laura at that moment. The were standing before a small flock of chickens, apparently engrossed.

"The best you could buy, sir," the poultryman was saying eagerly, "and a better price you will not find—"

"Henry!" Lady Laura said, in horrified tones. Her gaze travelled to Polly and a deep blush came into her cheeks. "Lady Polly, I thought—"

"I doubt Lady Polly wishes to hear your excuses now, Laura," Henry said, fixing his sister with a cold, quelling gaze. "You have used her most shamefully. As for you, Farrant—" Henry's gaze turned to the unlikely Romeo "—I should have expected better of you!"

Charles Farrant started to stammer apologies and Laura to cry quietly. The poultryman took his cap off and scratched his head at this unexpected turn of events. They were attracting quite a lot of interest. Polly touched Henry's arm. She had seen the Dittons, with their unerring instinct for scandal, approaching down the row of stalls.

"This will have to wait," she whispered hastily. "We must all pretend that we met up by chance, I think. Mrs Ditton!" She turned with a beaming smile to greet the lady. "How glad I am to have found you again, ma'am! And only see, Mr Farrant and Lord Henry are here as well! How the good weather brings people out of doors!"

Henry was smiling a little at such inanity, but he followed Polly's lead easily enough. "Farrant has told me that the Fairs here are renowned for their local colour, ma'am, and I thought to take a look. I am returned from Buckinghamshire only yesterday…"

The image of Susanna Bolt came into Polly's mind

again, incongruous amidst all the fresh air and sunlight. It could only serve to make her ill temper worse. Laura was sniffing a little and Polly took her arm, drawing her away from Miss Ditton's prying eyes. Any enjoyment had gone from the day.

"I'm sorry," Laura whispered as Polly hustled her back towards the carriages. "It was not that I did not trust you, but Charles said I was not to tell anyone! I have been very foolish…"

Polly's heart twisted with pity. She thought it most unlikely that Lady Laura would be permitted to remain in Suffolk now that this not-so-secret romance had been found to be flourishing, and Laura had not really done anything very bad. She looked at the girl's reddened eyes and noticed with a flash of irritation that Miss Ditton was almost running in her attempt to catch up with them. The tears could not be concealed. How then to explain them? Her talent for deception was being stretched to the limit.

"You should not believe all that the fortune-teller told you, Laura," she said loudly. "I might have known that she would upset you!"

Miss Ditton's avid face appeared over Laura's shoulder. "Oh, whatever can she have said?" She asked eagerly. "Dear Lady Laura, do tell!"

It was Lord Henry who answered, a hint of malice in his grey eyes. "She told my sister to beware of false friends, Miss Ditton, and to value true friendship above rubies!"

Chapter Ten

It was a sad little party that made its way back to Woodbridge. Charles Farrant and the Marchnights had gone their separate ways, with Lady Laura still sniffing into her handkerchief. Miss Ditton spent the entire journey speculating spitefully about Laura and Mr Farrant, pressing Polly to give details of the encounter between them and Lord Henry, certain that it was less good-humoured than Polly insisted. Polly's head ached. She had no wish to be obliged to lie even more and it only made Laura's treatment of her seem more shabby. She had liked the girl and considered her a friend. It was lowering to imagine that she had been used to further the clandestine romance. As for Lord Henry, she did not wish to think of him at all, for all her thoughts were melancholy ones.

It was with considerable relief that they reached the gates of Dillingham Court, and Polly insisted on leaving the Dittons' coach and walking up the lime avenue to the house. As she approached the carriage sweep, she was startled to see a travelling coach on the forecourt surrounded by what seemed vast amounts of luggage. Polly's spirits lifted and her step quickened. This had to be Peter and Hetty Markham, back from Kingsmarton. That must mean that the two of them were reconciled, which was a much-needed piece of good news.

Polly found the whole family assembled in the rosewood drawing-room. Miss Markham, a pretty girl with huge blue eyes and copious amounts of curling brown hair, was standing clutching Peter's hand and looking embarrassed as she responded to the Dowager Countess's slightly frosty welcome.

"Hetty and I are to be married in six weeks' time," Peter was saying as Polly slipped into the room. "We see no point in waiting any longer. After all, the wedding has already been delayed once."

The Dowager Countess blanched a little, startled into plain-speaking. "Six weeks? There will be a lot of talk, Peter! Everyone will say that you have anticipated your marriage vows and need to make a hasty match—"

Hetty flushed bright red and muttered something incoherent. For a fleeting moment she put her face in her hands, a gesture which Polly noticed with both concern and curiosity. Peter was standing his ground in the face of his mother's bluntness, although he too had reddened. There was a very curious atmosphere in the room, Polly thought. She took a chair unobtrusively by the fireplace and accepted a cup of tea from Lucille with a slight smile of thanks.

"Please, Mama!" Peter was saying carefully. "I suppose we must resign ourselves to being the subject of ill-bred remarks, but I do not intend to let my life be governed by it!''

Polly and Lucille exchanged a look. It seemed to Polly that Peter had grown in stature since he had gone away. There was a protective element in his behaviour towards Hetty that was very obvious and must surely augur well for their future relationship. Miss Markham, in contrast, seemed to have lost much of her natural ebullience and vivacity but perhaps this could be put down to an embarrassment at the rupture with Peter, now so fortunately overcome.

There was an awkward little silence that threatened to become prolonged. Polly hastened forward to kiss Hetty and draw her over to the sofa where she started to ask about the journey and enquire into Mrs Markham's health. Gradually Miss Markham relaxed a little and by the time the drinks were replenished, accompanied by some more of Mrs Appleton's delicious honey cakes, she was chatting almost as normal. It still seemed to Polly that there was something brittle in Hetty's manner and her eyes watched Peter almost constantly as if for reassurance. Polly, tired by the events of the day and the difficult scene at the Fair, noted Hetty's change of manner but felt too weary to think about it properly. It slipped to the back of her mind during the lively and enjoyable family dinner that followed, and it was only as she was brushing her hair before the mirror at bedtime that she remembered Hetty's tension and wondered at it. She could think of no explanation, however, and went to bed thinking that she must speak to Lucille about it. If anyone would know what was the matter with Hetty, it would be Lucille.

* * *

Polly would have been astonished to learn that a lone visitor called at Dillingham Court that night, long after she was abed. Medlyn had taken the visitor's card along to the study where the Earl of Seagrave sat up late, poring over old estate maps. He ushered the man into the Earl's presence and accepted his master's instruction that he should then go to bed. He asked no questions and in the morning all recollection of the visit had slipped his memory.

When their business was finished, the Earl offered his guest a second glass of brandy and sat back.

"So, how does your suit prosper, Harry?" he asked idly.

Henry Marchnight gave his lop-sided grin. "Very badly, I thank you! Your sister is now convinced that I am a hardened rake and lecher! She has me pursuing Lady Bolt from Richmond to Buckinghamshire! Never has the price of information been so high!"

"Lady Bolt ruining your reputation, is she?" Seagrave asked with spurious sympathy. "I thought she must have some information you wanted! I could not see you getting caught like that otherwise!"

Henry grimaced. "Would that Lady Polly had your discernment, Seagrave! But I can hardly blame her for jumping to the obvious conclusions! After all, I have deliberately made a name for myself as a rake and gamester. To plead innocence now, no matter how genuine, will cut little ice."

"Susanna Bolt is a deeply mercenary and unpleasant woman," Seagrave said absently, folding his map of Dillingham away. "Can she be caught in the same net that will trap Chapman, Harry?"

"I hope so." Henry drained his glass. "I plan it to be so! But there is another I am more anxious to catch…"

"An unholy trinity," Seagrave agreed. "I must confess I do not like it, Harry. Whilst he is free to come and go as he pleases, there is great danger."

Henry nodded. "I agree, but we cannot move against him until we are sure of Chapman. Until then, the risk must be run."

"He does not suspect you?"

"No." Henry permitted himself a grim smile. "His vanity is such that he suspects no one! And that will be his downfall!"

The following morning heralded another glorious, late summer day, with a sky as blue as cobalt and the sea as smooth and soft as silk. Polly, established with her easel in the shelter of a group of trees, watched as Peter and Hetty, and the rest of their party, strolled away down the beach in the direction of the small huddle of houses which constituted Shingle Street. They had had a delightful picnic lunch and now Miss Ditton had declared it time to call upon the poor fisher families who eked out a living in this isolated spot. Polly pitied the unsuspecting poor.

The settlement at Shingle Street had been augmented in the recent wars when a Martello Tower had been built as part of the coastal defences. The only other habitation in the vicinity was the romantically named House of Tides, the home of Lady Bellingham, former actress and black sheep of the county. Polly had intended calling on her ladyship, who had been a staunch friend of Lucille's before her marriage, but Miss Ditton had drawn back from the suggestion with distaste.

"Lud, to call on the actress? My mama would have a fit of the vapours if she heard I had been consorting with such a person!"

Polly had reluctantly abandoned her plans of the visit, not wishing to cause disagreement amongst the party and privately reflecting that it was probably unkind of her to inflict Miss Ditton's company on so likeable a character as Lady Bellingham. All the same, she was sorry.

It was very quiet and the breeze was pleasantly cooling. Polly became engrossed in her sketching, enjoying her solitude, and had no idea how long she sat there. Her attention was eventually drawn back to the present by the small scrape of stone on stone, a little distance away along the shingle beach. She put down her charcoal and listened. The noise came again. There appeared to be no one on the wide empty seashore, nor could Polly see anyone else nearby. The cries of children reached her faintly from the cottages where Miss Ditton was no doubt exercising her patronage, and she could just see Peter and Hetty in the distance, wandering hand in hand along the shore, engrossed in each other.

Polly got to her feet slowly and trod across to the edge of the springy grass. The small cliff sloped away steeply down to the shingle and cast a dark shadow. Polly squinted in the bright sunlight, then recoiled in surprise at the sight of a figure emerging from the shade a mere twenty yards away. It was Lord Henry Marchnight. He was dusting the sand

and shale from his hands and shaking more debris off his jacket. He had not seen her.

"Oh!" Polly's foot slipped as she stepped hastily backwards, sending a small shower of stones down onto the beach. In an agony of suspense she heard them bouncing off the rocks below and peered down to see Lord Henry, his eyes narrowed against the sun, staring straight up at her.

"Lady Polly!" Lord Henry took the steep cliff path with ease and arrived beside her barely out of breath. "How do you do, ma'am! I had no idea that you were there!"

"I have been sketching." Polly gestured towards the easel, its paper flapping in the breeze. For some reason she felt defensive, needing to excuse her presence. And Lord Henry was displaying all his habitual careless elegance and assurance, which was annoying since he had been creeping about on the beach in a most suspicious manner.

"But surely you are not alone?" Lord Henry looked round. "Where are the others?"

"Oh, they have gone to dispense charity to the villagers," Polly said, trying not to laugh. "Miss Ditton is calling on the poor."

"Good God, must she?" Henry looked disgusted. "But you prefer the solitary company of your sketch book? I cannot blame you, ma'am!"

They started walking slowly along the top of the cliff in the direction of the House of Tides.

"How is Lady Laura today?" Polly enquired hesitantly. She did not wish to pry, but was very afraid that there would have been unhappy repercussions as a result of the clandestine meeting at the Fair.

Henry sighed. "She is not at all well, I am afraid. My mother has forbidden her from ever speaking to Charles again and she has taken it very badly. Laura is young and headstrong…" He shrugged uncomfortably. "Mama has always considered her delicate, never realising that Laura's spirit is at least as strong as her own! When I suggested at Dillingham that you should not encourage Laura in her feelings for Charles it was not because I disapproved of the connection, but only because I knew how it could split the family! Indeed, I have tried to argue her case, but it was no use…" He shrugged again and fell silent.

Polly felt a rush of mingled relief and apprehension. She was glad to know that Henry was not motivated by the same regard for status and consequence as his parents, but like him she could see that Laura's love for Charles Farrant would set her on a collision course.

"Will Laura accept her mother's edict?" she asked carefully. "If not, perhaps Mr Farrant might be persuaded… But he seems as smitten as she… Oh, dear, it is so very difficult!"

Henry smiled at this masterly understatement. "I believe both of them are in earnest and neither will waver in their regard! By far the best course would be for my parents to accept the less-than-brilliant match, but I doubt they will see matters in the same light! I believe Mama will try to send Laura away." His gaze met Polly's. "Laura deeply regrets the way that she treated you yesterday, Lady Polly. She would not for all the world have risked your friendship, but she was foolish and her head was filled with romance—"

Polly made a slight gesture of dismissal. "I understand. I would not wish to lose Laura's friendship either and I am sorry that she is so unhappy."

They walked on a little in silence. The breeze was freshening, whipping Polly's hair loose of its pins and tugging at her skirts.

"No doubt you too will be leaving soon, sir," Polly said, a little coolly in case Lord Henry thought that the answer mattered to her. "Indeed, I am surprised to find you are still with us! You do not usually find our dull occupations diverting for more than a day or two at a time!"

Henry slanted a look at her. He was smiling. Polly found it most unsettling.

"Oh, I intend to be settled here for a while!" he said easily. "And in truth, there are far more exciting things happening here than, say, at Wellerden's houseparty! You would be surprised, ma'am!"

Polly felt vaguely irritated. Lord Henry always seemed to be singing the praises of Suffolk—then hurrying off to be elsewhere.

"You certainly seemed fascinated by whatever you discovered on the beach just now, my lord!" she said, a little snappishly. "What was it? A piece of driftwood? A message in a bottle?"

"I do believe you are essaying satire, Lady Polly," Lord Henry said admiringly. "But you should not mock me, you know! I was investigating a tale I had heard, which was that there is a secret passageway from the House of Tides out under the cliffs. I think I may have found the entrance! Would you like to see?"

"A secret passageway?" Polly was curious despite herself. "You mean—for smuggled goods?"

"No doubt that was what it was used for some years ago," Lord Henry agreed, "although there's precious little to be gained from such a trade now that the excise duties are so reduced. I imagine the passage to have been silted up for some time, but it is interesting, is it not? I must ask Lady Bellingham's permission to investigate further. Would you care to see the cave entrance?"

"I think not," Polly said severely. "To go in there with you would be the utmost folly!"

Lord Henry grinned. "Perhaps you are right, ma'am! Ah well, I see I must continue my investigations alone! And no doubt I should return you to your party now. They must be becoming anxious of your whereabouts."

There was no sign of the others as they retrod the springy turf path back to where Polly had left her paints and paper. Lord Henry viewed her drawings with undisguised interest.

"This is very pretty," he commented, pointing to a sketch of the tumbledown cottages, their washing blowing against the blue sky. "But this…" he paused "…this has real depth and passion. The earth colours, the texture… It is a very sensuous picture…" His gaze dwelt thoughtfully on her for a moment and Polly hurriedly covered the painting up. It was a country picture that she had drawn a few weeks previously, a study of the fields and woods about Dillingham, but instead of her usual pastels she had used oil paints and the effect had been startling. The rich reds and browns had given the painting a tactile quality, as though one could almost step into the picture. Polly was not quite comfortable with it.

The breeze was becoming fresher now and Lord Henry was frowning a little as he scanned the eastern horizon.

"I do believe we are in for a storm. Do you see those clouds massing out at sea? Where are your carriages, ma'am?"

Polly turned. "I think they must have gone down to the village to collect the others, sir. But it is only a step. Perhaps if I follow them down—"

The first drop of rain landed on her drawing paper, apparently out of the blue sky. It was followed by another and another. The wind had suddenly become strong. Polly bent to scoop up her scattered paints and paper and stuff them all into her portfolio. The easel blew over with a sudden crack, making her jump.

"We had best seek shelter," Lord Henry said, all hint of easy amusement gone from his tone. "No, it is too far to the village. The House of Tides is nearer. Hurry, please!"

Polly could understand his urgency. She had no coat to protect her, and already the rain was heavier. The sky over the sea had turned a leaden grey. She could not believe how quickly the weather had changed and now the air was heavy with the threat of thunder.

The first flicker of lightning touched the sky as they reached the edge of Lady Bellingham's land. Polly was almost in a panic now. She hated thunderstorms and the ones that rolled in from the sea could be particularly fierce.

"Not far now." Henry's voice was reassuring. "We will go in the back way, through the shrubbery, as it's closer."

He held the little gate open for her and they slipped through as the rain began to pour in earnest. Polly, clutching her soaking portfolio and box of crayons under her arm, wondered briefly what on earth Lady Bellingham would make of the arrival of two such drowned rats. She had only met her ladyship a couple of times for, though travelling copiously, Lady Bellingham was virtually a recluse when she was in Suffolk.

Henry helped Polly up on to the terrace with a hand under her elbow. The steps were slippery in the rain and she almost stumbled.

Then the French windows were flung open before them and Lady Bellingham's rich contralto tones, warm with amusement, said, "Well, upon my word! Apollo and Niobe! Or am I mixing my Greeks and Romans? I was never very good at mythology, alas!"

Polly, regardless of her dripping clothes, found herself engulfed in a huge scented embrace. Lady Bellingham's many colourful scarves wafted about her like a massive sheet.

"Dear child!" her ladyship said fondly. "How delightful to see you again! And Henry!" Now there was a roguish twinkle in her dark eyes, "You have been away too long, dear boy!"

There was a fearsome clap of thunder overhead. Polly jumped violently.

"Come in, come in!" Lady Bellingham urged, stepping back so that they could go into the drawing-room.

"We have come to throw ourselves on your mercy, Lady Bellingham," Henry said with a smile, pushing the soaking hair back out of his eyes. "Lady Polly and I were taking a stroll on the cliffs when the storm came up, and we thought to seek shelter here. Lady Polly has become separated from her party in all the confusion. I apologise for the imposition."

"Nonsense, dear boy, and you know it!" Lady Bellingham clapped her hands so that her bracelets jingled loudly. A fat white cat, asleep on a puffy sofa, raised its head briefly before closing its eyes again with the most perfect indifference.

"I adore excitement, as you know," she continued, eyes sparkling, "and I lead such a retired life usually. Your arrival is most timely for I was about to succumb to ennui. I shall rely on you for all the gossip in recompense!"

Her eye fell on Polly, dripping quietly on to the carpet.

"Dear me! I should not keep you talking or you will catch a chill! Now, I will take Lady Polly away to change her clothing and Gaston, my general factotum, will fetch some dry things for you, my dear Henry! Then he can go and see if he can find trace of your friends, my dear." She smiled at Polly. "I am sure we can reunite you all soon!"

She swept Polly out of the room, paused briefly in the hall to summon Gaston and give him her instructions, then whisked Polly off up the ornate staircase to a small bedroom decorated in the French fashion.

Polly stared at her reflection in the pier glass with something approaching horror. Her hair was straggling around her face, drying in wisps, and her clothes were sticking to her. She was not normally vain, but she could hardly bear to think of Lord Henry seeing her thus.

Lady Bellingham smiled understandingly. "Never mind, my love! I am sure Lord Henry finds your dishevelment attractive rather than otherwise! That was always *my* experience of gentlemen! And I can see that he admires you exceedingly!"

Polly blushed bright red. "Oh, Lady Bellingham, I think you must be mistaken. Lord Henry and I—" She broke off, quite unable to continue in the face of Lady Bellingham's amused cynicism.

"Fustian, my dear! Stuff and nonsense!" Lady Bellingham was busy pulling some enormous gowns out of the closet. Her voice was muffled. "You may pretend to be indifferent to each other, but you cannot cozen me! I have known Henry Marchnight for years and he has never truly cared for any young lady. But you—! Well!" She emerged with a huge lilac-coloured dress over her arm. Polly held it up in front of her. It was going to look like a tent. If Lord Henry found her attractive in that then the only explanation could be that his wits must have gone a-begging.

Chapter Eleven

Miss Ditton certainly found the outfit rather diverting when she and the rest of Polly's lost party were
shepherded into the drawing-room an hour later.

"La, Lady Polly, you are all the crack! You must
tell me where you buy your modes!"

"Miss Ditton, I presume!" Lady Bellingham
glided forward smoothly to greet her unwanted
guests. Her smile was all that was gracious, but there
was a look in those world-weary dark eyes that suggested that she had met Miss Ditton's type many
times before and knew precisely how to deal with
them. She welcomed Miss Ditton and her brother
coolly, Hetty with more warmth and Peter with almost as much enthusiasm as she had shown Henry,
who was now lounging before the fireplace watching
with amusement. He looked considerably more elegant in his borrowed plumes than Polly did in hers.
Polly wondered where Lady Bellingham had got
such stylish gentlemen's clothes from. She could
hardly imagine the lugubrious Gaston cutting a dash

in the slim black pantaloons, black jacket and snowy white shirt.

Gaston had found Polly's companions huddling in one of the cottages in Shingle Street. When the rain had started they had hurried to the carriages, intent on setting off back immediately until Peter had remembered Polly and had set out to look for her. This had delayed them sufficently for the road to become waterlogged, since it was scarcely more than a sandy track, and they had no choice but to inflict their presence on one of the glum village families until the rain stopped. This was not quite how Miss Ditton saw their predicament and she was loud in her condemnation of the noisome cottage and its smelly occupants.

"...and do you know, my dear Lady Polly, they actually had the animals in there with them!" She shuddered. "Apparently it helps them to keep warm!"

Polly caught Henry's eye just as he tried to repress a smile.

"Doubtless your presence incommoded the poor pigs considerably," Lady Bellingham said, with a suspiciously straight face. "They are not animals that take kindly to a disruption of their routine!"

The precise nature of Miss Ditton's difficulties now became clear. She could not snub Lady Bellingham, for she had no doubt that her ladyship was perfectly capable of turning her out into the rain if she chose. On the other hand, the Dittons had never acknowledged the former actress, even after the Seagraves had taken her up. Mr Ditton cleared his throat noisily, settling himself on the sofa.

"Extraordinary customs these inbred country folk have! Why, I remember—"

He broke off with a loud yelp. "Good God, ma'am, that creature has bitten me!"

Lady Bellingham smiled fondly at Horace the cat, who was moving more swiftly than anyone had ever seen in his attempt to get away from under Mr Ditton.

"Dear Horace," Lady Bellingham said sweetly. "Such a good judge of character! You are sitting in his place, I fear, Mr Ditton. He will not be quick to forgive!"

Fortunately a loud thunderclap interrupted this exchange and the ladies all exclaimed in dismay. The rain was still tumbling from a leaden sky. Lady Bellingham prosaically ordered tea and Henry sensibly suggested that Tristan Ditton and Peter join him in a game of billiards to while away the time.

The rain ceased for a while at about five, but Gaston gloomily reported that the road was still impassable by carriage. Henry suggested sending a messenger to Dillingham, Fenchurch and Westwardine to explain that they were marooned for the night, and the Dittons reluctantly agreed.

"I suppose staying here for the night is preferable to being set upon in the forest in the dark," Miss Ditton said discontentedly, staring out at the drenched garden.

"Preferable for you at least," Henry agreed blandly, smiling at her. Polly stifled a giggle. She had noticed how Henry's personality had undergone a subtle shift again as soon as they had company. He was still perfectly pleasant but the incisive edge had

gone. Once again, Polly puzzled over the curious in-
sipidity he could apparently assume at will.

"Perhaps, Miss Ditton, if you are very fortunate,
Lady Bellingham will lend you one of her night-
dresses," she said politely.

"Oh, my maid, Conchita, has just the thing for
Miss Ditton!" Lady Bellingham said cheerfully, ignoring Thalia Ditton's look of horror at being obliged
to wear a maid's night garments.

Lady Bellingham, revelling in her unexpected dinner party, did them proud with a meal of quail's eggs,
honey-roasted duckling and strawberries with cream.
Even Miss Ditton could not find fault with the hospitality. In the flickering candlelight they looked a
motley crowd. Peter had become soaked looking for
Polly earlier and had borrowed one of the late Lord
Bellingham's outfits. Unfortunately his lordship, like
his spouse, had been built on ample lines and had
also been several inches shorter than Peter. Polly felt
like a small girl who had been rummaging in the
dressing-up box and there was something distinctly
raffish about Henry Marchnight's appearance, with
no neckcloth and his tumbled fair hair. Polly thought
he looked most attractive but rather as though he had
spent a long night at the gaming tables.

It was, in fact, one of the most enjoyable aspects
of the evening that Henry spent so much time in her
company. The others played a few desultory hands
of whist and Miss Ditton insisted in entertaining
them at the pianoforte, but Henry gently monopolised
Polly's company and talked to her for most of the
evening. Nor was it idle chitchat—they discovered
and re-discovered their shared interests in music and

the theatre, reading, walking and the countryside. Polly did not want the evening to end.

Miss Ditton yawned loudly.

"Lud, how quiet it is out here in the middle of nowhere! I declare I would succumb to a fit of the megrims if I were forced to spend any time here! One could imagine all kinds of spectres and demons howling at the door!"

"They do say that Rendlesham Forest is haunted, Miss Ditton," Lord Henry said idly, "so it is fortunate you were not obliged to make your way back through the dark. A broken axle, a lost wheel, and you would be at the mercy of the spirits! They say that the black shuck, a huge black spectral dog, stalks its prey on stormy nights!"

Mr Ditton gave his excitable, whinnying laugh. "Or you would be at the mercy of more human predators! Is it true, dear Lady Bellingham, that there is a band of smugglers still at work in these parts, tapping on the window to signal the delivery of their goods, hiding brandy kegs in the churches…?"

Polly shivered as the shadows flickered. Out here, isolated on a stormy night, it was easy to believe almost anything. Hetty's eyes were huge and frightened as she clutched Peter's hand.

"I have never heard of it," Lady Bellingham said comfortably, leaning forward to put another log on the fire and smiling at Henry as he took it from her to place in the grate. "The smugglers are long gone from here, Mr Ditton. But by all means let us frighten ourselves with stories if we wish to be Gothic!"

Tristan Ditton looked put out by such determined common sense.

"Alternatively," Lady Bellingham beamed, "we could have crumpets and hot chocolate before we retire! Gaston!" She rang the bell vigorously. "Some refreshments, please!"

It was strange, Polly thought, how the room seemed to brighten and the atmosphere lift with Lady Bellingham's words. Her ladyship was now telling an enthralled Hetty about some of her experiences at Drury Lane Theatre.

"You should have seen me in *The Country Girl*, my dear, one of my greatest triumphs! Why, it was an innocent version of that old Restoration romp, *The Country Wife*, but to tell the truth I always preferred the bawdier version! I was perfect for the part, so natural and unspoilt, for I was a country girl myself, you see, and only nineteen years of age at the time! Ah, what a time it was!" And she shook her head reminiscently.

Polly tried to imagine Lady Bellingham as a country girl of nineteen and failed sadly. There was something so world-weary and disillusioned about Lady Bellingham, though that was not to say that she had lost her natural kindness. Polly was conscious, as she had been when speaking to Lucille, of the sheltered nature of her own upbringing, in comparison to those who had had to make their own way in the world. There were precious few similarities between the former actress and the current Countess of Seagrave, but one was that they had made their own luck, not been born with all the privileges like Polly had. Somehow it made her feel inadequate as well as fortunate.

Polly, returning to the turret bedroom she had used earlier, found the bed neatly turned down and a small fire burning in the grate. It looked warm and welcoming, but she could hear the thunder away out at sea and shivered. As soon as she was alone, all her nervousness had returned. On such a night it was all too easy to think of the miles of thick forest that cut them off from the town, the dense, secretive trees, the storm clouds harrying the moon. The bright beauty of the day had gone and the stark loneliness of the place created an eerie atmosphere.

There was a door in the corner of the bedroom, which Polly assumed must be the turret stair. Feeling rather foolish, she went across and checked that it was locked. There was no key on her side of the door, but the door did not move at all when she turned the knob. Satisfied, she climbed into the downy bed, convinced she would not sleep a wink.

Surprisingly, she fell asleep almost at once, to wake in the middle of the night with a feeling of suffocating uneasiness. The fire had gone out and the wind was pounding the corner of the house, whistling through the cracks in the windowpane. Out on the landing, a floorboard creaked. Polly stiffened, listening for footsteps. A sliver of light appeared at the bottom of the door, flickered and went out. Another board creaked.

Polly slid out of bed and opened her door a crack. She was conscious of a need to establish normality, certain that she would see nothing more than a servant tiptoeing about his or her business whilst the rest of the house slept.

There was no one on the landing. Then she heard the voices.

"Not tonight, at any rate… Yes, certain… He was

looking around earlier, but... No, no question of it.
They will not risk coming in and the tide is already
on the turn..."

Polly edged to the bannister and peeped over. The
hall was lit with dim candlelight, deeply shadowed.
Lord Henry Marchnight was standing in the drawing-
room doorway, brushing cobwebs from his clothes.
He was fully dressed.

Lady Bellingham, in the centre of the hall, was
clad in a dressing-gown of glossy, bright hue and
formidable respectability. Polly rejected her first reaction that this was an illicit lovers' tryst; it was ridiculous to assume an *affaire* between them, even
given her ladyship's preference for attractive young
men. There was something too watchful in Henry's
manner and too businesslike in Lady Bellingham's.
The grandfather clock chimed one suddenly and
Polly jumped. Henry, who had been turning to close
the drawing-room door, paused and his narrowed
gaze scanned the landing. Polly's heart was in her
throat. Would he see her in the shadows of the pillar?
And what would he do? What was his business, on
such a stormy night? Suddenly she did not wish to
know.

Lady Bellingham was yawning much in the manner of Horace the cat.

"I'm for bed, then," she announced, patting
Henry on the arm. "I am too old for all this excitement!"

Polly withdrew hastily to her room, closing the
door softly as Lady Bellingham started up the stairs.
She slid into bed, shivering a little.

Not a tryst then, so...what? A business transaction? But what could be so secret as to require so clandestine a meeting in the middle of the night? And what was it that Henry had said? Polly stretched out in the warmth, still puzzling. She remembered seeing Henry poking about on the beach earlier in the day and his mention of a secret passage linking the House of Tides to the sea. But…surely he was no smuggler, and what other purpose could he have for using such a route?

All Polly's previous suspicions came flooding back. He had been conveniently to hand to rescue them from the riot in London. Too conveniently, perhaps? He had carried a pistol when he had apparently been returning home from a ball. He was a man who habitually concealed his sharpness of mind beneath a bland exterior. And now he was up and about on a stormy night by the sea… But Polly's common sense was telling her that allegations of criminality were absurd, and something deeper told her fiercely that Henry was a man of integrity. Besides, there was Lady Bellingham's part in this. As smuggler's accomplice? The thought made Polly want to laugh.

She was just about to drift back into sleep when there was a tiny click and the door of Polly's room opened a crack. Through a gap in the bed curtains she saw the faint light increase as the door was pushed wider. Someone was standing in the aperture, listening. Polly froze. She leant out of bed and groped quickly and silently for something, anything to defend herself with. Her hand closed around the edge of the chamber pot. Without conscious thought, she ripped the bed curtains back and swung her arm in a wide arc. The pot made contact with something, there was a muffled gasp from the intruder, and Polly began to scream.

There was light and people everywhere, all of them talking at once. Polly could see Hetty's frightened face and Miss Ditton hovering behind her, avid and curious. Then Lady Bellingham came bustling forward in a monstrous bedcap and the vivid dressing-gown, and candlelight fell on the prone body of Mr Ditton, lying on the rug just inside Polly's doorway, clutching his head and groaning.

"Ditton!"

"Tristan!"

Peter Seagrave's exclamation and Miss Ditton's screech of horror coincided.

His jaw set, Peter plucked the luckless Mr Ditton off the floor and started to shake him.

"What the hell are you doing in my sister's bedroom, you loathsome cur?"

Miss Ditton began to cry noisily. Hetty rushed forward anxiously to ask if Polly was hurt. Polly sat down rather heavily on the edge of the bed, supported by Lady Bellingham's arm.

"I am quite well, I thank you, just a little shaken…"

Hetty was now trying to persuade Peter to let Tristan Ditton go, whilst Thalia was clinging to her brother's arm and pulling him in an opposite direction from Peter. Polly felt they might almost pull him apart between them.

"Oh, please let him go—" she started to say, only to find that control of the situation had been grasped firmly by Lord Henry Marchnight.

"A simple misunderstanding, I feel sure, Seagrave. I am persuaded that you would not wish to inflict any further injuries to Ditton's person! Why, his elegant night attire is quite ruined, I fancy!"

No one except Polly seemed to find it odd that Lord Henry's major concern should be for Mr Ditton's clothing, for they were all quite used to his preoccupation with sartorial matters. Ditton, released from Peter's cruel grip, drew himself up and exclaimed that the state of his silk dressing-gown was truly disgraceful, but not so shocking as the state of his nerves after an unwarranted attack.

Henry's ironic gaze then fell on Polly, still clasped within Lady Bellingham's protective arm.

"Not really unwarranted, Ditton," he drawled. "Seagrave did what any right-minded brother would do under the circumstances! Have you forgotten the agitation occasioned to Lady Polly at finding you in her room? An apology at least, dear fellow..."

Ditton, recalled to the demands of good behaviour, gulped a little, his Adam's apple bobbing. "Dear Lady Polly...of course...such a terrible mistake. I was looking for the closet and became quite lost in the dark...oh, dear, I am most abjectly sorry..."

"No harm done, eh, Ditton?" Henry observed, mercifully putting an end to this miserable monologue. "Except perhaps, to your head!"

The tension began to dissolve. Miss Ditton gulped noisily.

"Oh, Tristan, how could you be so foolish...?"

"Lady Polly...terrible mistake...abject apologies..." Mr Ditton was still stuttering. He was still looking a little stunned from Peter's treatment, his thin, foxy face a sickly pale colour and his grey eyes darting fearfully. He put a hand to his head. "Excuse me... Must retire..."

He wandered off along the landing, silk dressing-gown flapping, and Lady Bellingham started to shoo the others out of the room with a mixture of clucking and scolding.

"Come along, now! Back to your beds, all of you! Conchita!" She clapped her hands and the maid appeared apparently from nowhere, "Show these ladies back to their rooms! Good night!"

Peter and Hetty were disposed to linger until Polly reassured them with a pale smile.

"Truly, I am not hurt, only a little shocked. Oh, thank you, ma'am—" She accepted a glass of brandy from Lady Bellingham, then looked at it dubiously. "Must I indeed drink this?"

"For the shock, my dear," Lady Bellingham counselled. "It will help you sleep."

The grandfather clock chimed two.

The drink was very pungent and burned its way down Polly's throat.

"Poor Mr Ditton!" She started to laugh. "I imagine I gave him far more of a fright than he did me!"

"You were remarkably accurate with that chamber pot, my dear," Lady Bellingham observed. "One scarce knows whether to be grateful or otherwise that it was empty!"

It was only later, when Lady Bellingham had left her and the house had settled down once more into quiet, that Polly curled up and wondered how Lord Henry had managed to appear in his night attire.

Only minutes earlier she had seen him in the hall, fully dressed.

She was about to fall asleep for a third time that evening when she remembered the corner door. Some instinct prompted her to check that it was locked, although she had no reason to suppose otherwise. She dragged herself out of the bed again into the cold room. She shivered as she crossed the floor and turned the knob. The door swung smoothly open without a sound and the dark stair gaped below.

Chapter Twelve

All sleepiness fled from Polly's mind. The door, which had been locked when she went to bed, was now standing open. A faint draught, scented with sea salt, wafted into the room and the darkness yawned below. For a moment she stared, unbelieving, down the dark stair, then she slammed the door shut as though she almost expected an intruder to appear before her eyes. There was a heavy oak armchair in a corner of the room, and Polly made haste to drag it across in front of the turret door, barricading herself in as best she could. The silence of the House of Tides seemed to spread around her. There was no step on the stair, no turning of the knob, but it was a long time before Polly returned to bed and even longer before she slept.

"You look fagged to death, poor child," Lady Bellingham said next morning, "and no wonder! What a night of alarums and excursions!"

She had brought Polly's breakfast tray herself and now moved forward to draw back the curtains, letting in the bright sunlight and swathe of blue, rainwashed sky. Her dark, thoughtful gaze lingered on the heavy wooden chair which was still in place squarely against the door.

"Lady Bellingham," Polly said directly, "do you know where the key is for that door?"

For a moment she thought that her ladyship looked distinctly furtive. "The key? Is it not in the door, my love? I must confess I have not seen it this age, for we seldom use this room."

"The door was locked when I went to bed," Polly said, feeling a little foolish at airing her suspicions in the bright light of day, "but it was open in the middle of the night! I cannot understand it!"

Lady Bellingham's eyes seemed to hold a secret amusement. "Oh, no, my dear, I am sure you must be mistaken! The door is always kept locked!" And to illustrate her point, she turned the knob and gave the door a hearty push. It did not move.

"There now," Lady Bellingham said comfortably. "I am persuaded that you must have dreamed it, my dear, and no wonder with all the shocks there were during the night! Mr Ditton and his sister seem in an unaccountable hurry to leave this morning! But at least Miss Ditton will be unable to gossip about last night's rodomontade, since her own brother was the villain of the piece! Now, here is your dress, freshly laundered by Conchita, and you must join us down-stairs only when you are ready!"

After she had gone, Polly slid from the bed and checked the door herself. It did not move an inch. Polly ate her breakfast slowly, puzzling over the mystery, but she could come up with no explanation and eventually gave up, choosing instead to sit by the open window and look out at the fresh, blue day. The rain had left deep, water-filled ruts in the track, and Polly was surprised to see a carriage picking its way carefully through the quagmire. It paused at the gate, where the Dittons' coach rattled past it with rather more speed than was wise, then turned on to the forecourt of the House of Tides.

Polly hurried down the stairs. Lord Henry March-night was just coming into the hall, his hair tousled by the fresh breeze. Polly eyed him suspiciously. He looked remarkably wide awake for someone who had spent the best part of the night prowling around and, she suspected, up to no good.

"Good morning, Lady Polly! I hope you are re-covered from the trials and tribulations of last night! Sir Godfrey Orbison has just arrived—no doubt to rescue the susceptible Seagraves from the clutches of the wicked Lady Bellingham!"

Sir Godfrey's stentorian tones could already be heard haranguing an impassive Gaston at the door.

"Come to find out what the deuce is going on! Only arrived at Dillingham last night to find Cecilia Seagrave in receipt of a dashed odd message about the whereabouts of her family! Seagrave has been called away so I undertook to find out how everyone came to be marooned out here! Dashed lonely spot, what! Dashed odd place to live!"

"Sir Godfrey!" Polly called, running across the hall and hugging her godfather. "How are you, sir?"

"Sharp-set, miss, sharp-set!" Sir Godfrey said, smiling despite himself. "Sent out here on some outlandish wild goose chase before I even had my breakfast! What's going on, eh?''

''We were caught in a storm yesterday and had to seek shelter here,'' Polly said, catching his arm and turning him towards the drawing-room. ''Come, I must introduce you to Lady Bellingham, who was kind enough to rescue us!''

''No need, my dear. Sir Godfrey and I are old acquaintants!''

The drawing-room door had been thrown open with a flourish worthy of a great melodrama. Lady Bellingham, resplendent in a sapphire gown and diaphanous scarves, wafted forward.

''Godfrey!'' she said in throbbing accents. ''To think that we should meet again after all this time! You went away, you wicked man!''

''Bessie!'' Sir Godfrey had dropped Polly's arm as though thunderstruck and had hastened forward with the speed of a young man. ''My dear Bessie! You married Another!''

''Only because you had deserted me, you cruel deceiver!'' Lady Bellingham said, tapping him on the arm with her peacock fan.

''So much time lost!'' Sir Godfrey mourned, enthusiastically kissing her on both cheeks. ''So much to rediscover!''

Polly's jaw had dropped as she watched this tableau unfold.

''I think we are witnessing a great romance,'' a voice said in her ear, ''though Lady Bellingham seems uncertain whether this is to be a tragedy or a comic opera!''

Polly turned to see Lord Henry grinning as he

watched Lady Bellingham steer Sir Godfrey towards the drawing-room, looking up at him flirtatiously as she went. The elderly baronet seemed totally enslaved. Moreover he was willing, eager, to be swept away.

"Now that we have found each other again, Godfrey," Lady Bellingham said in throbbing tones, "I insist that you sample my hospitality for a little! The children—" she dismissed Polly and Henry with a wave of the fan "—can amuse themselves for a while! There is so much for us to talk on!" And she shut the door firmly behind them.

"Well!" Henry said, still smiling. "It seems Lady Bellingham has found yet another way in which to scandalise the neighbourhood and Sir Godfrey will be her willing dupe!"

"Their romance... It seems most unlikely..." Polly ventured.

"True..." there was a twinkle in Lord Henry's eyes "...but one must not consider romance to be the prerogative of the young! I have no doubt that those two had a most passionate affair—"

"Lord Henry!"

"Still so proper, Lady Polly?"

"Unlike you, my lord!"

Lord Henry's grin was broad now. "Perhaps you should hurry back to your chaste maiden bower, Lady Polly! Unfortunately, you are unlikely to have Sir Godfrey's escort, and your brother and Miss Markham are exchanging sweet nothings in the garden. So..."

Polly's lips tightened at his teasing. "Must you always make a mock of things, my lord?"

"On the contrary!" Henry's gaze was bright on her. "I consider love to be a very serious matter!"

"So I have heard! And seen! There are those who consider it to be your only preoccupation, my lord!"

"No, that's too unkind!" Henry's smile faded and his glance was a challenge now. "But you, Lady Polly—your attitude is a little different, is it not? You always seem to behave as though there was something shameful about love, or at the least something shameful about honest emotion. I suppose it is the result of so sheltered and restrictive an upbringing!"

Polly stared at him speechlessly. It seemed at least five seconds before she managed to exclaim, "Well upon my word, my lord! Your presumption is outrageous!"

Henry's look was a provocation in itself. "Is that so? Then tell me your own view of the matter!"

"It is true that I have had a protected upbringing, being the youngest and the only daughter—" Polly was so indignant that she needed no second invitation "—but I do not believe that I have suffered as a result either materially or emotionally! I consider myself to be a woman of sense! I do not know what type of woman you admire, Lord Henry, but if it is one full of die-away airs and affected sensibility then I must agree I do not conform to that style!"

"Yet on the surface you appear so prim and conventional," Lord Henry countered with every evidence of regret. "One has the impression that any suggestion of strong emotion would have you recoiling with the vapours!"

"Indeed!" Polly was now more cross than indignant. "I do not know how you have the effrontery to accuse me of a want of feeling! When we met in London you behaved like the greatest rake imaginable, and I did not hear you complaining that I was lacking in my response to you *then*!'' She broke off and clapped her hand to her mouth, but it was too late. The words could not be unsaid.

The expression on Henry's face would have silenced her anyway. There was amusement there and a dawning warmth, melting into a tenderness that made her catch her breath.

''You tricked me,'' she said, and it came out as a whisper. ''I should never have said that...''

''Yes,'' Henry also spoke softly, ''I'll admit I gave in to a perverse impulse to provoke you, for you sometimes seem so prim and yet I know you to be different...''

The hot colour flooded Polly's face. She took an instinctive step towards him, knowing that in a moment she would be in his arms.

There was a blast of fresh, salty air, then the main door banged in the breeze and Gaston came forward, clucking with disapproval.

''Morning, Polly! Morning, Marchnight!'' Peter, smiling with genial cheer, ushered Hetty into the hall, where Gaston fussed about taking her scarf and coat. Peter was chatting easily to the butler and seemed completely oblivious to the scene before him. Hetty, her face flushed pink from the cold air, looked from Polly to Henry and raised her brows very slightly.

Polly tore her gaze away from Henry's with an effort of will.

''I was just waiting for Sir Godfrey,'' she said, slightly at random and to no one in particular. ''He has come to escort us back to Dillingham, but it seems he is already acquainted with Lady Bellingham…'' She gestured vaguely towards the drawing-room door.

Henry was laughing openly at her obvious confusion and she was both charmed and annoyed by his teasing. He seemed suddenly so sure of his power to disturb her and with masculine arrogance was enjoying it. Despite Peter and Hetty's arrival, Polly still felt deliciously flustered and excited. She knew that Henry would have kissed her if the others had not come in and she felt out-of-proportion disappointed to have been denied the experience.

''Are you quite well, Lady Polly? You are looking rather flushed. Perhaps your experiences last night have overset you?'' Henry had taken her hand, a wicked smile on his face, eyes dancing. ''I hope you are quite well, for it is the Deben yacht race tomorrow morning and I quite count on your support to help me wrest the cup from Marcus Fitzgerald!''

''Oh, a race!'' Hetty clapped her hands, eyes shining. ''We shall all be there to cheer you on, Lord Henry!''

''There is a luncheon afterwards at the Queen's Head,'' Henry continued, ''and, of course, in the evening there is your mother's impromptu ball. A day of uninterrupted pleasure, which is what I like best!''

Polly gave him a repressive look which he met with one of limpid innocence. ''Shall we see you at the ball then, my lord?'' she asked demurely, trying to withdraw her hand from his.

Henry did not release her. Instead he raised her hand to his lips and pressed a lingering kiss on it.

"Certainly you shall. I hope you will save a dance for me, Lady Polly!"

"I should be delighted, sir." Polly cast him a look under her lashes. He was still smiling in that slightly challenging way, and for a moment her heart skipped a beat through sheer anticipation.

"Until tomorrow then, my lady," Henry murmured, letting her go at last. "I should be on my way to Fenchurch, I suppose. Your servant, ma'am. Miss Markham…Peter…"

"Oh." Hetty sighed soulfully, as they watched his tall figure stroll away towards the stables. "Oh, Polly, he really is so very charming…"

The drawing-room door opened and Lady Bellingham came out, deep in conversation with Sir Godfrey.

"…put up for the night at Farnforth," Sir Godfrey was saying, "at the Rose and Crown. Not a bad hostelry, but a little overcrowded…"

Polly was still gazing after Lord Henry's retreating figure, but spun around at a faint noise from Hetty. The other girl had gone chalk white, her hands to her breast as though pierced by an arrow.

"Gaston! A chair for Miss Markham!" Lady Bellingham, hearing Polly's exclamation of concern, had hurried forward to take control of the situation. "Conchita! My hartshorn! There now, my dear…" With infinite gentleness she helped Peter ease Hetty into the chair. "Have no fear, you will feel better directly…"

Hetty was drooping like a cut flower. She was still alarmingly pale, but her eyelids fluttered. Peter, kneeling beside her, was the picture of concern.

"The heat..." Lady Bellingham was saying excusingly, although it was still early and a very fresh day, "and the wedding preparations no doubt. You must take care not to overtax yourself, my dear!"

"Yes, ma'am," Hetty said submissively, and Polly saw a tear slide from the corner of her eye and make a trail down her pale cheek. For a moment Polly had the horrible thought that Hetty might not wish to marry Peter and that that was what was making her so unhappy. Yet Hetty was gazing at Peter with the concentrated regard that was surely a sign of love rather than dislike, and was clutching his hand as though her life depended on it. And there had been nothing in their behaviour to suggest anything other than they were both pleased to be marrying so soon. Polly frowned. She had discussed Hetty's strange behaviour with Lucille, but neither of them could understand why Miss Markham, normally so ebullient, had become so tense and woebegone. She was not ill. She should have been happier than ever before in her life. It made no sense.

Hetty was struggling to get to her feet, a little colour coming back into her face.

"I am so sorry... I cannot imagine what is the matter."

She saw Lady Bellingham looking at her with thoughtful concern and looked as though she was about to burst into tears. She scrubbed viciously at her eyes.

"We had better start for home, Lady B.," Peter said hastily, a protective arm around his betrothed. "It will be best for Hetty to rest. Shall we see you at the ball tomorrow?"

The atmosphere lightened as Sir Godfrey added his pressing persuasions.

"Dear lady, of course you must be there! You will be the belle of the ball, putting all others in the shade!"

Lady Bellingham acceded graciously to his invitation and they went out to the carriage in a flurry of repeated good wishes and invitations. Peter and Hetty sat very close together on the way home, Hetty's head against his shoulder, and Sir Godfrey sat in his corner of the carriage with a ridiculously fatuous look on his face. It was clear that he was dwelling on the delights of renewing his acquaintance with Lady Bellingham. Polly, despite the promise of encountering Lord Henry again the following day, began to feel decidedly left out. All the world, it seemed, was in love, but she was the only one who had no notion where it was leading.

Chapter Thirteen

"**Y**ou are in magnificent looks tonight, Lady Polly." It was not Lord Henry Marchnight but Tristan Ditton who bent close to Polly's ear, his sharp gaze appraising her with familiarity, his foxy face wearing an unpleasant smile.

Polly stepped back sharply. For a man who had retreated ignominiously only the two nights before, Mr Ditton seemed in very high spirits. Indeed, he was positively effusive in his greetings, as though no matter of embarrassment had ever passed between them.

"Save me a dance for later, fair one," he purred, before moving on into the ballroom, leaving Polly to puzzle over his strange and unwelcome behaviour.

The ballroom was filling rapidly as the guests gathered for the Dowager Countess's impromptu ball. Sir Godfrey, looking as pleased as a dog wagging its tail, was escorting Lady Bellingham. Polly suspected Lady Bellingham of deliberately playing to the gallery, for she was drawing a great deal of attention in a dress of rich ruby velvet and some staggering diamonds. The Farrants and Fitzgeralds were also out in force, but Polly's eye was drawn constantly to the door, awaiting the arrival of Lord Henry Marchnight. She knew, without the benefit of Mr Ditton's compliments, that she was looking her best. She had brushed her dark hair until the chestnut lights in it had gleamed with rich colour and the curls tumbled becomingly about her face. Knowing that pastel colours, the favourite apparel of the debutante, could make her look sallow, Polly had chosen a dress of eau-de-nil. The style was appropriately modest, but the cut flattered her neat figure and the material whispered softly as she walked.

The orchestra struck up for the first dance and Peter swept Hetty on to the floor, opening the dancing since Nicholas had chosen to sit out with Lucille. Hetty appeared to have recovered her spirits and was almost as vivacious as Polly remembered. Sir Godfrey and Lady Bellingham followed them onto the floor with barely concealed eagerness. There was less formality than at the London routs and balls, but the company was elegant nevertheless and, more importantly, was enjoying itself with gusto. Seeing Mr Ditton approaching her purposefully, Polly caught the eye of Charles Farrant, who had also been watching the door covertly for the arrival of the Marchnights. Charles could take a hint, and stepped forward to claim Polly's hand before Tristan Ditton could reach her.

"Mr Seagrave and Miss Markham make a very handsome couple," Polly heard Mrs Fitzgerald remark to her partner, further down the set. "I am so glad that match is to be made soon..."

As Charles Farrant swung Polly round, she caught sight of Tristan Ditton once more. He seemed to be ubiquitous. But this time Mr Ditton's attention was not on Polly, for he too was watching Hetty Markham with a peculiar, brooding intensity. A sudden shiver ran down Polly's spine. There was such a malevolent look on Ditton's face that it disturbed her.

A moment later, she forgot all about it. Lord Henry Marchnight was ushering his mother and sister into the ballroom, apologising graciously to the Dowager Countess for their late arrival. The light from the chandeliers gleamed on his carefully dishevelled fair hair and she caught her breath at the stark elegance of his evening attire. Then Henry turned and their eyes met across the room. Polly felt her pulse flutter as he held her gaze.

The dance concluded and Charles, who had also seen the Marchnights arrive, escorted Polly to Lucille's side, and hovered, looking hopefully across the room at Lady Laura. Polly tried not to laugh. Charles had the same eager look on his face as Sir Godfrey, as he contemplated the object of his affections. She hoped that the Duchess would allow her vigilance to slip and give Charles and Laura a little time together.

"Come and sit by me, Charles," Lucille said, taking pity on him and clearly thinking along the same lines. "I shall call Lady Laura over in a little while, when the Duchess's attention is distracted!"

Polly danced the next with John Fitzgerald and Nicholas Seagrave persuaded a blushing Lady Laura to join him on the dance floor. The Duchess beamed her approval. Sir Godfrey and Lady Bellingham were scandalising the guests by dancing every dance together, more amorously entwined than any younger couple. Several people looked horrified at this display, but Polly rather suspected that Lady Bellingham was deliberately putting on a show. Miss Ditton and Mr Bunlon looked decidedly more gloomy as they circled the floor together.

"Do you return to London for the Little Season?" Polly asked Laura neutrally, when the dance ended and they found themselves together in the group around Lucille. She knew that the younger girl was feeling some constraint in her presence, no doubt arising from the fiasco at the Fair, and she was anxious to break the ice.

Laura shook her fair head. "No, indeed, for Mama is making arrangements to send me away!" She bit her lip. "Dear Lady Polly, I am so sorry for the way I have behaved towards you at Cold Hollow—"

Polly put her hand on Laura's arm. It was hardly the place for heartfelt apologies, but Laura was certainly sincere. She was looking positively miserable.

"Say no more of it," she said decisively, with a warm smile to show that she bore no grudge. She raised her voice a little to attract Charles Farrant's attention.

"So you are to leave us, Lady Laura? I am so sorry! Where do you go?"

"Mama has decided that it would be good for me to visit my sister, Lizzie Ellerbeck, in Northumberland," Laura said, glancing through her lashes at Charles Farrant. "I wish that it were not so, but Mama is adamant that Lizzie requires company. She is increasing, you know, and no doubt Northumberland is a strange and lonely place to be all alone in Ellerbeck's medieval castle!''

"How Gothic!'' Lucille commented, with a smile. "You must make the most of your time amongst us then, Lady Laura, and dance every dance! Mr Farrant…''

Charles Farrant cleared his throat. "Er, yes, indeed… Lady Laura…if you would grant me the honour…''

"An awkward suitor,'' Lucille said with a smile as she watched them go, "but an honest one for all that! I do so hope that the Duchess will relent! Laura could do much worse…''

"Playing Cupid, Lady Seagrave?''

Extraordinarily, Polly had missed Lord Henry's approach, so absorbed had she been in the romance of Lady Laura and Charles Farrant. Lucille had the grace to blush.

"Oh, Lord Henry! Perhaps we should not encourage them, but it seems such a pity for their hopes to be dashed…''

Henry grinned. "Romance is most decidedly in the air tonight, is it not?'' He turned to Polly as though he had more pressing matters on his mind than his sister's future. The gravity of his salutation was belied by the wicked twinkle in his eyes and she felt the same breathless sense of anticipation that had come over her at the House of Tides.

"Dance with me,'' Henry said softly, persuasively, taking Polly's gloved hand and pulling her to her feet.

Lucille caught her husband's eye and smiled.

"Some of the company seem to have no need of Cupid's help," she observed lightly.

Polly was feeling the same melting excitement that had possessed her when she saw Henry enter the ballroom, but this time his proximity intensified the feeling. He drew her into his arms as the waltz struck up. She could not tear her gaze away from his, from that grave but concentrated expression in his eyes as he considered her face upturned to his. They did not speak throughout the dance, yet Polly was sharply aware of him all the time. The touch of his hand on hers, the brush of his body against hers gave her an acute physical consciousness of him. Polly was caught in so potent a spell she had no wish to break it.

When the dance ended, Henry did not escort her back to Lucille's side but to a love-seat in an alcove.

"Are you enjoying your day of uninterrupted pleasure, sir?" Polly asked lightly, smiling at him as she sat down. "I have not yet had the opportunity to congratulate you on your second place in the race today! I hope you were not too disappointed to secede the cup to Mr Fitzgerald!"

Henry laughed. "I have to concede to the better sailor! It's true I was disappointed—one is always aiming for the prize."

There was something meaningful in his gaze that made the colour come into Polly's cheeks. She hoped he thought her a prize worth winning.

"I was also disappointed that you were not able to join us for luncheon," Henry said, after a moment. "I understand that the Dowager Countess does not approve of the Queen's Head?"

Polly laughed. "No, indeed! We tried to persuade her that it is a respectable hostelry but I think she feels it is little better than an alehouse! But we did enjoy watching the race. It was a very beautiful day."

"Everybody seems most glad that the amusement is continuing here tonight," Henry said, looking about with a smile, "but then the Dowager Countess's entertainments are renowned!"

For a moment Polly thought of Mr Ditton, the only person present who did not appear to be enjoying the evening. She almost told Henry about Ditton's curious malevolence when he was watching Hetty and his peculiar familiarity with her, but then she dismissed the thought. Mr Ditton's foibles were nothing to do with her after all.

"I hope," Lord Henry said, turning back to her with a lazy smile, "that you have recovered from the events of the night at the House of Tides. It must have been a most disturbing experience for you."

"Finding Mr Ditton creeping into my bedroom in the dark was indeed unpleasant," Polly agreed tartly. "There were other events that night, however, that I found equally disturbing!"

Henry's lips twitched. "Indeed! Whatever could those have been?"

"A door that was locked which mysteriously became open before locking itself again," Polly said coolly, "and a meeting I witnessed between yourself and Lady Bellingham which led me to believe that both of you were engaged in the business of smuggling!"

There was a silence whilst the dancers spun before them and the strains of the music swept on.

"Three curious events in one evening," Henry said thoughtfully.

"Yes, and those were only the three I witnessed! Who is to say that there were not more!"

Polly saw the flash of amused appreciation in Henry's eyes.

"You have suspected me for a long time, I think," he said easily. "A smuggler, a malcontent, a rabble-rouser, the rich patron of a dangerous criminal, perhaps... What extraordinary deeds you have credited me with, Lady Polly! I wonder that you dare be alone with me!"

"We are not alone," Polly pointed out, still cool.

"We were when I came up the turret stair the night before last and unlocked the door into your bedroom!"

Polly bit her lip to prevent the gasp that was almost audible. She had sought to provoke him without believing that she would hear answers such as this. Her dark eyes kindled. "I might have known you had the key! Creeping around in the middle of the night, and into a lady's bedroom—"

"Yes, you have no idea how much I have wanted to be there," Henry said smoothly. "You were fast asleep and looking quite delightful with your hair tumbled all over the pillow! I was tempted—"

"Lord Henry!"

"Must you be forever interrupting my most ardent dreams, Lady Polly? Alas, that the reality is far colder than the fantasy! Or at least—" his tone dropped "—I used to think so..."

Polly fought to get a grip on matters before they slipped beyond her control. "Lord Henry, I believe that you owe me an explanation! *That* is the point at issue, not your fevered imaginings!"

"Well..." Henry looked around at the crowded ballroom "...it is too busy here for complicated explanations. If you will walk a little with me, I undertake to tell you all you wish to know. Or almost all," he added with a whimsical smile.

Polly eyed him with suspicion. "Truly?"

"Truly!"

"But can you tell me? Should you?" Polly suddenly felt uncertain. "Perhaps I do not wish to know after all—"

"Too late," Henry said laconically, pulling her to her feet. "You already know too much, Lady Polly! A little knowledge is more dangerous than the whole truth!"

At one end the wide ballroom doors led through to the winter garden, with its palm trees and warm, ferny twilight. They strolled slowly along the tiled path.

"Where to start?" Henry said thoughtfully. "I suppose the beginning is in London, with the arrest of Chapman at the gunsmith's and his subsequent escape. As you know, he is a dangerous malcontent and one of the most wanted men in the country. He has undoubted gifts of oratory and can stir up the populace to riot and revolt. He uses other men's discontent for his own ends, for he has no real interest in improving the lot of the common man. He has planned and executed more robberies with violence than I could tell of, and I have been hunting him down ever since he escaped."

Polly stopped and drew in a sharp breath. "Then you mean that you... You must work for the authorities—for the government?"

There was an atmosphere of intrigue conjured up by the intimate darkness and the watchful stillness of the warm night. They started to walk again, very slowly, neither of them paying much attention to their surroundings.

"Yes, I have worked for the government for the last five years, under many names and in many guises." Henry sounded very matter of fact, as though such an admission was commonplace.

"You mean that you are a spy?" Polly kept her voice level, finding it difficult to match his practical tone. She was astonished. Her images and perceptions of him had been plunged into a complete whirl.

"I suppose you could call me that." There was an element of amusement now in Henry's voice, although he did not smile. "I do not care for the word. It is too...melodramatic. I have done all kinds of work—whatever is required. In the recent wars I spent some time abroad, in both France and elsewhere. I also collected..." he hesitated "...information from sources along the south coast."

Polly knew what he meant. The smugglers who brought in contraband goods might also have very useful intelligence from the continent, but the business was dirty and dangerous. She remembered the times when Henry had vanished completely from Society, how the gossips and tattle-merchants always had him conducting some scandalous love affair, or wasting his patrimony on gambling. He had covered his tracks well. And yet the strength and integrity she had seen in him, the contradiction with his superficial lifestyle had always puzzled her. Now it took on new meaning.

"I thought…" she said hesitantly, "we all thought that you were simply…amusing yourself…"

"Hardly surprising, since that was precisely the impression I wished to give." Henry shrugged. "What better way to convince people that I was interested in little beyond women, gambling and the set of my neckcloth? Very few people know the truth of it, and only those I can trust completely."

Polly registered the implied compliment with a little glow of pleasure. "Then, all through the Season you were intent on finding Chapman?"

"Yes, indeed, at Hampstead Wells and during the riot and even at the the Royal Humane Society! A fine dance he has led me! And all the time, you were basely suspecting me of being the criminal!"

Polly blushed. "The riot…I see now why you were carrying the pistols! But you put your search aside to rescue us, which surely you should not have done—"

There was a harsh note in Henry's voice. "Do you think I could possibly have left you there unaided? Why do you think I intervened?"

Polly did not answer. She could feel the tension between them now and turned aside from the question. It felt too soon to consider it.

"But Chapman is not taken yet and you are here in Woodbridge…" Her eyes widened at the implication. "No, it cannot be that he is *here*!" She cast a swift look through the glass door to where the couples still swirled around the dance floor, as if expecting the felon to declare himself. Henry took her arm in a comforting grasp.

"No, he is not here, not tonight. But your deduction is as faultless as ever, Lady Polly! Chapman is close by and others I seek are closer still. You will do well to be vigilant until the matter is finally resolved!"

"I suppose your midnight foray at the House of Tides is all a piece with this," Polly said a little dazedly. She sat down on the cushioned bench by the ornamental pool and watched the candlelight reflected in the cool water. "The turret door in my bedroom at the House of Tides led down to the cellars and no doubt to the sea…"

"Yes." Henry shifted slightly on the bench beside her. "There are indeed compensations to my work, ma'am!"

"Outrageous! It mattered not one whit that I was asleep in there, I suppose!"

"It certainly made the business more enjoyable!"

Polly refused to let her attention be diverted by this.

"Why have you told me all this?" she asked.

Henry's amusement faded. He looked at her. There was such a clear, innocent look in her eyes. He knew he should lie to her, but he could not. This was important.

"For lots of reasons," he said, as lightly as he could. "Maybe I did not wish you to have such a low opinion of me any more! You suspected much already, but I wanted you to know the truth. It mattered to me.''

Polly could tell that he was utterly sincere. There was none of the teasing mockery that had been present a moment before. She could sense the tension latent in him as he sat, not touching her, but very close. His face was still in shadow.

Polly got up and moved across to the window, looking out across the silent gardens to the lake shimmering in the silver moonlight. His honesty had prompted her to say something herself, something that she had always wanted to tell him but had always held back.

''When you said to me—that night at Lady Phillips's ridotto—that I had played my part in making you what you had become, then I thought—'' She broke off. ''I had not really thought of it that way before, but I suppose my rejection of your suit five years ago must have had its effect on your actions. I am sorry, so very sorry, that I ever refused you. Matters could have been so very different—'' Her voice broke on a sob.

''It was very wrong of me to attribute any blame to you,'' Henry said swiftly. He had moved until she could sense he was very close behind her. ''I must take the responsibility for my own behaviour. I did not choose this path simply because you refused my proposal of marriage five years ago. There were many factors that influenced that decision, of which only one was seeing the reversal of my hopes of a life with you.''

Polly studied his reflection in the glass behind her. He was so close that she could feel the warmth emanating from his body, a contrast to the cold draught from the window and the emotion which was making her shiver a little.

"When you asked me to run away with you I was too immature to cope with the situation," she said slowly. "I did not really understand what love meant. Oh—" she made a slight gesture "—I thought I loved you and it was all very girlish and romantic, but the depth of feeling that would have given me the strength to go with you was lacking. I have thought about it so often... About what might have been had I had the courage to accept... I wish...I wish so much—"

Henry put his hand on her arm. "Lady Polly. Do not. Sometimes it is not good to be so honest. Sometimes it can only be painful..."

Polly swung round to face him. Her eyes were bright with emotion and the chestnut hair curled about her flushed face. Henry found himself wanting to kiss her very much, not with the calculated seduction of that night at Lady Phillips's ball, but with such genuine passion that it shocked him.

"I know now," he said, a rough edge to his voice, "that I miscalculated when I thought you incapable of deep feeling. I was wrong..."

Polly's mouth was just below his own. It was easy to put a hand to her cheek, then tilt up her chin so that their lips met, tentatively at first, then with a sudden flood of desire that threatened to carry them away. All the suppressed emotion and tension of their encounter was suddenly in the kiss, as Polly's lips parted in surprise and swift acquiescence and her arms slid around his neck to draw him closer. Henry knew a second's hesitation before he allowed himself to let caution go. Polly knew no such moment of doubt. She had been aware of the feeling building between them, the thoughts and emotions unspoken, the dizzy sense of awareness and anticipation. When he touched her, the love and expectancy had fused into one overwhelming need. She pressed closer, pliant against him, and Henry moved to draw her closer.

When he would have drawn back, Polly pulled him closer still, tangling her hands in his hair so that she could bring his mouth down to hers again.

Henry held her away from him, pressing a kiss against her hair, breathing hard.

"Seldom have I made such a mistake," he said, the rueful amusement audible in his slightly shaken tone. "Polly…"

Pressed close in his arms, feeling the thud of his heart against hers, knowing instinctively just how difficult it was for him to let her go, Polly had no incentive to help him. She wanted to show him just how far he had misjudged her. All the years of restraint could be unlearned very easily. She slid her hands under his jacket, relishing the hard strength of his body under her fingers, and when she heard Henry catch his breath on a groan, she raised her lips to his again.

Henry spun her round so that she was trapped against the wall. Polly could feel the cold through the thin silk of her gown but was barely aware of it. All her senses were concentrated on the heat of the sensuality between them. She wanted it to sweep her away. The explicit demand of the kiss eased into gentleness, then Henry's lips left hers to trace the delicate lines of her throat, to tease and caress the sensitive skin and rain kisses on her upturned face.

"Polly..." he spoke between kisses "...this has to stop... We cannot... This is neither the time nor the place. Until this business is over I am not free..."

Polly opened her eyes with reluctance. She felt intoxicated with kissing, aching with a need that could not be appeased. She understood that it had taken a tremendous effort of will on Henry's part to let her go, that he felt as shaken as she did. Nor could she misunderstand his last words. He intended to woo her properly when he could, to make a declaration... Her eyes lit up like dark stars and Henry smiled gently.

"I love you," he said softly, "and you may believe me when I say that I have never said that to anyone but you."

Chapter Fourteen

Despite his good resolutions, it was a considerable time before Henry let Polly go, whispering to her that she should go back into the ballroom as unobtrusively as possible and that he would follow as soon as he was able. Polly, dazed with kisses and happiness, almost floated into the room, convinced that everyone would immediately notice that something was different. No one seemed to do so, however. The supper dance was in progress. Lucille was still surrounded by a circle of family and friends at one end of the ballroom and looked up only briefly as her sister-in-law wafted past. Hetty and Peter were sitting together in an alcove, their heads bent very close together, their words and smiles for each other alone. Lady Bellingham and Sir Godfrey Orbison were still dancing together. Polly had paused when her arm was unexpectedly seized from behind.

"Lady Polly," Tristan Ditton hissed in her ear, "I must have speech with you. Immediately!"

Some of Polly's euphoria faded as she looked into Mr Ditton's thin, secretive face. It was all she could do to avoid shuddering. Once again, his look appraised her in the most unpleasant manner. Polly, fresh from the enchantment of Henry's kisses, found Ditton's behaviour deeply repellent.

"Perhaps some other time, sir," she began, as courteously as she was able. "I was about to rejoin my mother—"

"The Dowager Countess may spare you for a moment, I am sure," Ditton said insinuatingly. "There is a matter of supreme importance which we must discuss. I have been thinking of it ever since that distressing episode at the House of Tides and I feel it my honour and duty to offer you the protection of my name!"

Polly almost gaped at him. Henry's words of love were still in her mind and it was nearly impossible to accept that Tristan Ditton had just made her an offer of marriage. And yet he seemed quite serious. He drew her aside from the other couples who were jostling them as they made for the supper room, and in a moment they were in the deserted and dimly lit hall.

Polly struggled with her feeling of unreality.

"You do me great honour, sir," she said politely, "but there is no need. Everyone knows of the incident and realises it was entirely innocent."

In the darkness she thought she saw Ditton smile. "I had been led to believe that you were so proper a lady, so careful for your reputation, that you would not refuse me, Lady Polly! Was I then mistaken?"

Polly felt her temper rise at the insinuation that she had been in any way to blame. "I am sure that my reputation is as good as that of any lady," she said coldly, "but I feel no need to protect it from so imaginary a threat! It was a generous offer, sir, but I must refuse." Through the open ballroom doors she saw the Dowager Countess pass on her way to supper and took a step forward. Tristan Ditton put a restraining hand on her arm. A servant, scurrying across the darkened hall, gave them a curious look.

Polly's patience snapped. "What is all this about, sir? I have already said—"

Tristan Ditton put his thin face very close to hers.

"It is about a young lady who is not as careful of her reputation as you are of yours, Lady Polly! How do you think your brother would feel were he to discover that the lady he desires to marry has already been free with her favours? That Lord Edmund Grantley was before him?"

Polly recoiled a step in disgust, staring at him in disbelief. "You are loathsome, sir! How dare you insinuate—?"

"It is no insinuation." Ditton spoke with satisfied certainty. "I have heard the whole tale—that they were alone at the inn, that Grantley was boasting of deflowering Miss Markham, and that the innkeeper confirmed the next day that Grantley had succeeded! She had been with him all night! And if you do not agree to our betrothal, Lady Polly, I will make sure that every guest at this ball knows Miss Markham's disgrace!"

His eyes were burning with an excitement that sickened Polly. She was about to reject his words utterly when the memory of Hetty's arrival at Dillingham Court stopped her. With hideous clarity she remembered Peter's insistence upon an early wedding and Hetty's distress at the Dowager Countess's objections. Hetty, whose natural liveliness had been tempered by a mysterious unhappiness. Could it be true? Perhaps Peter knew and was trying to protect his betrothed the only way he could? Even worse, then, if he was prepared to make that sacrifice, for Mr Ditton to expose the truth before such a multitude.

Polly froze as an even more hideous thought occurred to her. What if Hetty were expecting a child? Her faint the previous day was now very suggestive of more than simple wedding nerves and exhaustion. How horrible would be her disgrace if it were true! The thought took a lot of the strength from Polly's response.

"You disgust me, sir! You wish me to consent to a betrothal on the grounds that you will denounce Miss Markham if I do not? You must be mad!"

"Not so!" Tristan Ditton caught Polly's arm in a cruel grip. "You will do as I ask, Lady Polly. Think of Miss Markham's dishonour, think of your brother's anger and disgust! And think of all these prurient gossips who will turn it into the biggest scandal in years! You cannot refuse me!"

"I cannot even believe it! You must be mistaken, or lying…" But Polly knew that her response lacked conviction and she saw Ditton smile.

"I have witnesses who can prove Miss Markham was at the Rose and Crown that night! She would crumble under the first accusation! Aye, and all the world would be there to see it!"

Polly's breath caught in her throat with the shame and horror of it. She could not think clearly. She knew she must be mad to even think of agreeing, but Ditton's hand was like a claw on her arm, his eyes burning into hers. Madness! She could not throw away her own future because of Hetty's behaviour. Then, through the open door she saw them, Peter smiling down into Hetty's face with such love, his hand covering hers as it lay on his arm... Polly remembered his unhappiness over the broken betrothal, how he had made a fool of himself with Lady Bolt, how he had got drunk through his misery on hearing the false news of Hetty's betrothal to Grantley.

"I am at the point where I need a rich wife," Ditton was saying conversationally, only heightening the horror of it all, "and you are both rich and well connected. I could never aspire to marry an Earl's daughter under other circumstances. Come, my dear, we could make a good match of it! What do you say?"

There were a hundred people at the ball, Polly thought with dread. If Ditton were to announce Hetty's downfall before them all, the effect would be too devastating to contemplate. If she could only buy some time, prevent the disclosure. She need never go through with it and she would be able to talk to someone, sort it all out, explain...

Polly's mind was a whirl of thoughts and images. Henry's face was before her, the scene between them in the conservatory suddenly so distant it seemed almost imagined. Or was this the unreality? Ditton was like a coiled spring, unpredictable, unstable.

"Very well," she said weakly, and heard his breath hiss with satisfaction, "but the betrothal must be kept a secret until I have had chance to tell my family—''

It had been a gamble and it showed at once how far she had underestimated him.

''A secret!'' Ditton exclaimed gaily. ''No such thing! I want to shout it from the rooftops!'' He had grasped her hand and was drawing her with hideous inevitability towards the supper room, where the chink of china and buzz of voices could be heard. Polly hung back, suddenly terrified.

''Oh, no! You cannot! I did not intend... We must wait—''

But her words fell on deaf ears.

''Come, come, my dear, do you think I shall give you the chance to cry off! Credit me with a little sense, I beg of you! What a sensation this will be—almost, but not quite, as good as telling the guests of Miss Markham's debauchery!''

Polly gave a faint moan.

''Oh, never fear,'' Ditton continued in the same light tone, ''I shall keep my part of the bargain for as long as you keep yours! And here we are—ready to break the news!''

A curious silence fell on the room when they entered. The tables, in long rows that stretched towards the picture windows at the end, were laden with a harvest supper and almost full. At the top table, the whole Seagrave family were chatting animatedly to the friends and neighbours around them. Worse, to their left, the Duchess of Marchnight, Lady Laura and Lord Henry were enjoying the repast. Henry's head had been inclined towards his mother as she expressed some view on the sweetness of the strawberries. He looked up as Polly came closer and the glad light sprang to his eyes, to be banished only slowly as he saw Tristan Ditton pulling her forward by the hand.

Ditton reached the top table and stopped. He addressed the Earl of Seagrave.

"Lady Polly has done me the honour of accepting my hand in marriage," Tristan Ditton said with oily complacency. "She has made me the happiest of men!"

There was absolute silence. The Dowager Countess put down her wineglass with a clatter that sent her dessert spoon spinning away.

"Polly? Engaged to Mr Ditton? What nonsense is this?"

Polly felt Tristan Ditton stiffen beside her. Afraid of his instability, convinced that he would suddenly blurt out what he had just told her, she hastened into speech.

"It is not nonsense, Mama! I assure you, I have consented to marry Mr Ditton. After all, we have known each other all our lives, and I esteem him greatly—" She broke off as she saw the look of contemptuous amusement cross her elder brother's face. Polly knew that she had started to rattle on out of nervousness, here in front of all these people. And, as yet, Nicholas had said nothing at all. Beside him, Lucille's face was a blank mask.

Fortunately, Tristan Ditton had been the only one convinced by her words. He beamed at the assembled group.

"Come, congratulate me on my conquest!"

Nicholas Seagrave stood up. The look of scorn in

his dark eyes was so swift it was barely noticeable, but Polly saw and understood. He would not make a scene in front of his guests, but the reckoning would come later.

"Thank you for your announcement, Ditton," Seagrave said pleasantly. "I shall look forward to having the opportunity to discuss the matter with my sister and…" his hesitation was barely perceptible "…her trustee, Sir Godfrey."

Ditton's lips curved in a sneer. Even he was not so thick-skinned to miss the lack of warmth in the atmosphere. He turned to Polly, his hand at her waist, pushing her forwards into the centre of the room.

"Come, my love," he murmured, "it is time to tell everyone of our tender romance! Speak up, lest your brother think you half-hearted! You know you must convince him!"

Polly could hear the threat implicit in his tone. His hand was hot and damp through the thin silk of her summer dress. Her skin crawled. She opened her mouth to say something, anything, that might help win the day, though she knew in her heart that the cause was hopeless. Then she met Lucille's eyes. The Countess of Seagrave had one hand resting lightly on her stomach where the faintest curve of her pregnancy was beginning to show. The other hand was on her husband's arm, in a gesture at once tender, supportive and united. And the look in her vivid blue eyes as she gazed at Polly was one of direct challenge. A sob tore itself from Polly's throat. Lucille had everything that Polly wanted, everything that she had thought at last she might achieve with Lord

Henry Marchnight, and here she was, smashing it to pieces before it had begun.

She looked at Hetty Markham and found herself trembling on the very edge of exposure. Hetty's disgrace would be her freedom, but then there was Peter…Peter, who had never been particularly sensitive but was looking at her with a mixture of puzzlement and concern, Peter who would be so hurt…

"You must excuse me…the heat…I feel so unwell…"

But before she could escape the pitiless stare of all those eyes, Henry's chair went clattering back. Polly saw the outrage and disgust on his face, the blazing fury as he turned his back on her and stalked out of the room, and then she fainted.

Somewhere beyond the locked door, Polly could hear the Dowager Countess's voice rising and falling like a peal of bells.

"It's madness, I tell you, complete madness! To throw herself away on that loathsome creature—well, really, Godfrey! Someone must speak to her! No, not you, Godfrey, you would only make matters worse! Oh, Lord, what are we to do?"

There was a rumble from Sir Godfrey, the words indistinguishable, then Polly heard Lady Bellingham's soothing tones. "Dear ma'am, I do not believe for one moment that Lady Polly wishes to marry Mr Ditton. Surely what is of concern is the reason she feels she must!"

Polly held her breath. She had great respect for Lady Bellingham's perspicacity.

"She has told us that it is that ridiculous business

the other night!'' the Dowager Countess was saying
tearfully. ''We have told her and told her that it is
of no consequence, but she insists that her reputation
is damaged! I never heard such a nonsense! The girl
has taken leave of her senses! And to pretend that
she holds him in esteem! It's utterly absurd!''

Polly heard the sound of a door closing across the
corridor, then Lucille's tones, soft and questioning.

''Lucille!'' the Dowager Countess expostulated.
''You must speak to Polly! At once!''

Polly tensed, awaiting the knock at the door. She
could hear Lucille's tones, a brief murmur in stark
contrast to the Dowager's histrionics, and then there
was silence. Polly waited, but no knock came. She
felt so relieved that she almost cried all over again,
for now she would at least be spared the necessity
of lying to Lucille, something she simply could not
bear to do.

She slipped off the bed, where her hot, furious
tears had soaked right through the pillow, and went
across to the open window. The cool evening breeze
from the sea was stirring the curtains, caressing her
swollen face with its gentle touch. Polly could not
bear to look at her reflection, both to avoid seeing
her ravaged face but more to avoid the shock of recognising the pain in her own eyes.

She had cried all night and for the better part of
the following day, until she had no tears left. She
had cried for herself, for her brother Peter, who had
inadvertently put her in this situation, and for poor,
feckless Hetty, whose obsession with glamour and
consequence had been her own—and now Polly's—
downfall. But most of all, Polly cried for the death

of all her hopes. She remembered the tenderness with which Henry had held her only the previous evening, the stupefied amazement on his face as Tristan Ditton had made his announcement, and the way he had turned his back and walked away.

She had been so foolish, believing that she could control Tristan Ditton, thinking it an easy matter to save Hetty's reputation and then somehow save her own future. Now she realised too late that even if she explained everything at once, the barrier she had placed between herself and Henry Marchnight could never be overcome.

The shadows were falling across the bowling green. Polly found it impossible to believe that it was only the previous day that the world had seemed so bright with promise. But now... She shut her mind to it. Soon—very soon—she would have to face the cumulative disapproval of her family again, for they had been promised for an assembly at the The Angel in Woodbridge, and Polly did not trust Tristan Ditton to hold his tongue were she to cry off.

She had seldom looked so ill as when she descended the stairs that evening. None of the family had been in to see her as she was dressing, a sure sign of their disapproval, and the pity on Jessie's face as she had viewed Polly's pale and swollen countenance was almost enough to send her back to bed. None of the frills and furbelows, the primping and tweaking, could make any difference. She looked dreadful.

All the Seagraves, Sir Godfrey Orbison and Lady Bellingham, were assembled in the hall awaiting her.

No one said a word. Polly thought that Nicholas looked as angry as when she had refused Julian Morrish—or possibly more so. His dark eyes were blazing and his mouth was drawn in a very tight line. The Dowager Countess and Sir Godfrey both looked as though they were about to pop with the effort of remaining silent, whilst Peter and Hetty looked both distressed and embarrassed. But it was Lucille and Lady Bellingham with whom Polly knew she had to be careful, for they were fully capable of guessing at least a part of what had happened.

By the time the party reached The Angel in Woodbridge, Polly felt that she had already reached breaking point. There had obviously been some agreement amongst the family that no one would mention her betrothal, for both Lucille and Nicholas, with whom she was travelling, avoided any subject that had even the slightest overtones of engagement, marriage or Mr Ditton. Polly found it rather sinister. Paradoxically, she found this silence, particularly on Lucille's part, made her desperate to confide in her sister-in-law. But Nicholas's dark gaze, resting on her with exasperated resignation, kept her silent.

It was clear that news of the unlikely betrothal had circulated around Woodbridge with the speed of wildfire, for dozens of their acquaintance hurried forward to offer congratulations, and those who had been at the ball were still talking about it. Miss Ditton fell on Polly's neck as soon as they entered the ballroom.

"Sister!" she said in raptures, "how delightful to see you! Mama is still *aux anges* and can speak of little else!" She stood back, and frowned at Polly's puffy, pasty face. "Good Lord, you look quite freak-ish tonight, my dear! I would have expected to see you happier!"

Polly, reflecting miserably on a life in which she had to tolerate Miss Ditton's malicious pin-pricks every day, could barely face the delight of her mother. Mrs Ditton was sitting, beaming, beside a potted palm. Her unctuous son, whose smile was twice as wide, was leaning on the back of her chair and accepting the congratulations of all who passed. As soon as she saw him, Polly began to feel physi-cally sick. There was such an aura of evil exuding from him that she wondered no one else could sense it.

Her torment had only just begun, however. Tristan claimed her for the first dance, and followed it up by pressing for the waltz as well. In vain did Polly pro-test that she did not care to dance. He swept all her objections aside.

"Nonsense!" he cried gaily, whilst his mother looked on indulgently at his ardour and the Dowager Countess of Seagrave looked considerably less en-thusiastic. "Nothing could be more appropriate! My dear Polly—my very dear Polly, you are mine now to flatter and tease and monopolise! What joy! What delight!"

"It is perfectly in order for you to dance the waltz, Polly," the Dowager Countess said, with the sort of weary patience which suggested that she thought it was probably Polly's just desserts.

Mr Ditton clasped Polly very close. His bony hands seemed to clutch her to him, pressing against her in a thoroughly unpleasant manner. And when she tried to ease away, he pulled her tightly against his sparse chest and hissed, "Do you forget that you must dance to my tune now, Lady Polly? One word out of place and Miss Markham's reputation dies forever! Aye, and your brother's happiness too! Smile, my dear!"

Unbidden, an old memory came into Polly's mind from when they had all been children together. Tristan had always been the one who took pleasure in torturing the frogs and toads they found in the woodland ponds, poking sticks at them, or worse. Polly could remember screaming at him to release a small bird that had fallen from its nest and was fluttering helplessly in his greedy, cruel hands. And now he was torturing her, and enjoying himself thoroughly in the process. She hated him. The bile was rising in her throat and a red mist hung before her eyes. The only way she could survive was to deaden all feeling.

Tristan Ditton stuck fast to Polly's side all night, acting the attentive lover to the hilt. At some point in the evening, the Marchnights had arrived and Polly's heart had leapt until she had realised that Henry intended to ignore her utterly. The only gentleman who did attempt to break Ditton's monopoly was an officer of the 21st Dragoons, who were stationed at Woodbridge Barracks. A number of them were at the ball, their redcoats making a bright splash of colour amongst the more sober black of the evening dress, and the young captain made eager play for Polly's hand in a country dance until Ditton told him to take himself off. Polly was embarrassed by Ditton's bad manners as she saw the captain back away in puzzlement and anger. Nor did her own fam-

ily evince any interest in her company. It was as
though they had abandoned her completely to the
Dittons. Never had she felt so alone.

"Polly, you are looking like the spectre at the
feast," Lucille said, under her breath, pausing briefly
beside her sister-in-law whilst Mr Ditton's attention
was temporarily distracted by his sister. Miss Ditton
was begging her brother to confirm that Lady Laura
Marchnight was looking positively sallow that evening and Lucille's clear gaze rested dispassionately
on the tittering brother and sister before coming back
to rest on Polly.

"Oh, Lord, Polly, I promised Nicholas that I
would say nothing, but when you told me last week
that you would marry the first man who asked, I
scarce thought—"

Polly took a breath to tell Lucille that she wanted
to explain, but Mr Ditton turned back to them and
the chance was lost.

"The supper dance!" Mr Ditton said, still burning
with the unpleasant glow of excitement that his torment of Polly engendered. "Lovely Lady Polly, do
me the honour..."

There was no possible way that Polly could eat
anything at all. The food at The Angel was very good
for a provincial assembly, but Polly, plagued by the
joint torments of Tristan Ditton's presence and the
sight of Lord Henry ostentatiously ignoring her, sat
miserably looking at the plate of strawberries and
playing with her spoon. Eventually she excused herself and slipped out of the dining-room. Not even
Tristan Ditton would insist on accompanying her to
the ladies' room.

Polly gazed at her reflection with complete lack of interest and tweaked a curl back inside her coronet with a weary hand. The temptation to stay in here forever was overwhelming. She would have to tell Lucille. She could not bear it... A shadow fell across the mirror. The candles wavered. Polly swung round, a hand to her throat.

She would never have thought it of him, but then she had consistently underestimated Lord Henry Marchnight. He did not care a rush for convention and would go wherever he pleased, even into the ladies' withdrawing-room. As she watched, he closed the door with great deliberation and came towards her.

"Good evening, Lady Polly," Lord Henry said, with icy courtesy. "I want to talk to you."

Chapter Fifteen

All of Polly's emotions flashed into immediate and vivid life, as though she had previously been moving through a dream. Although Henry was standing at some distance from her, she could feel the anger emanating from him, see the hostility in his eyes. Even as she grasped at the opportunity to speak to him and attempt to explain the dreadful dilemma in which she found herself, something in her quailed before the fury she saw in him.

She put out a hand towards him. "Henry! Oh, thank God! Please—it is not as you imagine—"

"No? Then how is it, my lady?" There was no gentleness in him now. He took a step forward and caught both her arms above the elbow. "Is it that Ditton could offer what I was not free to do? Strange, I did not think you the type to accept an offer for the sake of being married! Why, you have had many better chances! Morrish! Bellars!" He shook her slightly. "So perhaps it is that Ditton's type attracts you? But again, I could have sworn that was not so! Was his love-making prettier than mine, perhaps?"

Polly wilted in his arms. "Oh, do not," she whispered, unable to bear the anguish in his eyes. She put up a hand to his cheek. "Harry, it was not like that! I had no choice..."

There was a moment of complete stillness, when the fury still burned in Henry's eyes, then it faded and he slid his hands down her arms, clasping her cold hands in his.

"Polly, my love, you must tell me what has happened. I was so angry... I am sorry—" He broke off. "When I saw you tonight I knew something was dreadfully wrong. Tell me." He tightened his grip. "You must trust me..."

The easy tears stung Polly's eyes again and closed her throat. If Henry had remained angry, had reviled her, she would have withstood his hostility in stony silence, but this gentleness almost unmanned her.

"Oh, Harry, I cannot tell—" The tears choked her. She could not bear it.

Henry was still holding her tightly. "Ditton is compelling you into this offensive masquerade, is he not? But—" he frowned "—I cannot see by what means..."

"I cannot tell," Polly said again, unable to meet his eyes. "Oh, Harry, do not ask me—"

"It cannot be because of that foolish incident the other night," Henry continued, his tone hardening. "That would be a nonsense. So, Polly, what is it all about? Blackmail?"

His tone compelled her to look up and meet his eyes. She saw stark determination there, anger, puzzlement and an intentness to find out the truth. Her resolve weakened. But it would not be like confiding in Lucille—Henry would feel obliged to take some action, and to pour out Hetty's disgrace to him would be so unfair to her future sister-in-law. She could not break her silence and expose Hetty's guilt.

''It is not my secret to tell,'' she said piteously. ''But Harry, it is not *my* actions that have given Mr Ditton the means to exert his will...''

Henry frowned. ''Then—''

''It is Hetty!'' Polly said, and burst into tears.

''Miss Markham?'' Henry seemed astounded. ''Polly, you must tell me. Trust me—''

Polly gazed at him hopelessly. Surely he could see how desperate she was to tell him, that she trusted him more than anyone in the world, and yet...

Henry had forgiven her so much—the youthful immaturity that had stunted her first love for him, her foolish suspicions about his activities. But now he would believe that she did not trust him enough to confide in him, not understanding that a loyalty to her family kept her silent. Polly saw the look of withdrawal she dreaded come into Henry's eyes, and in that second, she realised that the most important thing was not to preserve Hetty's secret, but to entrust Henry with it. She started to speak, but another voice interrupted her before she had said more than two words.

''By all accounts, fishing in other men's pools is your favoured occupation, Marchnight!'' Tristan Ditton sneered from the doorway. ''An affecting tableau, but not one to which you have any right! Do not approach my promised wife again!''

All expression had been wiped clean from Henry's face. He turned to face the other man. For a moment it seemed that Ditton flinched back, although Henry had made no move towards him.

"Take care that you do not make her a widow, Ditton," he said softly, but with an edge to his words that made Polly shiver suddenly. "It will be my most earnest endeavour to see her so."

"Mr Ditton!" Barely had Henry brushed past Tristan Ditton without another word before Lady Bellingham was standing behind him in the passage and addressing him in tones of deepest displeasure. "You do realise that this is the ladies' withdrawing-room, sir? I assure you, you are the last person a lady would wish to meet when she takes refuge in here! Kindly retire!"

Mr Ditton flushed bright red and sidled off down the corridor.

"Routed!" her ladyship said with immense satisfaction. She closed the door behind her and turned her critical dark gaze on Polly.

"My dear, how very woebegone you look! Did you have the chance to speak to Lord Henry? I sent him along to you as soon as I was able, but I was afraid that that unpleasant Ditton fellow would get in the way! What a vulgar piece of work that man is!"

Polly was not sure whether to laugh or cry. There was something so bracing about Lady Bellingham's practical common sense that it made matters seem much less black.

"I was about to confide in Lord Henry when Mr Ditton came in," she admitted. "It took me a little time to pluck up the courage and by then Mr Ditton had already found us. Oh, dear! Lord Henry will think that I do not trust him—''

"Indeed, my dear, and it is of the utmost importance that he is made to understand!" Lady Bellingham said energetically. "Lord Henry loves you so very much that I imagine you have occasioned him a great deal of pain through this false engagement! If you do not act quickly he may not forgive you!"

"I did try," Polly said dispiritedly, "but I did not have enough time—''

"And no doubt he wasted some of it in berating you!" Lady Bellingham shook her head sadly. "Gentlemen are so predictable, but I have high hopes of Lord Henry's intelligence and perception. Surely he can see that you are being blackmailed?"

"Yes, but I did not have the chance to explain—'' Polly broke off. "How on earth did you know that, Lady B.?"

"Oh, my dear…" Lady Bellingham gestured widely "…how could you possibly have agreed to marry that horrid little man otherwise? For a while I could not imagine what hold he had over you, then I realised that it could be nothing to do with you personally—''

"You cannot know—''

"No," Lady Bellingham said serenely, "I do not know the precise truth. All I know is that you are protecting someone else for the best of motives." She took Polly's hands. "But I do urge you, my dear, to reconsider. You may find that what you have been told is very far from the truth…''

Polly stared. "I wish I could believe you, ma'am," she said sadly, "but all the details fit the case. You do not think that I would have agreed to the betrothal otherwise? Oh, I do not know what to do—''

The door opened and a young lady peered in a little dubiously. Lady Bellingham took Polly's arm and steered her out into the corridor.

"Come, we must see if we can find Lord Henry for you. I cannot deny that I am consumed with curiosity to know the truth, but Lord Henry should be the first to hear! You must tell him, and at once. If necessary, I shall occupy that repellent Mr Ditton by telling him exactly what I think of him. That should distract his attention! In fact, I think I shall do that anyway!''

Lady Bellingham's plan was destined to be dashed, however. Neither Lord Henry Marchnight nor Tristan Ditton could be found when they re-entered the ballroom.

Looking about, Polly thought that the company seemed to be thinning rapidly. The officers of the 21st Light Dragoons seemed to be vanishing from before her eyes.

"Oh, this assembly is so tediously dull!'' Miss Ditton yawned. "Mama, let us retire! Where can Tristan have got to?'' She looked about her, vexed. "I hope he will not mind if we take the carriage! It is so thoughtless of him to disappear just as we require his escort!''

As far as Polly was concerned, Ditton could not be far enough away. She endured Miss Ditton's pretence at an affectionate farewell embrace, winced as she was addressed as "Sister', and retreated thankfully to Lucille's side. She had already decided that she would seek a private audience with her sister-in-law as soon as they reached Dillingham Court. She could carry the secret of Hetty's disgrace no longer.

The journey home was almost as dreadful as the one to the assembly. Lucille, Polly and Nicholas sat in silence whilst Polly ached to burst out with the truth. Other melancholy thoughts also occupied her mind. A few moments more and she would have told Henry everything, but now he would think that she did not trust him enough to confide. And it had been true...doubt had kept her silent until it was too late.

Polly took no notice as the carriage lurched along the dark lanes from Woodbridge to Dillingham. It was only when they came to an abrupt halt in the middle of nowhere that she looked up in surprise. Nicholas opened the window and stuck his head out. A cold mist was blowing in from the sea, wreathing around the trees, creeping into the carriage. Polly shivered. She was uncertain of their precise location as she had not been paying attention, but the night was cold and as desolate as only the empty Suffolk nights could be.

"John? What the devil's going on?" Nicholas demanded.

"There's a barricade across the road, my lord," the coachman responded. "Army business, apparently, though here's one can tell you what's going on—"

"What's happening, Lieutenant?" Nicholas Seagrave demanded of someone beyond Polly's vision. "Why have we stopped?"

There was a murmur of conversation and then the soldier stepped around the side of the carriage, his red coat vivid in the misty darkness. His broad smile dispelled some of the tension gathering inside, where Lucille and Polly were just starting to worry.

"Oh it's you, my lord! Please accept my apologies for stopping the coaches—a precaution only—but there has been some trouble down on the mud-flats…" He grinned suddenly, dropping all formality. "You'll be glad to know, sir, that the operation has been a success and both parties taken as we planned—"

"Nicholas? What is happening?" The Dowager Countess's voice reached them imperiously from the door of the carriage she was sharing with the others. "Why have we stopped in this godforsaken place?"

The young Lieutenant turned hastily to apologise. "In just a moment we should be able to allow your journey to proceed, ma'am…"

"Did you take the ship as well?" Nicholas asked.

"We did, sir! The *Laribee* was hanging about outside port for the best part of the day, but she showed the revenue cutter a clean pair of heels when they went after her! When darkness fell she came in close again and put a boat out at the mouth of the creek, but we were waiting for them before they got to the rendezvous! The crew swore blind that they were innocent, but we found a tidy stock of brandy in the hold. It was to be an exchange, a man out and the cargo in, only the men on the beach started to quarrel and under cover of the noise and darkness—"

He broke off at the sound of marching footsteps on the road. Polly, leaning forward to peer into the darkness, drew back with an exclamation as a posse of soldiers, mudstained and filthy, marched past the carriages with two prisoners under escort in chains. One was utterly unknown to her, but the other—

"Tristan Ditton!" The Dowager Countess's astounded tones cut the air. "You have Tristan Ditton there under arrest! What on earth is going on—"

"Do close the carriage door, Mama," Nicholas said hastily. "We may progress now. Questions must wait until we are back in the warm, I think." And he drew back into the coach. They started to move again, but not until Polly's astonished gaze had taken in every detail of Mr Ditton's extraordinary appearance. Gone was the dandified, exquisite simpering over his shirtpoints, and in his place was a snarling monster, straining helplessly against the chains that held him. For a moment his furious gaze picked her out and pinned her with his anger before he was dragged past. Polly shivered violently and, as the carriage picked up speed, she burrowed as far under the rugs as she could in a vain effort to get warm.

"Tristan Ditton!" The Dowager Countess was still expostulating loudly as they all entered the hall at Dillingham Court. "If I had not seen it with my own eyes, I doubt I should have believed it! And you—" she swung around accusingly on her elder son "—you appear to know all about it!"

Nicholas Seagrave was grinning broadly. "Oh no, this is Harry Marchnight's show, not mine! I merely offered my help when he asked! You will have to ask Harry for the explanation!"

"Harry Marchnight!" The Dowager Countess was beginning to resemble a parrot in her repetiton. "What in the name of all that's holy can Harry

Marchnight have to do with this? Why, I like Harry above all people, he is the most charming of men and he did us a great good turn in London, but—''

She stopped suddenly. ''And you, Polly! What do you know of all this? The betrothal to Tristan Ditton—''

Polly had not been listening to her mother's exclamations. She had suddenly realised with a feeling of sick horror and indignation that her brother had known of Ditton's criminality and yet had said nothing, had done nothing to rescue her from the travesty of her engagement to him. Worse, only a night ago, Henry Marchnight had sworn to tell her the truth and had done so, but had neglected the most important part—that Tristan Ditton was the real villain.

''How dare you?'' Her words cut across whatever Lucille had been saying to the Dowager Countess. She glared at Nicholas. ''How dare you and Henry Marchnight play your games and think it entertaining? You could have saved me—*one word* from you and I would have known—'' Her voice broke and she started to sob.

''You must see that I could not, Polly.'' Nicholas had come across to her and tried to put an arm around her, but Polly pushed him away furiously. ''The situation was so fraught with danger that, if Ditton had had any hint that all was not well, he might have run before we could trap him—''

Polly did not want to hear him. She turned away and stumbled up the stairs to her room where, for a second time, she locked herself in and cried as though her heart were breaking.

Chapter Sixteen

By the time that a pale dawn was breaking over Dillingham Court, an exhausted Polly had thought about her situation twenty times over and had been forced to admit that Nicholas had been right. Had she known of Tristan Ditton's connections with Chapman, had she been told he was a criminal, she would never have been able to treat him with the cool courtesy she had usually meted out to him. It would have been impossible to behave normally in his presence. Nevertheless, Henry's behaviour rankled. She had been chastising herself for lack of trust in him; it was difficult not to feel that he had shown a similar lack of faith in her.

As for Hetty's secret, it seemed to Polly that it would be best to keep silent on that score now that Ditton was taken. There was no way of knowing if he had spoken the truth and it seemed to Polly that least said was soonest mended. She knew that it would be difficult to avoid the perceptive questions of Lucille and Lady Bellingham and the more forthright ones of the Dowager Countess, but with the wedding only five weeks away she was determined to hold her peace. Ditton could not constitute a threat any more and it would be pointlessly distressing to rake up the story. Henry was the only one to whom she had confided that she was being blackmailed through Hetty, and Polly thought rather wearily that Henry was unlikely to be able to press her on the matter since she would never be alone with him ever again. Polly was too tired and too resigned to try to delude herself that matters could ever be the same between her and Henry. For a brief time everything had been perfect, but now it was spoiled beyond re-demption.

Polly slept fitfully and woke late, going down to breakfast determined to put a brave face on matters. The fact that everyone else had eaten and the room was empty helped her gather her courage. However, she almost fell at the first hurdle when she emerged from breakfast to find Henry Marchnight being ush-ered into the drawing-room. The Dowager Countess, on espying her daughter about to bolt up the stairs, seized her arm in a vice-like grip and marched her into the room.

''There you are, Polly! Lord Henry is come to tell us all about Mr Ditton's activities! I am sure we are all agog!'' She peered at her daughter's face rather critically. ''Dear me, you are as wan as a December morning, my love! The shock of it all, I suppose! Medlyn, some tea if you please!''

''Mama!'' Polly began, in an agonised whisper, but the Dowager appeared to be suddenly afflicted by deafness. She took a seat on the sofa and com-pelled Polly to sit down beside her. The whole of the family was assembled, Peter and Hetty on the window-seat, Lucille, Nicholas and Henry in scattered armchairs set in a circle.

There was a pause whilst the tea was brought in by two footmen and placed before the Dowager Countess. Polly felt almost stifled with nerves. Even more galling, she had known before her mother spoke that she looked dreadful; it seemed that every time Henry saw her now she was looking wan and pasty, a far cry from his own careless elegance.

''Tristan Ditton as Chapman's protector!'' the Dowager Countess exclaimed, breaking the silence and passing Henry strong tea in a china cup. She bestowed a warm smile upon him. ''It is scarcely to be believed! Why, I always found him a loathsome man, but never suspected… Nicholas!'' She appealed to her elder son. ''Did you ever imagine Tristan Ditton a criminal? Before you knew him to be so, of course!''

''No, Mama,'' Nicholas Seagrave said obligingly, ''I am ashamed to admit that I had no notion! I always found him deeply offensive but had no idea that he had the ability to run a criminal operation!''

''Extraordinary!'' the Dowager opined.

''Ditton was certainly intelligent enough to appear stupid,'' Henry said drily, ''but with too little self-control to resist boasting about his achievements! My suspicions were first aroused by the gloating excitement with which he spoke of Chapman in London, and kept insisting that the man had a rich protector. I soon saw that he thought himself invulnerable. But his vanity was his downfall.'' He shook his head. ''His contacts in Suffolk made this the perfect escape route for Chapman. Ditton had been dabbling in smuggling for a number of years when he needed the money——he even used his carriage to transport smuggled goods under the noses of the militia! And, of course he cultivated that foolish, foppish attitude which led one to believe that he was nothing but a dandy.''

''No doubt you recognised that deception since you practised it yourself!'' Polly put in a little pointedly. She gave Henry a very straight look as his thoughtful gaze transferred itself to her. It was very difficult for her to swallow her resentment and hear him out courteously. She found that she felt very angry.

Everyone seemed to be looking at her and to distract attention she fiddled with her teacup and only succeeded in spilling the liquid and drawing even more attention to herself. The Dowager Countess pursed her lips and filled another cup for her daughter.

''How did you know that Ditton intended to try to smuggle Chapman out of the country, Henry?'' Lucille asked curiously when the commotion had subsided.

Henry shifted a little in his chair. ''I received the intelligence that Chapman was to be helped to escape abroad and then matters made perfect sense,'' he said. ''Ditton was spending a lot of time down here and Suffolk has the ideal coastline for smuggling. Goods, men...'' he shrugged ''...there are so many deserted beaches, mudflats, creeks... It should have been easy for him, but I was watching him all the time and in the end, of course, he gave himself away by quarrelling with his allies and allowing the Dragoons to capture them all!''

"That night at the House of Tides..." Polly began, drawn in despite herself.

"Yes—" Henry smiled a little "—Ditton was certainly on the prowl that night! It was one of the nights when the tide was right to bring a boat in, but in the end the weather was against it. It was Ditton's bad luck to be marooned at the House of Tides that night, and my good luck that he was so close by! Like me, he knew that there was a passageway from the cellars to the sea and he decided to explore.'' Henry gave Polly an expressive look. "The spiral staircase in your room there led directly down to the cellars. I imagine Ditton had heard mention of that too. Certainly his explorations took him into your bedroom and into direct confrontation with your chamber pot!''

There was a rustle of laughter from everyone. Polly had to make a conscious effort not to smile. She did not want to forgive Henry so easily and she could feel her defences weakening. It was so fatally easy to like him, to feel that warmth melting her hostility.

Lucille shivered a little, sobering abruptly. "Poor Mrs Ditton—and poor Thalia! I could almost find it in my heart to feel sorry for them!''

"Lucille! That horrid Miss Ditton!'' Hetty raised her brows. "How can you spare them your sympathy?''

Lucille smiled a little sadly. "Only think what it must be like for them now, Hetty! Mrs Ditton was always so proud of her offspring and she has precious little to be proud of now! A son in prison and a daughter who will no doubt be abandoned by her fiancé! They will be forever moving now, trying to conceal their notoriety, looking over their shoulders, afraid that someone will give their shameful secret away. Tristan has brought them to that and I pity them.''

''And to think that Lord Henry knew all the time that Tristan Ditton was a criminal!'' Polly said, an edge to her voice. Everyone looked at her again. The words had come out more loudly than she had intended, but she was so angry she could not contain them.

''You told me much of the truth about your activities, Lord Henry,'' she said coldly, aware that everybody was listening but speaking for Henry alone, ''that night at the ball. But the most important part you chose to neglect—''

''As did you, my lady,'' Henry said gently, holding her gaze, ''when I pressed you to tell me the means by which Ditton compelled you into the betrothal. Would you care to enlighten us now that all is safe?''

Polly caught her breath. Against her will her gaze slid to Hetty and away again. She had not thought to speak of this in company.

''I think not, sir.'' She cleared her throat. ''The matter is closed now that Mr Ditton is under arrest. It need concern us no further.''

''Perhaps you still consider yourself bound by the betrothal?'' Henry asked, for all the world as though he genuinely believed it might be so.

Polly reddened with a combination of embarrassment and annoyance at his persistence. "Certainly not!" she snapped. "But the matter is no longer relevant—"

"Nonsense, Polly!" The Dowager Countess could be most obtuse when she chose to be. "You may speak freely, my love! We are all positively consumed with curiosity and will not rest until we know!"

Polly, who had found herself incapable of tearing her gaze away from Henry's look of challenge, forced herself to face her mother instead.

"No, truly, Mama, it will not serve—"

"I think you should speak out, Polly." Surprisingly it was Lucille who spoke up now, gently but firmly. "You may find that what you believe—what you have been told—is not the case. At the very least, I do not believe that the truth can be hidden any longer."

Polly stared at her. "Lucille? But—how can you know?"

"Tell us," Lucille repeated, and her tone was inexorable.

Polly allowed herself to look across at Peter and Hetty, who were sitting opposite her on the sofa. Peter looked vaguely puzzled but the delicate colour had already started to come into Hetty's face, as though she sensed what was to come. Polly took a deep breath.

"Very well, if it must be so. Mr Ditton came to me on the night of the ball. First he suggested that we should become betrothed to protect my good name from the scandal caused by his presence in my bedroom that night at the House of Tides. I thought this ridiculous and told him so. He then dropped all pretence of respect and affection." Polly looked briefly at Hetty again. This was so very difficult. Everybody was quite silent, waiting for her to continue. Lucille was willing her on with a look of combined sympathy and determination.

"Mr Ditton told me," Polly said very clearly, "that he had information injurious to Hetty's reputation and that he would make it public—announce it in the ballroom—if I did not immediately consent to an engagement between the two of us."

"Oh!" Hetty had gasped even before Polly finished speaking, pressing one hand to her mouth, her cheeks scarlet and her eyes wide with horror. Polly watched as Peter moved closer, taking her hand in a comforting hold.

"Mr Ditton must have told you what that information was in order to gain your consent," Lucille observed, coolly. "And it must have been convincing. You would not have believed it else."

Polly's eyes flew to her face. "Yes, indeed, but— Lucille, I cannot!" She threw another look at Hetty, who had turned her face into Peter's shoulder. "Hetty, I am so sorry! I did not wish to tell—"

Peter's face was grim. "You should finish Ditton's tale, Poll!"

"How can I?" Polly appealed to them. She felt sick at what was happening. Hetty looked like a broken butterfly, her tumbled curls brushing Peter's shoulder, her face hidden. Polly had a horrible vision of Peter pushing her away, repudiating her when he knew the truth. Yet Peter was holding her so tenderly, whispering words of comfort, almost as though he knew...

"You know!" she said, almost accusingly.

"I know the truth," Peter said harshly, "but what is the tale?"

Astonishingly, whilst Polly groped for the words, it was Henry who answered. "My guess is that Ditton told Lady Polly that Miss Markham had spent a night alone at an inn with a man, and that the man was Edmund Grantley."

This time it was Polly who gasped. She stared at him in astonishment. "How could you possibly know—?"

Across from her, Henry said bitterly, "I would guess further that Lady Polly could not bear for her future sister-in-law to be ruined, but most of all she could not see you hurt and disillusioned, Peter. Perhaps she thought that you might already know and that you were protecting Miss Markham by offering her marriage. In either case, Lady Polly knew that you loved Miss Markham sincerely and would be dreadfully injured by the disclosure. It was misplaced loyalty that kept her silent—and impelled her into the betrothal."

Polly could not speak. Hetty was crying quietly in Peter's arms and Polly wished she could follow suit. Her mother's face was stiff with shock and horror, Nicholas looked almost as grim as his brother, and it was Lucille who came across to Polly in a rustle of silk and put an arm around her.

"I did what I thought was right!" Polly said. It seemed to her that the words came out too loudly, rattling the china, making her listeners wince.

"Of course you did," Lucille said soothingly, hugging her close. "It is just that Mr Ditton's story was not true. Oh, if only you had confided in someone—" She bit her lip, clearly thinking that this was hardly the time for recriminations.

The Dowager Countess, who had been viewing Hetty's sobbing figure with a mixture of concern and doubt, turned to Lucille, her face clearing.

"The tale was not true, you say? Ditton invented it? But—"

Nicholas Seagrave stirred slightly. "Peter," he said thoughtfully, "there is nothing for it but to tell the truth."

Hetty gave a little whimper. "Oh, must we, indeed? I cannot bear—"

"Yes, you can, my love." Peter put her a little away from him, giving her an encouraging smile so full of love and warmth that Polly felt a huge lump in her throat. This was very different from her imaginings, from the denunciation and horror that she was certain would greet her revelations.

"It is true," Peter said grimly, "that Edmund Grantley took Hetty to the Rose and Crown at Farnforth and imprisoned her there. There is no doubt his intention was to seduce her. He had taken her driving that afternoon and Hetty had become concerned at the distance they had gone from home. It was dusk when they pulled into the yard at Farnforth, and Grantley's intentions soon became clear to her." He glanced down at Hetty, who was still held close to his side, her eyes cast down, her face now as pale as it had been scarlet before.

"He kept her locked in one of the chambers for

several hours whilst he drank below," Peter continued savagely. "Several people heard Grantley boasting drunkenly of the ripe little bird he had waiting for him upstairs. All might have fallen out as he had planned had I not chosen to put up at Farnforth that night."

"You!" It was the Dowager Countess whose stunned accents spoke the word and conveyed that she had already understood the rest of the story.

Peter sat up a little straighter and took Hetty's hand in his once more. She was still very pale, but a light burned in her eyes. Watching her, Polly understood. Hetty was safe in the knowledge that Peter loved her above all things and that his love would never falter. He would not desert her to the condemnation of the world.

"It was too late to travel on to Kingsmarton that night, and Farnforth was conveniently on my route," Peter confirmed, meeting his mother's eyes very directly. "Hetty heard my arrival, heard me talking to the ostler, and recognised my voice." He looked at her and smiled. "She smashed the window and shouted to me for help. Grantley was still downstairs and I...persuaded him to take himself off. It was quite a mill." There was grim amusement in Peter's voice. "Then I went to find Hetty. She was desperately upset and frightened."

There was a pause whilst everyone filled in the missing bits for themselves. Polly could imagine Hetty's overwhelming relief at her rescue, the breaking of the tension after such terror, Peter's fear for her and his feelings on finding her unharmed... An irresistible passion could quite easily sweep one away. Moral frailty, perhaps, but entirely understandable. Looking up, she caught Henry Marchnight's eyes upon her, accurately reading every thought and looking very interested. Polly blushed and looked away.

"I think you all know already," Peter said gently, "how much I love Hetty and how honoured I am that she will be my wife. None of that has changed and I would marry her tomorrow if I could! I wish with all my heart that I had never done anything that endangered her reputation but—" he shrugged "—such things happen and it is pointless to deny it. Poor Hetty has been through agonies of regret and remorse but I feel she has done nothing of which she should be ashamed. I can only repeat that I love her with all my heart."

"A good thing that you are to marry so soon!" The Dowager Countess said trenchantly, conveniently forgetting that it had been her most ardent hope to see the marriage at St George's, Hanover Square, the following spring. "But the scandal, Peter! Whatever can Mrs Markham have thought when Hetty did not return that night?"

"Mama was most distressed," Hetty confirmed, speaking for the first time and just managing to overcome her embarrassment. "Fortunately, my aunt and cousins were from home, so knew nothing of the scandal, and when Mama saw that it was Peter who had rescued me and that we were…" she blushed "…betrothed once more, her fears were put to rest."

The Dowager Countess snorted. "A fine protector, indeed, who takes advantage—" Aware of where her words were leading her, she broke off again. Her eye fell on her younger son, defiantly looking back at her, and she softened slightly. "Well, well!" She looked as though she were about to say "No harm done!", but quickly changed her mind.

"What I do not understand," Lucille said, a frown on her forehead, "is how Tristan Ditton came to know of this—or at least to know enough to make up so damaging and scurrilous a story."

Now it was Henry's turn to look a shade embarrassed. "I can see that there is nothing to be done but tell you the rest, Lady Seagrave—I was hoping to spare you this, for a little time at least—" He broke off and sighed heavily, seeing the look of blank incomprehension on all their faces. "It was Lady Bolt who told Ditton about the episode at the inn."

"Lady Bolt!" Several people spoke at once.

"It does not surprise me that she is spreading slanderous gossip," the Dowager Countess observed.

"But she was at Wellerden with you when Peter was at Farnforth!" Polly exclaimed and found that everyone was looking at her again. She turned bright red as Henry looked at her with quizzically raised brows. "I mean...I understood that Lady Bolt...that you..."

Henry's smile mocked her. "Just as you understood that I had arranged a tryst with Lady Bolt at Richmond? It was only business, I fear, contrary to all appearances! It is true that Lady Bolt and I were briefly at Wellerden's houseparty, though not together in any sense of the word," he added drily. "In fact, Lady Bolt left only a day or two after Peter did. Her intention, I believe, was to join the Duke of

Garston at the Newmarket races. I imagine her route took her through Farnforth—I know it did, for she stayed at the Rose and Crown only the night after Peter was there. The landlady there knows Lady Bolt and also knows of her connection with the Markham family. She was bursting to tell her ladyship this prime piece of gossip and no doubt she was rewarded for the information.''

"And Mr Ditton?'' the Dowager Countess pressed.

Henry gave an ironic smile. "This part might be amusing were it not that the behaviour of Ditton and Lady Bolt was so damaging. You may know that the two of them are old…'' he cleared his throat "…old friends. In recent times they have been in a different business together. Lady Bolt has lent Ditton considerable sums of money, has become involved in several illegal gaming rackets with him and has even, I suspect, benefited from his and Chapman's criminal activities. The extent of her involvement is something on which she is currently being questioned. She was arrested this morning.'' He turned back to Lucille. "I am sorry if the news occasions you any pain, Lady Seagrave.''

"I shall bear it with fortitude,'' Lucille said, straight-faced. "But we digress. Did Lady Bolt pass on the gossip to Ditton?''

Henry nodded. "She did. She wrote to him immediately. She knew that he loved scandal and she was also sure that he might find the information useful at some point in the future. Of course, she was correct.'' He glanced briefly at Polly, who looked away.

"The piquant part, however, was that Lady Bolt did not approach the subject directly. She liked to hint and tease, and at no point did she tell Ditton whom the gentleman was by name. He, knowing that Miss Markham had recently been courted by Grantley, made the obvious assumption. I know, because I have seen and destroyed the letter. Ditton was carrying it last night."

"So you knew that as well!" Polly was so affronted she thought she might burst. "You knew why I had agreed to the betrothal even though you pretended you did not!"

"I only knew about the letter after Ditton was arrested," Henry said calmly, "and I could not be certain that that was the means he used to compel you to marry him. There might have been something else!"

Polly was not to be pacified. "I do not believe you! Of all the cruel tricks! Oh! You are despicable—"

"Polly!" The Dowager Countess's shocked tones mingled with Lucille's more tempered reproof. Henry did not seem much put out. Polly thought he was almost smiling and she felt she could have slapped him had she been closer.

"The tea has gone cold," Lucille observed prosaically in an attempt to calm the atmosphere. "Nicholas, would you pull the bell for some more? Henry, will you stay?"

Henry Marchnight got to his feet. "No, ma'am, I thank you. I have work to do. I am not sure—" his gaze touched Polly's face briefly "—whether I shall return to Suffolk."

"But you must come to the wedding!" Hetty said hopefully. She seemed to have almost recovered her spirits now that the dreadful truth had come to light and no one, not even the Dowager, had condemned her as a fallen woman.

Henry smiled. "I should be very glad to do so if I can," he said, "and I wish you both very happy!"

There was an awkward silence after Nicholas had gone out to see Henry to his curricle. The Dowager Countess made some comment about the weather, indicating that the topic of the past fifteen minutes was now effectively closed. Hetty ventured a remark about the wedding arrangements and soon everyone was chatting about the rival merits of orange blossom or hot-house lilies to decorate the church. For a fantastical moment it seemed to Polly as though the whole episode had never even occurred. She was left to marvel at the swiftness with which the most enormous of family secrets could be swept successfully under the carpet.

Chapter Seventeen

"**Y**ou are my only hope now, Polly!" The Dowager Countess fixed her daughter with tragic dark eyes. "I had every expectation of seeing Hetty and Peter married in London, but of course that is out of the question now! I was never more shocked in my life! And Hetty the daughter of so respectable a man! There must have been some sad lack of guidance in her upbringing—perhaps the influence of that dreadful Cyprian," the Dowager added thoughtfully, brightening at so plausible an explanation.

"I feel, Mama, that you should be laying the blame at Peter's door if you must apportion it anywhere," Polly said firmly. "He is the seducer, after all!"

"Yes, and in such a low place as that inn!" the Dowager mourned.

Polly hid a smile at the thought that Peter's behaviour would have been more acceptable had he chosen more salubrious surroundings.

"I do feel that Hetty should show a certain reticence," the Dowager continued. "Why, she behaves as though nothing has happened! It shows a certain unsteadiness of character!''

Polly thought that Hetty's ebullience sprung more from relief than a want of feeling. ''I am persuaded that Hetty's feelings are all that is proper,'' she said. ''She is very young, Mama, and is understandably excited about the wedding. Now, in what way am I your only hope?''

''Why, for a fashionable wedding, of course!'' Happily, the Dowager was now diverted. ''First Nicholas and Lucille marry in that hole-in-the-corner fashion, and now Peter… But you will not disappoint me, I know! It is what your father would have wanted—''

Polly was looking vaguely confused. ''But, Mama, I have no intention of getting married—''

''No intention!'' The Dowager Countess laid aside the linen she had been folding for Hetty's trousseau. ''But surely it is as good as arranged? I assumed that Lord Henry was only waiting until he could wash his hands of this sordid affair with Tristan Ditton! Surely—''

''You are mistaken, Mama.'' Polly got up hastily. In the five weeks since Henry Marchnight had left Suffolk, she had had ample time to reflect on what had happened and resolve that she could never explain to her mother why such a match was now impossible. ''There never was an understanding between Lord Henry and myself—''

Polly steeled herself against the memory of that brief time when they had been in such perfect accord. ''And I would be astounded were he even to return to Dillingham for the wedding next week!'' she finished with relief.

The Dowager raised her dark brows.

''Now there you are fair and far out!'' she said triumphantly. ''I have had the most delightful letter from Lord Henry, engaging himself for the wedding and the breakfast! He will be escorting his mother and sister. Oh, and the Vereys are also coming up from London! Is that not fine? Perhaps,'' the Dowager said, brightening, ''it will be almost as good as a Society wedding, after all!''

Lord Henry did not come to the wedding. The Duchess of Marchnight, accompanied by the Vereys and stately in Dowager purple, explained graciously that her son had been detained on business but hoped to join the wedding party later in the day. Polly was acutely disappointed. She tried not to lose interest in the proceedings as a radiant Hetty wafted up the aisle on Nicholas Seagrave's arm to be joined in holy wedlock with his brother.

The service went very smoothly. The Dowager Countess cried becomingly into a large lace-edged handkerchief and Mrs Markham sniffed slightly less elegantly in the pew opposite. Hetty and the Dowager both wore expressions of faint relief as she floated down the aisle again, this time on her husband's arm. A happy end to a potential scandal, Polly thought with a smile. Now that they were safely married and Hetty had the protection of Peter's name, the whole unfortunate episode could be allowed to slip into the past where it belonged.

* * *

The wedding breakfast at Dillingham Court seemed interminable to Polly. Had Henry been there she would have been consumed with nerves, but as it was, she felt both disappointed and let down. Eventually they rose from table to take a rest before the evening dance and supper for the Seagraves' tenants and the villagers. Polly felt out of sorts. Misery had prompted her to eat too much and the meal weighed heavily on her stomach. She lay down in the cool of her room and allowed herself to doze.

She was awoken by the sound of hooves on the gravel outside and voices raised in greeting. Hurrying across to the window, Polly was in time to see Henry Marchnight hand his reins to one of the grooms as Nick Seagrave came forward to shake his hand and lead him up the steps into the house. That put a different complexion on the evening. Polly, lethargy forgotten, rushed to the bell and rang energetically for Jessie.

By the time she was ready, the dancing had already started in the Long Barn. Peter was energetically twirling his bride around in a spirited country dance whilst the villagers, made merry by drink and good food, roared their encouragement. The older folk had retired from the fray, but the Vereys had remained and Lady Laura Marchnight seemed to have persuaded the Duchess to allow her to stay. Polly was immediately swept into the dance by Simon Verey.

Henry was dancing with Therese Verey and Polly attempted the difficult manoeuvre of trying to see his face whilst executing the complicated steps of the dance. She could read nothing there. Nothing of encouragement or liking or interest. He did not even glance in her direction. She sighed inwardly. Perhaps they were back as they had been a few short months ago, mingling at the same social events but apart, almost strangers. It seemed intolerable and yet she might have to learn to live with it.

Then Simon Verey was steering her across the floor towards Henry and was saying, "You must grant Lord Henry a dance, Lady Polly, for he has ridden all this way solely for that privilege!"

Henry gave him a droll smile.

"What a good friend you are, Simon, giving all a fellow's secrets away!"

Simon smiled imperturbably, gravitated back to his wife's side, and Henry took Polly's hand with grave courtesy.

"Will you dance, Lady Polly? Good manners might compel you to accept after that introduction!"

"I need no compulsion, sir," Polly said, looking up into those steady grey eyes and feeling a little dizzy. Hope and fear were warring within her. Did they have another chance?

They danced in silence. The country jigs and figured dances favoured at such rustic gatherings hardly leant themselves to conversation. All about them the chatter and laughter ebbed and flowed, the tankards of ale were drained and replenished, but Polly was only conscious of Henry's eyes following her through the movement of the dance and the brief touch of his hand on hers.

"You have been good enough to grant me this dance, Lady Polly," Lord Henry said when the music ended. "Will you go further and grant me a private interview? There are matters we must discuss—"

"Lord Henry!" It was Hetty, bright-eyed and beaming with happiness, who was at his elbow. "Oh, I am so glad you were able to be here!"

She stood on tiptoe as Henry bent to kiss her cheek and wish her happy. Polly wondered fleetingly how Hetty had managed to achieve such an easy friendship with him. But then, Lucille had also found him both friendly and charming. It seemed that she was the only one who had difficulty in achieving such intimacy and that was only because she could not escape that powerful attraction he held for her. As Henry had said only a few months before, they could never be comfortable with each other.

"You must not be angry with me, Lord Henry," Hetty was continuing sweetly, "but I am come to take Polly away! She has promised to attend me this evening and my new Mama..." she nodded towards the Dowager Countess "...tells me it would be fitting for me to retire now! It seems a shame..." for a moment Hetty looked at the revellers a little enviously "...that I must miss the party!"

Henry stepped back with a slight bow. "Then I shall hope for an opportunity to continue our conversation later, Lady Polly."

Polly hoped that her disappointment did not show as sharply on her face as she felt it inside.

It was much later that she was able to rejoin the party. Hetty had retired to bed with becoming modesty and there was only a small moment of awkwardness when both mothers clearly felt they should make mention of what to expect on the wedding night, only to remember that this was hardly necessary. Mrs Markham had become quite tearful now that her only fledgling was married and had to be dosed with medicinal brandy in the library. As Lucille had been too tired to stay late, this duty fell to Polly, who patiently listened to Mrs Markham's rambling tales of Hetty's childhood. Eventually Mrs Markham hauled herself to her feet a little unsteadily and went off to bed and Polly cut through the empty ballroom, where the chandeliers still blazed, and out through the conservatory.

It was very dark on the terrace. The sound of music and laughter still drifted through the trees from the Long Barn, and the torchlight glowed faintly. As Polly closed the conservatory door behind her, a slight figure came hurrying along the terrace and almost collided with her. There was a muffled exclamation, then the figure put back the hood of its cloak and revealed herself to be Lady Laura Marchnight.

"Oh, Lady Polly!" Laura gasped. "How you startled me! I did not see you there!"

She cast a swift look around. "Please could you pretend that we have not met? Indeed, it is of the utmost importance, for you see, I am eloping!"

She brought the words out with a certain flourish and in the moonlight her eyes were bright with excitement.

"Mr Farrant—" Polly began.

"He is waiting with the carriage at the end of the lime drive!" Lady Laura interrupted excitedly. "He was a little unhappy with the plan, but I persuaded him! Mama was quite immovable over the scheme to send me to Northumberland and I knew I should not see my dearest Charles for an age were I to comply! Oh, dear Lady Polly, say you will not betray me!'' She caught Polly's hands in a desperate grip.

''Of course not,'' Polly said hastily, giving Laura's hands a reassuring squeeze. ''But are you certain that you are doing the right thing? Your family will be very displeased by a runaway match—''

''If I am Charles' wife I shall have my whole happiness,'' Laura said confidently, her eyes shining like stars, ''and though it grieves me to go against the wishes of my family, I cannot lose that which is most precious to me! Wish me joy!'' She reached up to give Polly an impulsive kiss. ''I am so happy!''

''I wish you all the luck in the world,'' Polly said, a lump in her throat at such transparent happiness. ''Now, you had best begone before anyone else sees you!''

Laura paused on the edge of flight, fumbling in the deep pocket of the coat. ''Oh, I almost forgot! I was going to leave this with a servant, but perhaps you would be so good... It is for Henry, but please do not give it to him until the end of the evening. I could not bear for him to worry about me, but rather that than that he should catch up with us!''

The letter was crisp and smooth between Polly's fingers. She watched Laura's hurrying shadow disappear along the colonnade. Polly was not sure how long she stood there alone in the darkness, but it was long enough for the glow of the carriage lights to fade away between the trees.

''Do not give it to him until the end of the evening...'' She did not want to break her word to

Laura, but even less could she lie to Henry or keep a secret from him. She thrust the letter into the bodice of her dress and walked slowly across the cobbled yard towards the barn. There had been a break in the dancing whilst the guests partook of supper and Polly spotted Henry quickly, deep in conversation with Nick Seagrave. As she hesitated to approach them, Henry looked up and their eyes met. Seagrave said something, smiled and sauntered away, leaving Henry alone.

"My lord, I must speak with you... There is a very urgent matter—" Polly was amazed to find that she was out of breath, sounding quite shaken. "It concerns your sister—"

Henry's attention sharpened. He took her hands in a strong grasp.

"Concerning Laura? What is it? You are shaking, Lady Polly! What can be the matter?"

Polly glanced around instinctively. Most of the guests were preoccupied with the serious business of eating and drinking, but a few glances were being cast their way.

"Not here," she said softly. "I have a letter for you. It is a delicate matter..."

Henry nodded, offering her his arm. "Perhaps you will be good enough to show me your father's sculpture collection before supper, Lady Polly? I have heard tell that it is very fine."

It was dark outside and not secluded enough for a private conversation. They re-crossed the courtyard hastily and went in through the long library doors. The library was in near darkness, only one branch of candles throwing its shadowy light over the sculpture which was indeed accounted very beautiful. Henry shut the door behind them and Polly moved to light some more candles. From a purely practical point of view, Henry would hardly be able to decipher his sister's script in the gloom. Her hands shook a little as she lit the wavering flame and turned back to him. Henry was standing with his back to the door and Polly felt once again the little leap of her heart that his presence always caused.

"Here." She took the letter from the bodice of her gown and passed it over, still warm from the contact with her skin. "You will be wanting to read it in peace, I am sure, my lord—"

But she was not to get away so easily.

"Just a moment—" Lord Henry said, sounding preoccupied. He had already unfolded the missive and scanned its brief contents, but when he looked up at Polly, his gaze was intent.

"When did Laura give this to you?"

Polly glanced at the clock. "No more than fifteen minutes ago, my lord."

"Then why does she imagine that I will be reading it several hours hence?" He tapped the letter. "She states quite clearly here that she will have been gone for several hours, yet you say it is only fifteen minutes! I could catch them up quite easily if I chose!"

"Yes." Polly struggled a little, wishing she had beaten a retreat sooner, "that is…she asked me to give it to you in a little while but—" She broke off with a slight gesture. "I thought that you should know at once—" Polly stopped again. This was coming out all wrong and Henry was frowning deeply as he watched her.

"Why?" he demanded. "Were you so determined that I should put a stop to this? I have not forgotten your aversion to elopements!"

"No!" Polly was stung. "It is unfair of you to bring that matter up between us again, my lord! I wish Lady Laura every good fortune! But I could not just stand by with your letter for a few hours and then give it to a servant to pass to you and pretend that it had not been in my possession all the time! I just hoped that you would make the right decision—" She broke off. "Truly, my lord," she finished, a little desperately, "it is best that I leave you to consider matters."

"No," Henry said firmly, "I do not think so." He was leaning on Seagrave's beautiful inlaid walnut desk and was still frowning. "There is a mystery here which I feel must be unravelled. Laura gave you the letter and asked that you give it to me in a few hours' time, to give them a good head start. You say that you wish them well and indeed it must be so, for in here—" he flicked the letter as it lay on the desk "—she also says that you advised her most kindly to follow her heart." The look he gave her was sardonic. "I cannot believe you to have indulged in such double-dealing, Lady Polly, that you advise my sister to elope and then immediately give her away! Pray, sit down and explain the matter to me!"

Polly glanced across at the door. It seemed so much easier just to run away, except for the conviction that Henry would probably run after her and bring her back, and cause a scandal in the process.

The deepening smile on his face suggested that he had guessed her thoughts—all of them. She sat down on one of the elegant gilt sofas and tried to marshal her thoughts.

"It is true that Lady Laura confided in me her feelings for Mr Farrant," she admitted, "and also that I was aware of the objections of her family to the match. You and I have discussed as much! I do not know what part your sister has assigned to me in all this, but I freely admit that my advice to her was that she should do what she thought was right. She has more determination than I ever did at her age— she knew what she wanted and now she has taken it, and I wish her all the luck in the world in her choice!"

"Then why did you pass me her letter so swiftly?" Henry asked. "You must know that I could stop them if I chose." He had come round the desk and taken the chair opposite Polly's, watching her all the while. Polly was intensely conscious of his intent gaze resting thoughtfully on her face. She prayed that it was too dark for him to read her expression. This was the most difficult part.

"I did not wish to deceive you," she said candidly. "Whilst I wish your sister success and happiness, it was more important to me that you should know of her actions and choose for yourself. If you decide to go after them I shall be very sorry, but I will still feel that I did the right thing in entrusting the letter to you now rather than later."

There was a little silence. Polly's face was growing hot under that unrelenting scrutiny. "A little late in the day to be speaking of trust between us," Henry said drily. "You must forgive me, Lady Polly, if I find it difficult to accept that you are finally trusting me with information in the belief that I will do the right thing. There have been other occasions, arguably more important, when you did not show any such confidence in me!"

Polly clasped her hands together tightly. "If you are speaking of my engagement to Mr Ditton then I can only concede that you are right, my lord. However, if we must indulge in recriminations, allow me to say that you are hardly blameless yourself!"

Henry smiled slightly. "Your point, Lady Polly! But it is a little different. I would have done anything I could to save you from Ditton."

"Almost anything," Polly said sweetly. "Let us not rake over the past, my lord, for we shall only quarrel! It seems that you cannot forgive me my lack of trust and I resent that you did not fully confide in me! Untrusted and untrustworthy both! But will you go after your sister?"

Henry shook his head slowly.

"No, I will not. I never opposed the match, although I cannot deny that it will cause a great deal of trouble. But..." he sighed "...it is not my choice to spoil Laura's happiness!"

Polly let out a long, unsteady breath. "Oh, thank you!"

"And," Henry added, with the ghost of a smile, "as long as neither of us admits that we knew of the elopement only fifteen minutes after it occurred, we may avoid any censure!"

For a moment they were drawn into a tenuous alliance. Polly felt hope and despair stir in equal measure. Was this how it was always to be, forever wanting more, hoping for more, when Henry had made it clear that he could not forgive her lack of faith in him and she had just demonstrated that she still blamed him for telling her only half a story?

It seemed heartbreaking.

"I must go," she said, a little uncertainly. "Mama will be wondering, and I have had no supper..."

Henry stirred a little in his chair. "I shall bid you farewell then, Lady Polly. I am returning to London tomorrow. Perhaps you will be in Town for the Little Season?"

"Perhaps," Polly echoed dully. She felt her spirits sink like a stone. There would be the Little Season and then the following Season and the year after, forever in Lord Henry's company, forever set apart from him, summers in Brighton, or Bath, or Dillingham, becoming the spinster aunt, wearing the willow forever...

She swallowed hard. "Good night, my lord," she said.

Chapter Eighteen

There was a curious air of quiet about Dillingham Court the following day. Both Lucille and the Dowager Countess stayed in bed resting, but Polly found herself full of a restless energy that compelled her out of doors. After breakfast, she took her watercolours down to the lake and sat in the summerhouse trying to paint, but somehow she could not transfer the pretty pastoral scene onto her paper and tore up her efforts in a fit of temper. It seemed that she would not find solace for her broken heart through her painting.

The lake was very calm under the blue sky of early autumn, but the air was warm and the sky was heavy with gathering rain. The light was interesting and Polly was frustrated that she could not convey it onto paper. She put down her brush and leant her elbows on the railing, watching the distant clouds roll towards her. With a sigh, she pushed her paints to one side. A quiet walk was almost always enjoyable, although she would have to be careful that she did not get caught in the rain.

She took the path that skirted the lake, walking slowly down towards the River Deben. The breeze whispered softly in the grass and stirred the leaves on the trees. It seemed almost unnaturally quiet. The river was running quickly, little eddies pushing at the muddy bank and lapping at the soles of Polly's shoes. She could see the roof of the fishing-house a little further downstream, and wandered towards it. The skies opened almost as suddenly as they had done that day at Shingle Street, and the rain began in a steady downpour. By the time Polly reached the fishing-house, she was drenched and hurried towards the shelter it provided. The door swung open with one touch of her hand and, as before, she stepped into the dim interior.

Unlike the last time, the pool was empty. The mermen and mermaids watched her with blank eyes. There was total silence. Polly paused. A completely insane idea took hold of her. She had gone seabathing with the Dowager Countess at Brighton the previous summer and had enjoyed the fresh sensation of the cool water. Of course, the pool was not like the sea, but it would be most refreshing and she was already soaked through. Without further thought, she stripped off her dress and, wearing only her chemise, eased herself into the plunge pool. The chill of the water made her gasp, but once she had become accustomed to it, it was immensely invigorating. Closing her eyes, she floated on her back, listening to the drumming of the rain on the wooden roof above her head and enjoying the curious sensation of being immersed in water whilst it poured down outside. She could feel her hair floating free of its pins and almost laughed aloud. How delightful to feel so free from inhibition, to indulge herself, relish the sensation... She was almost happy.

She opened her eyes, gasped, swallowed what felt like a gallon of water and almost choked. Through streaming eyes she could quite clearly make out the laughing face of Lord Henry Marchnight as he stood beside the pool looking down at her. As she struggled to regain her breath, he crouched down by the pool's edge and caught one of her arms, holding her above water.

"Dear me, Lady Polly," Lord Henry said mildly, "just when I thought it impossible that you could surprise me, I find myself being utterly astounded!"

To Polly's relief, Lord Henry behaved with perfect chivalry. He made no comment about her state of undress but found her a huge, soft blanket to wrap about her and cover her modesty. Then he almost undid all his good work.

"You will find me an adequate lady's maid, I am sure," he said with a grin. "I have had some practice at such things!"

The colour flooded Polly's cheeks and she pulled the blanket closer. "I am in no doubt as to that!" she said tartly.

Henry was still grinning unrepentantly as his gaze took in her tousled hair and pink face.

"You look utterly delightful, Lady Polly! Perhaps you would care to join me on the balcony whilst you dry off?"

Before Polly had chance to demur and effect a discreet withdrawal, he had scooped her up in his arms and carried her up the ladder and out on to the balcony. There was another blanket and a couple of cushions on the bare boards and the remains of what looked like Henry's breakfast. For a long time they sat together under the shelter of the eaves, watching the rain upon the river. Neither of them spoke. Polly was possessed by the most extraordinary feeling of peacefulness and did not wish to break the spell. Eventually the rain retreated and the first streaks of pale blue sky appeared again. She stirred.

"Whatever are you doing here, Harry? I thought that you had gone..."

Henry gestured towards the rod and line lying discarded on the edge of the balcony. "I was fishing—until you came to disturb the peace of my retreat!" He hesitated. "Truth to tell, I was thinking..." He shot Polly a glance. "I was coming to see you later, but you have beaten me to it."

The sun came out suddenly, swirling across the dark river water and dazzling them.

Polly suddenly found that she could not meet his eyes.

"What were you coming to discuss with me?" she asked shyly, tracing a pattern in the dust with one finger. "I thought—last night you intimated that there was nothing more to say."

Henry shifted a little, leaning back against the wall. "Yes, that was wicked of me. I could no more lose you now than I could cut out a part of myself. Please—" suddenly there was raw feeling in his voice "—tell me that we may put all the misunderstanding and misery behind us and that you will marry me."

At last Polly was able to look at him, but with astonishment rather than anything else.

"But I haven't had chance to explain why I did not tell you—" she began.

"I don't need explanations." Henry took her hand in his and drew her closer. "I knew last night that you trusted me enough for me to be the first one you came to with a secret. That is enough for me. I know that you must love me as much as I love you."

"Harry—" Polly's voice broke. "I believe you are almost too forgiving…"

His strained face broke into a smile. "Do you feel that I should castigate you for the business with Tristan Ditton? I had felt that we had grown closer over the past few months and the business with Ditton did set me back." He grimaced. "I did not understand—still do not, to tell the truth—why you could not confide in me. You must have known that I would not have shamed Miss Markham by making the knowledge public, and yet you did not trust me—"

The pain in his voice caused Polly to look up at last. "I wanted to tell you," she said hesitantly. "That night at the assembly, I was on the verge of telling when Tristan came in and put a stop to our conversation. I know I should have trusted you more—all those times I doubted you, the foolishness over the smuggling, my suspicions over your activities in London—you must think me so stupid!" Her voice broke. "I don't know why I could not commit myself, Harry… I was so close to trusting you, yet I always held back, perhaps because I have loved you for so long that I could not bear to take the final risk and gamble on losing it all! I found it very difficult to forgive myself for refusing you all those years ago!''

Henry slid an arm around her and pulled her to him so that her head rested comfortingly against his shoulder. ''I must take my share of blame,'' he said, very softly. ''I fostered the impression of a wastrel and a rake, which is scarcely the kind of behaviour that would encourage a gently bred girl to rely on me! I could have warned you about Ditton—I knew you would not tell anyone, but I was afraid that you would not be able to behave naturally in his company if you knew he was a criminal. If I had to take the same decision now, I would have to do the same...''

''I know,'' Polly said softly. Henry looked so wretched that she touched his cheek. ''You did the right thing. When I was thinking about it all last night, I remembered how you had risked the whole endeavour to save me in the riot in London. You must have cared a great deal to do that for me...''

They sat quietly for a long time, Henry's arm warm about her, his cheek rough against the smoothness of hers.

''Polly,'' Henry said at last, his voice muffled against her hair, ''you have not yet agreed to marry me!''

''Oh!'' Polly turned to him and their lips met with a tenderness that was both sweet and instinctive.

''I assume,'' Henry said, much later, ''that that is an acceptance. I should not allow another rejection anyway!''

Polly snuggled closer to him. ''How much time we have wasted! When may we be married, Harry?''

''In the interests of making up for lost time,''

Henry said seriously, ''I suggest the wedding should be very soon. Tomorrow, perhaps?''

Polly sat up and stared at him in confusion. ''Tomorrow? But how—''

''I thought, perhaps, that you might be persuaded to elope with me.''

Polly looked at him for a long time. ''You mean— to come away with you now?'' she asked, a little breathlessly. ''But—''

She saw the faint look of withdrawal that came into his eyes. ''I understand if you do not wish to do so—''

''No!'' Polly put out a hand quickly and touched his. It was suddenly essential to make him understand. ''Henry, listen. I will gladly go with you. I would follow you anywhere, or do anything you asked.'' The tears gathered in her eyes. ''Oh, I am so very *happy* to have the chance to run away with you!''

Suddenly they were both laughing like children, tumbled back once more in each other's arms.

''I had not intended to go to Gretna,'' Henry said after more kisses had been exchanged, ''but my home at Ruthford is but a day's journey from here, and I have a special licence and a priest who would be very happy to marry off another of the Marchnight brood! Indeed, I imagine he would be particularly glad to officiate at my wedding since he has been deploring my bachelor life this age!''

Polly stood up. ''I had best return to the Court and gather my belongings. Oh!'' She looked down at the blanket still clutched about her. ''I had forgotten— my dress is still by the pool! I can hardly return to the house like this or we would have to be married even sooner to avoid Mama falling into the vapours!'' She looked suddenly shy. ''Will you help me down the steps, Harry?''

Henry got to his feet. ''Of course—but take care that the blanket does not slip!''

He tactfully stepped outside whilst Polly was donning her dress again, and gave her a critical look-over when she emerged into the sunshine.

''Not bad, although I do not think it would stand the scrutiny of a discerning eye! You could always tell them the truth, of course!''

Polly came close to him. ''I should like to be able to tell Lucille and Nicholas where I am going,'' she said, a little hesitantly. ''I know it seems strange, but...''

Henry gave her a brief kiss. ''If you wish to do so, let it be so. I am confident they will not stop us.''

Polly had one last question. ''Henry...'' She did not quite raise her gaze to his. ''If we are to be married tomorrow, what happens tonight?''

When she finally looked up into his face it was to see a mixture of amusement and speculation that made her blush all over again.

''What do you think?'' he said.

It was just over an hour later that the Earl of Seagrave, striding in at the door of Dillingham Court, was distracted by the sound of his own mother in strong hysterics. Hastening into the drawing-room, he found the Dowager prostrate on the sofa and Lucille hovering with a bottle of smelling salts whilst the Dowager's maid tried ineffectually to calm her mistress and Peter and Hetty stood helplessly by.

"Nicholas!" the Dowager Countess said, immediately sitting up and recovering at the sight of her elder son, "Do something! Your sister is eloping with Lord Henry Marchnight! I have seen them with my own eyes—the carriage has been gone but five minutes!"

Nicholas Seagrave strolled over to the table and poured himself a glass of wine. "But, Mama, I thought that you liked Lord Henry! You have been forever praising him these months past!"

There was a snort of laughter from Lucille, quickly suppressed. Peter bit his lip and Hetty turned a smile into a sort of cough.

The Dowager looked outraged. "Like him! Of course I like him! He is precisely the sort of man I would wish to marry Polly! But what is that to the purpose, pray? She is to be married at St. George's, Hanover Square! I have it all planned!" The Dowager wrung her hands. "The foolish chit told me that they were running away together, and when I told her that there was not the least need to do so, she told me that there was every need! I have no notion what she meant!"

Nicholas's eyes met Lucille's and they exchanged a smile of complicity.

"*Do* something, Nicholas!" the Dowager besought again.

Nicholas crossed to his wife's side and took her hand. "But Mama, there is nothing more I can do! I had already met them at the gates and offered them the use of my travelling carriage! Harry assured me that they should make Ruthford late tonight and are to be married in the morning!''

The Dowager Countess gave a muffled squeak. ''Tonight! But Polly is unchaperoned! Even if they are to be married tomorrow, what is to happen tonight?''

There was a brief silence. Peter and Hetty studiously avoided each other's gaze. Nicholas Seagrave raised his eyebrows.

''What do you think?'' he said.

It was early evening when they reached Ruthford. Polly had fallen asleep on the journey, her head resting on Henry's shoulder, and awoke just as the carriage pulled up in front of the house. She had a confused impression of mellow stone and part-timbering before Henry ushered her up the steps and into the hall, handing her over to his housekeeper, Mrs Owen, to show her to her room. They ate alone in a small but tastefully appointed dining-room and, after the meal, took a turn along the terrace as dusk was falling. Away to the west the clouds were building and Polly shivered at the sound of distant thunder.

''I have spoken to Father Beckham and he is very happy to marry us in the morning,'' Henry said conversationally. ''You are very quiet, Polly. I hope...'' he took Polly's cold hand in his warm one ''...that it is not a sign that you have changed your mind!''

The warmth of his touch helped to reassure Polly. ''It is just that it seems so strange,'' she said excusingly, ''and so unexpected, for all that I have been wanting to marry you these five years past! And suddenly we are alone...''

"Yes." Henry tucked her hand comfortingly through his arm. "It is bound to seem a little strange at first. Perhaps we should retire to the drawing-room and I shall read my paper and you may essay a little needlepoint, and we shall be like any old married couple!"

Polly laughed. "I had no idea that marriage to you would be such a dull affair, my lord! Perhaps I should change my mind—"

"Too late," Henry said cheerfully. "You are compromised beyond redemption, I fear, and..." he drew her closer "...should there be any doubt I should be happy to confirm that I had seduced you thoroughly!"

"I wonder how Hetty and Peter ever came to—?" Polly broke off, blushing rosily. "Well, no doubt I should not speculate..."

"Were you shocked when the truth came out?"

Polly considered. "Not shocked, precisely, at least not at what they had done. It was...understandable. But I was surprised and perhaps a little—"

"Envious?" Henry's grey eyes held a spark of mischief. "A pity then, that we are to be so respectably married on the morrow!"

"There is always tonight," Polly said, casting him a look under her lashes.

Their eyes met in a long moment of tension, then Henry shook his head reluctantly.

"For once in my life I am determined to behave in an honourable fashion!" he said.

It did not seem, however, that Henry's scruples prevented him from kissing Polly goodnight in the most thorough way imaginable. They made slow progress back inside and up the wide wooden staircase, entwined as they were in each other's arms. They stopped again outside Polly's bedroom door.

"What marvellously discreet servants you have, Harry," Polly observed. "No doubt they are accustomed to melting away as soon as you appear with a lady who is not your wife!"

"Minx!" Henry pulled her into his arms. "They are all well aware that tomorrow you will become Lady Polly Marchnight!"

He kissed her gently, lovingly. It was not what Polly wanted. She parted her lips beneath his, rejoicing as she felt the kiss turn from sweetness to sensual demand. Henry, that notorious rake, had exercised endless self-control in his dealings with her and she was determined to make him lose his restraint.

"I protest," she said against his lips, "that your reputation is undeserved, Harry! You are no rake—"

In reply, he turned his mouth back to hers driving out all thought with the explosive demand of his lips and his hands. When he finally let her go, Polly had to lean back against the door frame to steady herself. Henry stood back very deliberately.

"Enough! I must go—"

Polly had her hand on the doorknob and the door was already half-open. As Henry turned away she said, very softly, "Henry, I am afraid of the thunder. Don't leave me…"

She saw him hesitate, and smile, before he took her arm, drew her through the doorway, and closed the door very firmly behind them.

* * *

Neither of them heard the thunderstorm that raged about the house, being too concerned with the storm within. At some point during the night, when the thunder had died away, Henry stirred and raised himself on one elbow.

"The storm has gone," he said softly. "Would you wish me away, madam, now that you need be afraid no longer?"

Polly could hear the smile in his voice. She reached out to pull him to her. "I have not mentioned it before, my love, but I am afraid of the dark. I fear you must stay with me until the morning!"

In the light of the new day, Polly woke again and spoke drowsily.

"Henry? Do you still wish to marry me?"

Henry leant across to kiss her. "More than ever now, my love! Who would have thought that marriage would promise to be so enjoyable!"

Polly glanced across at the clock. Somehow they had never managed to draw the bed curtains.

"At what hour is the wedding?"

"At ten o'clock, the earliest that I thought that we could respectably arrange it..." Henry's kisses were becoming more persuasive, more determined. Polly pushed him away.

"That would be the ten o'clock that was a half hour ago?"

Henry sat bolt upright. "Good God! It cannot be ten-thirty already?" He put his head in his hands. "How could I miss my own wedding as a result of

being in bed with my future wife? Father Beckham
will be saying prayers for my immortal soul!''

Polly leant across to give him a consoling kiss. ''I
am persuaded that he knows you so well, Harry, that
he would expect no less of you!'' she said.

* * * * *

MONTANA MAVERICKS HISTORICALS

Discover the origins
of Montana's most popular family...

On sale September 2001
THE GUNSLINGER'S BRIDE
by Cheryl St.John
Outlaw Brock Kincaid returns home to make peace with his brothers
and finds love in the arms of an old flame with a secret.

On sale October 2001
WHITEFEATHER'S WOMAN
by Deborah Hale
Kincaid Ranch foreman John Whitefeather breaks all the rules when
the Native American dares to fall in love with nanny Jane Harris.

On sale November 2001
A CONVENIENT WIFE
by Carolyn Davidson
Whitehorn doctor Winston Gray enters into a marriage of
convenience with a pregnant rancher's daughter, only to
discover he's found his heart's desire!

MONTANA MAVERICKS
RETURN TO WHITEHORN—WHERE LEGENDS ARE BEGUN
AND LOVE LASTS FOREVER BENEATH THE BIG SKY...

Harlequin Historicals
Historical Romantic Adventure!

TRAVEL TO A LAND LONG AGO
AND FAR AWAY WHEN YOU READ
A HARLEQUIN HISTORICAL NOVEL

ON SALE SEPTEMBER 2001

THE MACKINTOSH BRIDE
by Debra Lee Brown

A young clan leader must choose between duty and desire
when he falls in love with a woman from a rival clan.

THE SLEEPING BEAUTY
by Jacqueline Navin

A fortune hunter enters into a marriage of convenience
to a beautiful heiress with a mysterious secret.

ON SALE OCTOBER 2001

IRONHEART
by Emily French

A brave knight returns from the Holy Land and
is mistaken for a noble lady's betrothed.

AUTUMN'S BRIDE
by Catherine Archer

FINAL BOOK IN THE SEASONS' BRIDES SERIES.
When a nobleman is wounded by brigands, a young
woman loses her heart while nursing him back to health.

Harlequin invites you to walk down the aisle . . .

To honor our year long celebration of weddings, we are offering an exciting opportunity for you to own the Harlequin Bride Doll. Handcrafted in fine bisque porcelain, the wedding doll is dressed for her wedding day in a cream satin gown accented by lace trim. She carries an exquisite traditional bridal bouquet and wears a cathedral-length dotted Swiss veil. Embroidered flowers cascade down her lace overskirt to the scalloped hemline; underneath all is a multi-layered crinoline.

Join us in our celebration of weddings by sending away for your own Harlequin Bride Doll. This doll regularly retails for $74.95 U.S./approx. $108.68 CDN. One doll per household. Requests must be received no later than December 31, 2001. Offer good while quantities of gifts last. Please allow 6-8 weeks for delivery. Offer good in the U.S. and Canada only. Become part of this exciting offer!

Simply complete the order form and mail to:
"A Walk Down the Aisle"

IN U.S.A	IN CANADA
P.O. Box 9057	P.O. Box 622
3010 Walden Ave.	Fort Erie, Ontario
Buffalo, NY 14269-9057	L2A 5X3

Enclosed are eight (8) proofs of purchase found in the last pages of every specially marked Harlequin series book and $3.75 check or money order (for postage and handling). Please send my Harlequin Bride Doll to:

_____

Name (PLEASE PRINT)

_____

Address   Apt. #

_____

City   State/Prov.   Zip/Postal Code

_____

Account # (if applicable)   **097 KIK DAEW**

HARLEQUIN®
Makes any time special ®

Visit us at www.eHarlequin.com

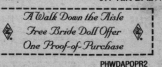

A Walk Down the Aisle
Free Bride Doll Offer
One Proof-of-Purchase

PHWDAPOPR2

COMING
SOON...

AN EXCITING
OPPORTUNITY TO SAVE
ON THE PURCHASE OF
HARLEQUIN AND
SILHOUETTE BOOKS!

*DETAILS TO FOLLOW
IN OCTOBER 2001!*

YOU WON'T WANT TO MISS IT!

PHQ401